A PERFECT LIFE

A Perfect Life is an impossible dream—

but real life can be whatever you make of it.

PRAISE FOR DANIELLE STEEL

"Steel pulls out all the emotional stops. . . . She delivers."
—*Publishers Weekly*

"Steel is one of the best!" —*Los Angeles Times*

"The world's most popular author tells a good, well-paced story and explores some important issues. . . . Steel affirm[s] life while admitting its turbulence, melodramas, and misfiring passions." —*Booklist*

"Danielle Steel writes boldly and with practiced vividness about tragedy—both national and personal . . . with insight and power." —*Nashville Banner*

"There is a smooth reading style to her writings which makes it easy to forget the time and to keep flipping the pages."
—*The Pittsburgh Press*

"One of the things that keeps Danielle Steel fresh is her bent for timely storylines. . . . The combination of Steel's comprehensive research and her skill at creating credible characters makes for a gripping read." —*The Star-Ledger*

"What counts for the reader is the ring of authenticity."
—*San Francisco Chronicle*

"Steel knows how to wring the emotion out of the briefest scene." —*People*

"Ms. Steel excels at pacing her narrative, which races forward, mirroring the frenetic lives chronicled; men and women swept up in bewildering change, seeking solutions to problems never before faced." —*Nashville Banner*

"Danielle Steel has again uplifted her readers while skillfully communicating some of life's bittersweet verities. Who could ask for a finer gift than that?" —*The Philadelphia Inquirer*

PRAISE FOR THE RECENT NOVELS OF DANIELLE STEEL

A PERFECT LIFE

"A classic Steel story, with a mother and daughter keeping up appearances as they overcome tragedy and learn a thing or two about themselves." —*Library Journal*

"It's the lessons learned by the mother-daughter duo about love, loyalty and family that bring them closer together than ever before in Steel's latest heartwarming page-turner."
—*Closer Weekly*

POWER PLAY

"[A] biting critique of the corporate gender gap . . . Steel expertly handles a well-paced morality tale while creating three starkly different heroines who share a common moral compass." —*Publishers Weekly*

"In peak form, Steel examines the effects of power on the lives of male and female CEOs in this insightful, all-too realistic novel . . . to dramatize just how differently men and women handle corporate power and personal responsibility." —*Booklist*

"Connecting two powerful CEOs through their children's romantic involvement, the author uses her signature low-key . . . style to examine personal and professional morality. Appealing fare from Steel." —*Kirkus Reviews*

WINNERS

"[*Winners*] will leave readers crying and cheering."
—*Booklist*

FIRST SIGHT

"A novel about love, in all its heartbreaking and splendid forms." *—Kirkus Reviews*

"Steel is one of the world's most popular authors, and this poignant romance is sure to thrill her many loyal fans and reach many new readers, too." *—Booklist*

"Steel deftly stages heartstring-tugging moments."
—Publishers Weekly

UNTIL THE END OF TIME

"[A] heartwarming love story that will have readers believing in forever." *—Publishers Weekly*

"This story of romance through hardship and across decades has a spiritual appeal." *—Kirkus Reviews*

"Clever and sweetly dramatic." *—Booklist*

THE SINS OF THE MOTHER

"*The Sins of the Mother* is classic Danielle Steel at her best. . . . Here, she allows us a glimpse into the price that the rich and famous pay for their success and touches our heartstrings with the emotional stories behind those choices. Steel's latest novel allows readers to journey across the world without ever leaving their easy chairs and provides a feel-good read that will leave them with a smile on their faces."
—Bookreporter

"As always, Danielle Steel has created an exceptional story of the rights and wrongs within a family and the road to healing. *The Sins of the Mother* is an unforgettable novel!"
—Fresh Fiction

FRIENDS FOREVER

"Like many of Steel's previous novels, *Friends Forever* is phenomenally written and leads the reader through a story filled with beautiful people doing extraordinary things."
—*Examiner*

"A page-turning drama portraying a tight group of childhood friends who must face heartbreak and disappointment in the circle of life . . . The five main characters bring a superb blend of rich personalities to the mix, creating a well-orchestrated symphony of pure literary pleasure. Her most compelling novel to date, *Friends Forever* is exactly what Steel's fans have come to expect. . . . Pure brilliance."
—Fresh Fiction

BETRAYAL

"There is definitely a dark side to fame and fortune, and Danielle Steel has captured the imagination of her readers in a brilliant, heartbreaking, emotional story."
—Entertainment Focus

"In this can't-put-it-down page-turner, Danielle Steel reveals the dark side of fame and fortune. . . . A story that in the end will remind us that if we hold fast to our values, faith, courage and conviction we will overcome any deception, disappointment and the pain left in its wake and emerge smarter, stronger, empowered." —*Book Peeps*

"I could not put this book down. . . . Steel has a knack for writing about real-life issues and invoking an emotional bond with her characters." —My Reading Rainbow

HOTEL VENDÔME

"Danielle Steel fans have come to expect a certain standard when reading the novels penned by their favorite author. When they pick up *Hotel Vendôme,* they won't be disappointed. . . . As they turn the pages of this novel [they] will enjoy taking refuge in the high-class world where the movie star, world leaders and other celebrities mingle with warm and friendly staff to create a well-rounded cast of characters who delight and entertain. Who wouldn't want to book a suite at the Hotel Vendôme?"—*Bookreporter*

"[The] tale of a young girl growing up in a posh hotel with her kind father . . . As the story unfolds, both father and daughter find themselves transformed." —*Kirkus Reviews*

"[Steel] always delivers." —*Publishers Weekly*

HAPPY BIRTHDAY

"*Happy Birthday* reminded me exactly why I've been a Danielle Steel fan for decades. Fascinating, lovable characters who aren't afraid of their imperfections, world-class settings, and storylines that simply swept me away."
—*Bookreporter*

"In Danielle Steel's latest novel . . . the queen of 'feel good' stories once again brings her legions of fans a wonderful tale of hard times, complications and love."
—*Las Vegas Review-Journal*

"In this enticing novel, readers meet three different characters who reach a turning point when they mark an annual rite of passage." —*OK! Magazine*

44 CHARLES STREET

"A warm, cozy tale about the triumph of love, friendship, and second chances."

—*Publishers Weekly*

"This book is classic Steel—lots of emotion, friendship, romance, heartbreak, tragedy, and danger. Her countless fans are guaranteed to find it impossible to put down."

—*Booklist*

LEGACY

"This inspiring story [is] about a frustrated woman who rediscovers her passion for life during a genealogical quest. . . . A doubly absorbing romantic adventure."

—*Publishers Weekly*

"In Steel's latest . . . a restrained anthropologist discovers her wild side while researching the life of a beautiful eighteenth-century Sioux Indian. . . . The two women's stories are compelling." —*Kirkus Reviews*

FAMILY TIES

"A sweet story about the importance of family . . . Annie and the kids are all endearing characters . . . making for a breezy summer read." —*The Parkersburg News and Sentinel*

BIG GIRL

"There is something in Steel's work that readers cling to—that makes them identify with characters."

—*The Washington Post*

"A moving story about a woman who is able to face the pain from her past in order to move on into her future no matter what the setbacks may be, this is an uplifting book . . . with a winning main character."
—*The Parkersburg News and Sentinel*

"What makes *Big Girl* fascinating is its chronicle of Victoria's struggles with her weight, a subject Americans aren't quite sure how to talk about right now." —*The Miami Herald*

SOUTHERN LIGHTS

"A veteran of exploring . . . family dynamics . . . Steel's many readers will, of course, devour this." —*Publishers Weekly*

"A woman's past comes back to haunt her as her court case gets more dangerous. . . . This is a great story of complex characters from Steel, of one woman's pain and her trying to move through it." —*The Parkersburg News and Sentinel*

MATTERS OF THE HEART

"Danielle Steel has crafted a modern-day tale that is deliciously suspenseful. . . . A haunting roller coaster [ride]."
—*The Oklahoman*

"A smart and thoughtful read that boasts well-drawn characters. . . . [This] twisty thriller will keep you reading."
—*The Arizona Republic*

"The isolated-woman-in-danger theme gives the novel a modern gothic feel. Steel's fans will be delighted by this story of a woman seduced by a man who is too good to be true."
—*Booklist*

A MAIN SELECTION OF THE LITERARY GUILD AND THE DOUBLEDAY BOOK CLUB

By Danielle Steel

COUNTRY • PRODIGAL SON • PEGASUS • A PERFECT LIFE
POWER PLAY • WINNERS • FIRST SIGHT • UNTIL THE END OF TIME
THE SINS OF THE MOTHER • FRIENDS FOREVER • BETRAYAL
HOTEL VENDÔME • HAPPY BIRTHDAY • 44 CHARLES STREET
LEGACY • FAMILY TIES • BIG GIRL • SOUTHERN LIGHTS
MATTERS OF THE HEART • ONE DAY AT A TIME • A GOOD WOMAN
ROGUE • HONOR THYSELF • AMAZING GRACE • BUNGALOW 2
SISTERS • H.R.H. • COMING OUT • THE HOUSE • TOXIC BACHELORS
MIRACLE • IMPOSSIBLE • ECHOES • SECOND CHANCE • RANSOM
SAFE HARBOUR • JOHNNY ANGEL • DATING GAME
ANSWERED PRAYERS • SUNSET IN ST. TROPEZ • THE COTTAGE
THE KISS • LEAP OF FAITH • LONE EAGLE • JOURNEY
THE HOUSE ON HOPE STREET • THE WEDDING
IRRESISTIBLE FORCES • GRANNY DAN • BITTERSWEET
MIRROR IMAGE • THE KLONE AND I • THE LONG ROAD HOME
THE GHOST • SPECIAL DELIVERY • THE RANCH • SILENT HONOR
MALICE • FIVE DAYS IN PARIS • LIGHTNING • WINGS • THE GIFT
ACCIDENT • VANISHED • MIXED BLESSINGS • JEWELS
NO GREATER LOVE • HEARTBEAT • MESSAGE FROM NAM • DADDY
STAR • ZOYA • KALEIDOSCOPE • FINE THINGS • WANDERLUST
SECRETS • FAMILY ALBUM • FULL CIRCLE • CHANGES
THURSTON HOUSE • CROSSINGS • ONCE IN A LIFETIME
A PERFECT STRANGER • REMEMBRANCE • PALOMINO • LOVE: *POEMS*
THE RING • LOVING • TO LOVE AGAIN • SUMMER'S END
SEASON OF PASSION • THE PROMISE • NOW AND FOREVER
PASSION'S PROMISE • GOING HOME

Nonfiction

PURE JOY: *THE DOGS WE LOVE*
A GIFT OF HOPE: *HELPING THE HOMELESS*
HIS BRIGHT LIGHT: *THE STORY OF NICK TRAINA*

For Children

PRETTY MINNIE IN PARIS

DANIELLE STEEL

A PERFECT LIFE

A Novel

Dell • New York

A Perfect Life is a work of fiction. Names, characters, places, and incidents are the products of the author's imagination or are used fictitiously. Any resemblance to actual events, locales, or persons, living or dead, is entirely coincidental.

2015 Dell Mass Market Edition

Published in the United States by Dell, an imprint of Random House, a division of Random House LLC, a Penguin Random House Company, New York.

DELL and the HOUSE colophon are registered trademarks of Random House LLC.

Originally published in hardcover in the United States by Delacorte Press, an imprint of Random House, a division of Random House LLC, in 2014.

This book contains an excerpt from the forthcoming book *Undercover* by Danielle Steel. This excerpt has been set for this edition only and may not reflect the final content of the forthcoming edition.

ISBN 978-0-345-53095-0
eBook ISBN 978-0-345-53096-7

Printed in the United States of America

www.bantamdell.com

2 4 6 8 9 7 5 3 1

Cover photograph: Shobeir Ansari/Getty Images

Dell mass market edition: June 2015

To my beloved children,
Beatie, Trevor, Todd, Sam, Victoria, Vanessa,
Maxx, and Zara,

May your lives always be as close to perfect as you wish them, and may your dreams turn out to be even better than you hoped, with myriad large and small miracles along the way.

And to my darling Nicky, I hope your world is peaceful and perfect now.

I love you all so very, very, very much.

Mommy/d.s.

"L'amour n'a pas d'age."
Love has no age.

"True love is like a special language:
You either speak it, or you don't."
—LALEH SHAHIDEH

A PERFECT LIFE

Chapter 1

Crowds of students began congregating outside Royce Hall Auditorium at UCLA two hours before Congressman Patrick Olden was scheduled to speak, an hour before they opened the doors. He had been invited by an enterprising professor, who taught a class on citizenship and public service, open to juniors and seniors. But once the congressman accepted, he had sent out notices to all political science majors, and the auditorium was expected to be full. They were estimating that two thousand students would be there. And judging from the number of people waiting for the doors to open, there might even be more. He was a popular congressman, with a liberal voting record dedicated to the underdog and was known for championing minorities, including women, and sympathetic to the issues of youth and the elderly. And he had four kids of his own. He was married to his childhood sweetheart, and everybody loved him. The students were excited to hear him speak that day.

The crowd was orderly once the doors were open, on a brilliantly sunny, warm October day. Olden was scheduled to begin addressing them at eleven, with time set aside for questions from the audience after his speech. He was scheduled to have lunch with the chancellor afterward and fly back to Washington that afternoon. Getting him there at all had been a major coup. It wasn't for a commencement address, or a law school graduation, it was just a class, and all of them were thrilled to have him there. Luckily it had dovetailed with his plans and a meeting with the governor the day before, and a dinner in his honor to receive an award. Pat Olden was a beloved figure with both young and old.

One of his own kids, his oldest son, was at USC, and he had breakfast with him that morning. Patrick Olden appeared on the stage less than ten minutes late, while they waited backstage for the crowd to settle down. He stood at the podium with his warm smile, his eyes sweeping the crowd. You could hear a pin drop in the room when he began, and students without seats sat cross-legged in the aisles, and stood at the back of the room. They paid rapt attention to everything he said about government today, and what their responsibilities would be if they chose a career in politics. He talked about his own college days and explained what he was trying to do on the various committees he was on, and went into considerable detail. He had already been in office for three years, had done considerable good with the bills he proposed, and this was not an election year for him. He sounded earnest and sincere, and the audience hung on his every word and greeted him with thunderous applause when he was through. He looked pleased. He was the perfect role model for them. The professor who had invited him opened the question and answer period, and a hundred hands shot into the air. The questions were pointed and intelligent and relevant to what he had said. They were twenty minutes into it when a boy in the third row stood up as soon as the congressman pointed at him, and looked him in the eye with a welcoming smile.

"What's your position on gun control now?" the young man asked him, which was a topic he hadn't touched on that day and didn't want to. He was gentle but firm in his views in favor of gun control, but it was a sensitive issue that had had no place in his talk, advising them about careers in government, and it was a subject he had chosen to avoid. The boy who asked the question had neatly combed blond hair, was clean-shaven, and was wearing a blue shirt and an army surplus jacket. He looked orderly and well-groomed, but didn't smile back when Pat Olden smiled at him, and someone said later that the boy looked unusually pale, as though he hadn't seen daylight in a long time.

Pat Olden began answering his question with a serious expression. "I think you all know how I feel about it. Despite the provision in our Constitution that gives us the right to bear arms, I think that terrorism is an important factor today that can't be ignored. And guns too easily fall into the wrong hands. I feel," he said, and before he could finish his sentence or reiterate his position, the young man in the blue shirt and army jacket pulled a gun out of his pocket and, barely pausing to take aim, shot him squarely in the chest, and then followed with a shot to his neck. The congressman fell forward across the podium and then slid to the ground gushing blood, as students throughout the room began to scream. Security guards rushed forward, along with two bodyguards who had accompanied him. People began running toward the exits, others crouched on the ground, as the boy with the gun shot the girl sitting next to him in the head, and then shot randomly into the crowd, while guards in uniform rushed toward him and he killed two of them when they approached. The seats on either side of him were empty by then, and he ran swiftly across them shooting at other students trying to run from the room. He shot three in the back and another girl in the head. There were bodies lying everywhere as a crowd on the stage was ministering to the fallen congressman. There was blood all over, as people continued to scream in terror and grief watching their classmates being killed. And knowing exactly what he was doing, the shooter saved the last round for himself. A university guard in uniform was within a foot of him and was about to grab him, as the shooter hesitated for only a fraction of a second, deciding whether or not to kill him, and then shot himself in the head, and ended the carnage he had begun only minutes before. The entire episode had taken exactly seven minutes, and eleven students and two guards lay dead, eight more had been injured, and the congressman was unconscious, covered in blood as paramedics rushed him from the auditorium on a stretcher. There were already a dozen emergency vehicles outside and more on the way, as university police attempted to control the crowd, to no avail. Several of them had been trampled on the way out and were injured too. All you could hear was crying and screaming in the room, as two thousand students had attempted to escape.

Police had rapidly surrounded the lifeless form of the shooter, and a policeman checked his pockets for ID. Moments later paramedics took him away. His brain was smeared across the seats around him.

It took hours to get injured students to hospitals by ambulance, remove the dead, clear the area, and begin to calm everyone down. Two of the victims died on the way to the hospital, which brought the student death toll to thirteen. It was a scene of carnage and grief, which, sadly, was not entirely unfamiliar in the world of campus violence today. It was an event that had happened before. All network programming was interrupted, with on-the-scene reports of the shooting at UCLA. Congressman Olden was listed as in critical condition, hovering between life and death from the wounds in his chest and neck, and he was in surgery at last report, while surgeons fought for his life.

Within an hour, the identity of the shooter was on

the air. He was a pre-law student who had dropped out the year before, and had a history of mental instability. He had evidenced signs of mental illness for a year before he left school. He had refused treatment while at UCLA and had previously been admitted to a psychiatric hospital while in high school. He had been reported in college for threatening an ex-girlfriend with a gun when she dated someone else, but he had never injured anyone before. He was nineteen, currently living in an apartment by himself, and working at a pawnshop, where he had bought the gun he had used that day. And his parents weren't reached for comment until later that afternoon. His mother was incoherent with grief as police led her from her home for questioning, and his father was reported to be away on a fishing trip. Neighbors, when asked to comment, said he was a nice boy, always polite, although a little strange. He was obsessed with computers, rarely left his place except for work, and seemed to have no friends. He had been a loner all his life. And the portrait of him painted by those who knew him, teachers, co-workers at the pawnshop, neighbors, all presented a classic image of a mentally disturbed boy who had somehow slipped through the cracks of treatment and run amok, killing sixteen people that day, including himself, and injuring seven others including the congressman. It was a wanton waste of life, and police believed that he had gone there to kill Pat Olden, for his stance on gun control, since he had been armed and taken a seat in the third row.

The campus was closed immediately, classes stopped as news got around, and crying students congregated everywhere, with their arms around each other, mourning lost friends.

Pat Olden's wife, already on a flight to Washington that morning, after the awards ceremony the night before, was told what had happened to her husband. She was on a chartered plane, which landed in Denver. Pat Olden was still in surgery but was not expected to survive, and his wife called their four children while on the ground before they headed back to L.A. Their oldest son, at USC, was already at the hospital, waiting outside surgery. He had been in class when he heard, and a friend at UCLA sent him a text even before it hit the news.

Everyone was in shock, and by late that afternoon, another of the victims had died from his wounds, a member of the university police. It was one of the worst shootings of its kind, compared to others in recent years, and events like it were precisely why Pat Olden was opposed to guns, readily available, and too often in the wrong hands in today's world. The boy in the blue shirt had proven him right, yet again.

Blaise McCarthy sat in her office at the network in New York, watching the images of crying, hysterical students, and the reruns of what had happened, from a video taken on someone's phone, which was a crazy jumble of visuals captured while the person who had recorded them hid under a seat at the back of the room. All you could really see was people running, and hear horrible screams and gunshots as the shooter took his victims down.

She was serious as she watched, when her assistant, Mark Spencer, walked into the room, with a stack of reports on the stories she was covering the next day. Blaise had been an anchor on morning news for years, but had moved on and had her own segment on the show now, to cover the most important aspects of the news. She did editorial pieces, and in-depth interviews of important famous people that were legendary. It was a long way from where she'd started, as a weather girl in Seattle, fresh out of college at twenty-two. Twenty-five years later, she had become the most famous woman ever to cover the news, and an icon in the business. And Mark had worked for her for ten years. He was a quiet, somewhat nervous man, who tried to anticipate her every thought and need, and had deep respect and affection for her. He was a perfectionist, who took pride in doing his job well. He loved her values, as well as her talent.

"You going out there?" he asked her, fully expecting that she would, but she surprised him and shook her head. Blaise had a mane of red hair, finely chiseled features, huge green eyes, and a famously cleft chin, all of which had been caricatured for years. She had a distinctive face, a great figure, and she looked easily ten years younger than her forty-seven years.

"There isn't enough for me to cover yet," she said

succinctly, with an unhappy look. Like Pat Olden, she was in favor of gun control, although she knew it would never happen. The lobby against gun control was one of the most powerful in the country, despite incidents like this. Blaise knew Pat Olden and liked him and his wife, and she was sorry to hear what had happened to him, and she knew he had young kids. And worse, Blaise always felt sickened by tragic incidents like this one, where so many innocent people got killed. It was so senseless. She hated the stories about mentally ill students who slipped through the cracks and then went on rampages. And afterward everyone cried about what they should have seen and should have done. But they didn't, and no one woke up until it was too late.

"It's all in the hands of local reporters," she explained to Mark, "and they're doing a good job. The kind of piece I'll do on it won't make sense until the dust settles a little, maybe in a few days. Besides, I have to go to London tomorrow night," she reminded him, which Mark knew well, since he had organized the trip for her, meticulously, as he always did. She was going to be interviewing the new British prime minister in two days, and an oil magnate in Dubai the day after. Blaise never stayed in one place for long. She had interviewed every head of state and royal on the planet, every major movie star, noteworthy criminals, politicians, and everyone worth knowing about all over the world, both in and out of the news. Her specials were remarkable and unique, and her editorial comments on her segment of the show every morning cut to the bone. Blaise McCarthy was beautiful, in an interesting way, and more than that, she was smart. She had character and guts, she had been to war zones and palaces, attended coronations and state funerals. Blaise McCarthy was simply one of a kind, and Mark knew that when she did the piece on the UCLA shooting, it would be more than just about a congressman and a number of students who'd been shot. It would be an important statement on the world today. Her coverage of 9/11 from Ground Zero had reduced everyone to tears each time it ran. She had won countless prizes and awards over the years. There was no subject she hadn't touched. The audiences loved her, and the ratings reflected that. Blaise McCarthy was the gold standard in her business, and thus far was untouched. No one dared argue with success, and although they sent up trial balloons from time to time, trying out a new face on the news, grooming them for her spot, they didn't even come close. But she was always aware that they might try to fill her shoes one day. She didn't like to think about it, but it happened in her business. And it could to her one day too, and she knew it.

She had no illusions about network news. It was a cutthroat world. And she knew that no matter how good she was, one day she'd be gone. But for now, for today, she was safe. It was a battle to stay on top that she fought every day. She was never afraid of hard work. She thrived on it. Part of her success was that she worked harder than anyone else. She always had, right from the beginning. Blaise had been in love with her work and her career, from the very first day. Aside from her early days right out of college at the local station as weather girl in Seattle, which had seemed frivolous and embarrassing to her, from then on, once she got to reporting news, first in Seattle when she got her first promotion, then when she moved to the affiliate in San Francisco two years later, and four years after that when she got her first really big break at network news in New York at twenty-eight, every step of the way had been exciting for her. Not a moment of it had been boring. And she had been willing to sacrifice anything and everything to keep her career moving forward, and to protect it once she got to the top. Blaise never took her eye off the ball. She was a genius at what she did, and what she chose to cover, the angles she saw, the subjects she interviewed. The choices she had made had made her who she was. Being as famous as she was had never been her goal, but excellence in everything she did was. Blaise had never slipped, not for a minute. The ratings had never stopped loving her, and even when changes at the network rocked the boat at times, Blaise had stayed solid. Unmovable, indefatigable. She had more energy than ten people half her age all put together. And at forty-seven, she looked great. In a business where youth and beauty were prized, people had long since stopped caring about her age, and lucky for her, she didn't look it. She took decent care of herself, but most of the time, all she thought about was work. She was tireless, and a great part of the year, she was on the road, interviewing important, famous, powerful, fascinating people, and doing what she did best.

Blaise glanced at the television behind where Mark was standing as he heard the announcer say that two more of the shooter's victims had just died. But Congressman Olden was still alive and remained in critical condition, still in surgery at Cedars Sinai L.A. while his family waited at the hospital. His other three children had come to L.A. that afternoon. And his wife, Rosemary Olden, and their four children were standing by in a private room the hospital had set aside for them.

The anchorman said that the bullet had gone through his neck and exited on the other side, fracturing several vertebrae. There was some speculation about whether he'd be paralyzed if he survived, but no one seemed to know. The bullet the shooter had shot into his chest had cost him a lung, but miraculously hadn't touched his heart. There was a slim chance he might survive.

Blaise looked somber as she put some research about the British prime minister in her briefcase and got ready to leave for the day.

"Salima called," Mark told her as Blaise stood up and grabbed her coat. Salima was Blaise's nineteen-year-old daughter. She had been away at school since she was eight. Blaise felt guilty about it at times, but they had a good relationship anyway. Salima was a kind, gentle girl, who was proud of her mother and respected the determined way she worked. Blaise couldn't be any other way. She loved her daughter, but she could never have been a full-time hands-on mother, and had never pretended to be, nor tried. Her assistant talked to her more often than Blaise. Mark loved her honesty about it. Blaise never tried to pretend she was something she wasn't. And her maternal instincts had never been as acute as her work ethic.

"How is she?" Blaise asked, with a worried look, referring to her daughter.

"She was very upset about the shooting at UCLA."

"Who isn't?" Blaise knew that her daughter shared her own concerns about violence on campuses and gun control. And Blaise was suddenly grateful that Salima attended a small community college in Massachusetts, and wasn't likely to be caught in a tragedy like the one at UCLA. "I'll try to call her tonight," but they both knew that she would only place the call after she finished her research for the segment the next day. It was how she operated, and Salima knew it about her too. Work always came first.

Blaise left her office then, and got into the town car waiting for her outside, provided by the network. It was in her contract, and she had had the same driver for years, a kind-hearted Jamaican man with a warm smile. He drove her to the office, and back, every day.

"Good evening, Tully," she said easily, as he turned to smile at her. He liked working for her, she was always reasonable and polite, never made crazy demands on him, and never acted like the star she was. She could have been a real monster, but she wasn't. She was thoughtful, hard-working, and modest. She was an avid sports fan, and they talked baseball scores in spring and summer, football in winter, basketball, or hockey. She was a rabid Rangers fan, and so was he.

"Evening, Miss McCarthy, I see you're going to London tomorrow. Going to interview the queen?" he teased her.

"No, just the prime minister." She smiled at him in the rearview mirror.

"I figured it was something like that." He loved driving her, and watching her on TV. They talked about the shooting at UCLA then. He was an intelligent man, and she was always interested in his point of view. And like everyone else, he had a lot to say about violence in the country today. He had two kids in college himself.

He dropped her off at her Fifth Avenue apartment twenty minutes later, and the doorman touched his hat as she walked in. She rode up to the penthouse, let herself into her apartment, and glanced into the refrigerator at the salad and sliced chicken the housekeeper had left for her. Blaise led a quiet life, and with the exception of important benefits, political or network events, she rarely went out and had few friends. She had no time to maintain friendships, and whenever she was home and not traveling, she worked. Friends didn't understand that, and eventually fell by the wayside. She had a few old friends left over from the early days but never saw them, and there hadn't been a man in her life in four years.

Her first big love had been her only one, when she was still in Seattle, where she had grown up. Her mother had been a schoolteacher, and her father a butcher. She had gone to City College, and they had led a simple life, and she had no siblings. There hadn't been much money growing up, and she never thought about it. She hadn't dreamed of success then, fame or riches, and had only thought of following her father's advice to work at something she loved. And she found that, once she started reporting the news. She was twenty-three years old then, and Bill was a cameraman, who spent most of his time on location, sent by the network. She was still doing weather then, her first job on TV. They fell madly in love, and she married him three months after she met him. He was the kindest man she'd ever known, they were crazy about each other, and he spent most of his time reporting from war zones. Six months later he was dead, shot by a sniper, and a part of her had died with him. From then on, all she had cared about was work. She took refuge in it, it grounded her, and gave her something to live for when Bill was gone. She had never loved any man that way again, and in time she realized that their relationship probably wouldn't have survived her career either. Her meteoric rise to success in the twenty-three years since then had pretty much precluded all else.

She met Harry Stern when she was working in San Francisco, two years after Bill's death. She interviewed him when he bought the local baseball team. He was twenty-two years older than she was, had already had four wives, and was one of the most important venture capitalists in Silicon Valley, and he had done everything possible to woo her, and was fascinated by how aloof she was. She told him she was too busy working to date. And she knew that her heart still belonged to Bill. Harry didn't care. He thought she was the smartest, most beautiful girl he'd ever met. It took him a year to convince her, wining, dining, and spoiling her every chance he got. There was no man more charming than Harry, and even now, at sixty-nine, he was just as handsome, and he and Blaise were good friends. He had had two wives since her, and had a fatal attraction to young girls.

Six months after they married, Blaise got her big break with the network in New York. It hadn't even been a debate for her, or a struggle to make the decision. She had told Harry from the beginning that her career came first. She had always been honest with him. She loved him, but she was never going to sacrifice an important opportunity for a man, and she hadn't. She had accepted the offer from the network while Harry was on a trip, and he came home to the news that Blaise was moving to New York. They were bicoastal from then on, and it worked for a time. She came home to his palatial house in Hillsborough on weekends, when she could get away. Or he flew to

New York. She got pregnant with Salima three months after moving to New York, and didn't slow down for a minute. She worked until the day Salima was born, left for the hospital from her office, and was back on air in three weeks. Harry flew in on his plane for the delivery, and just made it. But he already had five children from his previous wives, and never pretended to be an attentive father, and still wasn't. He saw Salima once or twice a year now and had had two more children since. He had eight in all, and he regarded it as the price he paid for marrying young women. They all wanted kids. He was happy to oblige them, and support them handsomely, but he was an absentee father at best. Salima had been disappointed by it when she was younger, but Blaise explained that it was just the way he was. And Blaise loved her daughter, but there were always a dozen projects and people vying for her time. Salima understood, it was how she had grown up, and she worshipped her mother.

The marriage to Harry had lasted five years after they became bicoastal, and then they both gave up. The relationship had dwindled to nothing by then, except for a warm friendship and occasional late-night calls between California and New York. There had been no hostility, no arguments, and they waited five more years to get divorced, when Harry wanted to get married again. Until then, he claimed that still being married to Blaise kept him out of trouble. Until he found a supermodel, who convinced him to get divorced and marry her. Blaise had gone to their wedding, and over the years she had wanted nothing from him, except child support for their daughter. They had been legally married for eleven years, but really only lived together full time as man and wife for less than one. And Blaise was thirty-eight when they got divorced.

Her relationships had been inconsistent from then on, as she flew around the world doing specials, and her career continued to climb. There had been a brief affair with a baseball star, which had been silly, they had nothing in common. A romance with a politician, which elicited considerable interest in the press. An important businessman, a famous actor. There was no one she cared about, and she never had time. The affairs would end, and they would move on to someone else before she even noticed. And she didn't care. They were window dressing in her life, and a distraction, and nothing more.

Her last affair, at forty-one, had been different. When Andrew Weyland took over as their news anchor, he was movie-star handsome and had every woman in the building going weak at the knees. As far as anyone knew, he was married, and Blaise had been the first one he told he was getting divorced. He asked her to keep it quiet, so it didn't wind up in the tabloids, and literally days after he shared that with her, he asked her out. She hesitated only for a minute, and although she wasn't immune to his looks either, what she loved best about him was how smart he was. Andrew was brilliant, funny, witty, he had a light touch about everything except love. And their relationship had rapidly grown intense. He was the most seductive, appealing, breathtaking man she had ever met. She fell head over heels in love with him, and when he proposed to her a year after they started dating, she said yes, without hesitation or regret. Even Salima loved him, he had a wonderful way with everyone, even kids. And with both of them in the same business, and dedicated to their careers, it seemed like the perfect match. He was kind and understanding, and even funny, about everything she did. Where other men had been annoyed by her intensity about her work, Andrew admired it, never complained about how busy she was, and gave her great advice.

Blaise knew, during the year she went out with him, that he still shared a house in Greenwich with his wife and children. He often went there on weekends to see his kids, and had reasonably explained that until the house sold, they were living separate lives under one roof. He had taken an apartment in the city, and most of the time, he stayed with her. And she was away a lot of the time anyway, so the weekends he spent in Greenwich with his children didn't bother her. She understood. And only once, when they started talking marriage, and she questioned him about the details of the divorce, and how advanced they were toward the final settlement, did she see a shadow cross his eyes. It was the first clue she had that something was amiss. The first of many. From there the truth unraveled slowly, a lie here, a small discovery there, like a surprise ball one gives to children, where the prizes fall out one by one. But in this case, they weren't prizes, they were lies.

Almost everyone at the network had long since figured out that Andrew wasn't getting a divorce, he was still very much married to his wife, who had no idea what he was up to with Blaise. In fact, she knew as little as Blaise, who had been so busy with work, and traveling so much, that it had never occurred to her to doubt him, or look beyond what he said. His explanation for not having seen a lawyer yet, when she discovered that no papers had been filed, was that they were only "inconsequential administrative details" he was planning to take care of but hadn't yet. There was no divorce. He was simply cheating on his wife and having an affair with Blaise. And while Blaise remained discreet about their relationship for over a year, so as not to jeopardize his "settlement," he was telling his wife that he was staying in town to work. He had the best of both worlds. The services of a detective told Blaise all she needed to know. Andrew was spending his weekends with his wife and children, and his weeks with her. His friends in Greenwich considered them a happy couple, and his wife had thought that he and Blaise were only friends at work.

"And how were you going to pull off getting married?" Blaise asked him when she learned the truth. "Tell her that you were going away for a weekend? Commit bigamy?" Blaise was heartbroken. Eventually someone talked, and it wound up in the tabloids, with photographs of his wife and children. Blaise got labeled a homewrecker and spent three months dodging the press while they stalked her outside her apartment and as soon as she left work. Andrew was a liar and a cheater. The relationship she had believed in and relied on was a total fraud. The man she loved and trusted didn't exist. She had opened up her heart and fallen hard, but Andrew had never planned to get divorced. He had conned her all along, and she had bought it hook, line, and sinker. She had believed him completely. It never dawned on her that he was lying, because she wouldn't have. And when Harry read about it, he called her to tell her how sorry he was. He knew she was a decent person, and it wasn't like her to go out with married men. When she ended the affair, she cried for months. She was devastated.

The whole affair had lasted sixteen months, and she had been so shaken by it that there had been no one since. She liked to say now that she was single by choice. She had no desire to risk her heart again. And worst of all, he still called. He had never apologized for the lies he told her, but he sent her e-mails and texts telling her how much he loved her, how much he missed her, but never how sorry he was. And he spent a good two years after she left him, trying to get her back into bed, knowing it would make her vulnerable to him again. She was smart enough not to fall for it. She still missed him, and what he had appeared to be, but she never believed his lies again. He still claimed that he and Mary Beth were about to get divorced, which was clearly a lie. And after her, she knew that he had cheated with several other women. Apparently, his wife was willing to forgive him anything. Blaise wasn't, and she only had one near slip when they wound up staying at the same hotel in London, and she agreed to have a drink with him. She had too much to drink on an empty stomach, and almost fell for the irresistible charm again. And at the last minute, she remembered who he really was and ran. She would never have admitted it to him, but she was lonely, and often thought of the good times they'd had, and something still stirred in her when she heard from him, wanting to believe that some part of it had been real. But in her more lucid moments, she knew that nothing was. Andrew Weyland was a liar to the core. It had been a relief when he had switched to another network and moved to L.A. And of course his wife and kids went with him. He claimed that after Blaise ended it with him, he no longer had the heart or the motivation to pursue a divorce. He made it sound as though his not getting divorced was her fault, which wasn't true either. Andrew lied as he breathed.

She still heard from him from time to time, and in the absence of anyone else in her life, sometimes she talked to him. He was familiar if nothing else, and she could always talk to him about the network. He was smart and funny, and she was at no risk of falling for him again. It was just nice to hear his voice no matter what he said. And foolish as she felt about it at times, he filled a void that no one else had since they broke up. And invariably she was depressed after they spoke.

She felt like a fool and a loser for falling for his lies during their affair. She'd been good enough to sleep with and cheat on his wife with, but nothing more. He had used her, just as he did everyone in his life. And it had been just bad enough, and painful enough, to make her shy away from getting involved with anyone again. Once again, as she always had before, she found refuge and solace in her work.

Blaise walked into her office at home and turned on the lights. She left her briefcase next to her desk, went to grab the salad in the kitchen, and brought it back to her desk to go over her research for the next day. It was exactly what she had asked for, and she was engrossed in it, as she planned her editorial for the morning segment. And by the time she glanced at her watch, it was ten o'clock. Too late to call Salima, since she always went to bed early, in her peaceful country life. Blaise felt guilty, as she walked into the kitchen to put her plate in the sink. She knew she should have called her and promised herself to call the next day before she left for London. Somehow there was just never enough time, except for work.

She stood thinking of her daughter, as she looked out at the view of Central Park. It was a beautiful apartment that she had bought nine years before, when she and Harry had finally gotten divorced, and given up their brownstone on East Seventy-fourth. The penthouse on Fifth Avenue suited her to perfection, a big spacious living room with a handsome view, her comfortable bedroom done in pale pink silk, the home office she spent most of her time in, a huge bathroom in white marble with an enormous tub, and a dressing room. There was a second bedroom down the hall from her suite, which was Salima's room, whenever she was home from school. There was a state-of-the-art black granite kitchen, with a dining room big enough to give dinner parties in, which she never did and never used, and behind the kitchen two maids' rooms, which had been unoccupied since she'd moved in. All she needed was a housekeeper to come daily—Blaise didn't want anyone living there with her. She was used to her solitude and privacy. She had been willing to give that up when she was planning to marry Andrew, and all of that seemed light-years away now. He had been out of her life, except for his random phone calls, for four years.

The apartment had been photographed by every major decorating magazine when she did it. And nine years later it looked just as perfect and pristine. She was hardly ever there. Blaise lived in a seemingly perfect world, in comfort and luxury, far from the simple life that had begun in Seattle. She was famous, celebrated, successful in a competitive milieu, where few people lasted, and careers usually ended early. But by sheer grit and talent and perseverance, Blaise had risen to the summit and stayed on top. It was an enviable life, one that others longed for and dreamed of, and would have snatched from her if they could.

What they didn't see was the solitude, the loneliness, the private moments devoid of people to love and support her. They had never felt the betrayals she had lived, at the hands of men like Andrew Weyland, or the false friends who had fallen by the wayside, the people who had wanted to ride on her coattails or use her in some way. It was in fact a lonely life, and she smiled when she went back to her desk, and glanced at a magazine Mark had marked for her and slipped into her briefcase. It was a brief profile of her in some magazine that had done a puff piece on her. Above a photograph of her they had gotten from the network was the heading in bold letters: A Perfect Life. And that's what it appeared to be. Only Blaise herself knew different. It was no more perfect than anyone else's life, and in many ways it was harder. Every day was a constant fight so as not to lose what she had, or the ground she had fought so hard to gain. She was alone on the mountaintop, and had been in hotel rooms all over the planet, sick in places no one would want to go even if they were well. And she spent her life getting on and off planes. No one really knew what went with the life they envied, or the price she'd paid. It was far from a perfect life, as Blaise knew only too well, but no matter how hard or how solitary, Blaise wouldn't have traded her life for anything in the world.

Chapter 2

The alarm went off at four o'clock, just as it did every morning. Without opening her eyes, Blaise reached her hand out and turned it off. She lay there with her eyes closed for a few minutes and forced herself to get up. It was still dark outside, and on Fifth Avenue, you could already hear the rumble of cars and trucks. She loved knowing that New York never fully slept. There was always someone awake. She found that comforting as she walked into her bathroom, pulled up her bright red hair, and held it with an elastic so she wouldn't get it wet. She had washed it, as she always did, the night before. The hairdresser on the set would do it when she arrived, and the makeup artist she always used did her makeup every morning, as she took a last look at her research.

She slipped into the enormous bathtub with the view of the park, and sat relaxing for a few minutes in the warm water, before she had to rev up her engines and start the day. This was usually the last moment of peace she had, and that night she would be on a plane.

At a quarter to five, she was in the kitchen, and put on water for tea. She went to the front door and got the newspapers. She always tried to get a good look at *The New York Times* and *Wall Street Journal* before she went to work. And then she checked online for anything that might have happened since. Anything even more recent than that would show up on her desk at work before the morning news, and Mark would make sure that she saw it if it was breaking news.

The shooting at UCLA was on the front page, and she saw as she read it that Pat Olden was still alive. The article said that he was on a respirator, clinging to life by a thread. She couldn't help wondering, if Pat survived, how severely he would be impaired. It seemed inevitable that wounds like the ones he had sustained would take a serious toll. And she wondered how his wife and children were. The shooting was going to be the main focus of her morning editorial, followed by a financial piece that she had carefully researched about a recent upturn in the stock market and what it meant.

She ate a single piece of whole wheat toast, along with her tea. It was too early to eat anything else. And there was fruit and a spread of breakfast food she didn't eat when she got to work. There was always food for the on-air talent, and for the guests on morning shows. But Blaise was restrained about what she ate. She had worn a dark blue blazer, and white silk shirt, gray slacks, and high-heeled shoes. She liked a more casual look when she did the morning news. She saved her more fashionable clothes for her interviews and specials. She had already picked a good-looking black suit to wear for her interview with the British prime minister in London the following day. She had packed the night before, and her two small bags were in the front hall. She was going to pick them up after work when she came home to change. When she took overnight flights, she wore slacks and comfortable clothes. It was all routine to her.

It was twenty to six by the time she finished reading both papers. She went to brush her hair, made sure her outfit looked right, picked up her handbag and briefcase, put on a coat, and at five minutes to six she was downstairs. Tully was already waiting for her, and he smiled broadly when she got in.

"Morning, Miss McCarthy. Did you sleep well?" he asked.

"Yes, thank you, I did. How about you?"

"Pretty good. I stayed up too late, watching one of those old films." He told her it was *Casablanca,* and they both agreed it was a good one. And until recently, when the season ended, baseball had been their main topic. Blaise was an ardent Yankees fan, and so was Tully. She gave him baseball tickets whenever she could, and Tully loved it. She had even gotten him tickets to the World Series.

He dropped her off at the network a few minutes later. There was no traffic at that hour, and it was a straight shot downtown. And by six-twenty she was in her office. Mark was waiting for her with the highlights for the morning news. She glanced over them and saw with relief that Pat Olden hadn't died. If he had, Blaise would have dedicated the segment to eulogizing him, and she was prepared for that too, just in case. But with the incident at UCLA, the main theme of her editorial that morning was about violence on college campuses, and untreated mental illness. There had been too many incidents recently like the one at UCLA the day before, with students who had been identified as mentally ill earlier and managed to shun treatment, with dire results later on. It was both tragic and frustrating when it happened. She put the finishing touches on her editorial and left for hair and makeup, where she spent forty minutes under bright lights getting camera-ready and bantering with the two women she saw every morning. Both women were young and had small kids at home. Once in a while they asked about Salima, and she said she was fine. Blaise was very private about her daughter. She asked about their children too, and as always, she looked terrific when they finished.

She was ready at seven-fifteen, and at her desk on the set at seven-twenty, looking competent and serene, and like a woman in control of every situation. Blaise McCarthy was every inch a star. She was serious as she went on the air, as soon as she got the signal, and then smiled, wishing her viewers a good morning.

"I know we are all shocked around the country, at

the tragedy at UCLA yesterday, and I would like to express our sorrow and deep sympathy to the families of the victims of the shooting. And it's even more distressing to note that this is a theme we've all heard before. A troubled young man, exhibiting signs of mental illness, who then falls through the cracks of whatever system, and manages to avoid treatment. And then suddenly, tragedy occurs. I would like to ask each of our universities what they are doing to prevent situations like this from happening again. How can we protect other students from mentally ill students among them? What can we do to insist on treatment, for their sakes as well? What are we doing about better security? Why was there no metal detector at the door to the auditorium at UCLA yesterday, and if there was, what did they miss? The shooter was armed when he walked in. Which of course brings us to how I feel about gun control, and many of us do.

"I honestly believe that those who are against it are misusing our Constitution to support their position. This isn't a matter of civil liberties, but of keeping our citizens safe. Freedom of speech will not kill you. The right to bear arms will. We need to make that distinction and not be afraid to limit rights that once made sense but no longer do. If you doubt it, take a good look at what happened yesterday, at what happened to Pat Olden, what his life will be like now, if he recovers, and the life of his wife and kids. Yesterday countless lives were forever changed. Not just the people who were killed and injured, but their families, their loved ones. We can't let this happen again, and again, and again. And above all, we must find a way to treat mentally ill students, once identified, and not let them slip through the cracks in our system. We owe them more than that, and the people they may ultimately injure. And yesterday proves once again that what we are doing now is not working. We need better fail-safe systems for treatment in place."

There was a moment's pause as she let her message sink in, and then she went on to discuss the stock market upturn, which had been worrying many knowledgeable people on Wall Street. Was it happening too fast and too soon after a recent slump, and what did it mean? Blaise put forward several theories that were quoted from experts. She always touched on a variety of timely topics. She had a full twenty minutes on the air, and then with a slow smile, which they showed in close-up, she looked into the camera and wished everyone a good day. You had the feeling when she said it that she was speaking just to you. The piercing green eyes looked straight at the viewers, and she spoke to each of them, and then they cut to commercial as she took off her mike, stood up, and left the set. Several of the producers told her the segment was very good. She had made her point on all the relevant issues in a provocative and practical way, not to panic viewers but to inform them and encourage them to think. She had touched on violence, mental illness, and Wall Street that morning, all key issues in the news. Blaise's pieces and editorials were always interesting and geared to both women and men. They were intelligent, but she also respected her viewers and gave them credit for having a brain. Her comments were aimed at anyone who was willing to think. And her interviews and specials were even better, because the choices she made of interview subjects were so good, and the questions she asked, gently but probingly, were on topics everyone wanted to hear. And she made her viewers feel they were right in the room with her. She had a knack for making her subjects relax and open up. She had an easy style and wasn't afraid to make them laugh. It put everyone at ease, and she got a lot more out of them that way. And then she'd move in on some controversial angle and pin them down. She wasn't just good at what she did, she was great.

"Good job," Charlie Owens, the executive producer, said as he whizzed by Blaise on the way to a meeting, as Blaise headed to her office to check her e-mail and the research for the interview with the prime minister for a last time. And when she did, it was all there. She spent the rest of the day working on an interview she would do in Dubai, and requested more research right up till the last minute before she left. She was meticulous and thorough, which were among the many reasons why both network and viewers loved her.

"Do you have everything you wanted?" Mark asked as she put the last file in her briefcase.

"I'm all set," she said as she put on her coat and smiled at him. He was as detail-oriented as she was, which was why they got along. He didn't find her annoying, he thought she was brilliant. It was six o'clock. It had been a long day, the usual twelve hours, which seemed normal to her. Mark worked overtime every day, and was happy to do so. "See you in three days," she said, smiling at him. "I'll call you if anything comes up." They were using a British cameraman for the interview with the prime minister, and he was flying to Dubai with her, with a soundman and crew, for the interview there.

"Try to sleep on the plane," Mark said with a solicitous look. He worried about her. She pushed herself too hard, harder than anyone he knew, but she seemed to thrive on it. The more she worked, the more energy she had. She had noticed it too. It was one of the secrets of her success, that and the fact that she didn't need much sleep. When people scolded her for how little sleep she got, she always reminded them that Margaret Thatcher had slept three hours a night, which shut them up. She loved doing what she wanted and staying up late at night, which was one of the reasons she liked living alone, and said she was "single by choice." And by now, she was convinced that was true. She was lonely at times, but she didn't want a relationship anymore. Occasionally, she missed having someone to talk to at night, particularly if something good happened at the office, or something very bad. But other than that, she was fine.

"I always sleep on the plane," she reminded Mark. "In fact, it's harder to stay awake." The flight from

New York to London was seven hours, and she had to be fresh the next day so she would be sure to sleep for most of the flight. She was meeting with the prime minister three hours after she landed, just enough time to go to the hotel, bathe and dress, and be at 10 Downing Street for the interview. There wasn't a minute to spare.

"Don't forget to eat," he admonished her, knowing that she often did. Blaise ate and slept little when she was excited about a project.

She waved at Mark as she headed for the elevator, grateful for all his help before she left. He was incredibly efficient. Traffic was heavy, and it took her forty-five minutes to get home, unlike the morning. She closed her eyes and leaned her head back against the seat, as Tully expertly threaded his way through the other cars, and she thanked him when she got home. "See you at eight-thirty," she reminded him. She had to be at the airport at nine-thirty, for an eleven-thirty international flight.

"I'll be here," he promised, and she went upstairs to the silent apartment, turned on the lights, and glanced at the park. It was nearly seven, and she wanted to shower and change, and have something to eat. She wanted to call Salima before she left, but she knew Salima would be having dinner then, so she waited till after her bath. Salima answered the phone on the first ring. An electronic ID system told her who was calling by voice, so she could hear it anywhere in the room and know who was on the line. She beamed the moment she heard it was her mother, and bounded across the room to pick up the phone.

"Hi, Mom," Salima said, sounding happy. Much to Blaise's amazement, there was never a tone of reproach in her voice for the many times her mother hadn't called, only pleasure when she did.

"Hi, sweetheart. What have you been up to?" Blaise said, smiling when she heard her.

"Just school," Salima said, sounding even younger than she was. And the timbre of her voice was very much like her mother's. People often got them confused on the phone when she was home for vacation. "Are you going to L.A.?" She was hoping her mother would do more on the UCLA story, but Blaise still felt it wasn't ripe for her. It wasn't time for an on-location editorial, only news. She had an unfailing instinct for that, for doing a story at the right time. And she knew this was premature for her.

"No, I'm going to London tonight, to interview the new prime minister."

"That's cool." She sounded disappointed. She thought that the UCLA piece was better, and the piece on the prime minister seemed dull to her.

"And I'm going to Dubai tomorrow night, to interview a Saudi prince who is a major oil company executive. He's supposed to be a very interesting guy. There's a rumor that his brother is a terrorist, but no one knows for sure."

"Are you going to ask him?" Salima loved the idea and laughed at the thought.

"Probably. I'll see how it goes. I'll be back after that. I'll just be gone for three days."

"I'm fine, Mom," Salima reassured her. It was she who always reassured Blaise, not the reverse.

"I'll come see you when I get back. How's school?"

"Boring. I'm trying to get all my required classes out of the way. They're awful. I only have one elective this term."

"What is it?"

"History of Italian Renaissance music," she said, sounding delighted, and her mother groaned.

"Oh my God, now *that* sounds awful. I'd rather take math," Blaise said with feeling, and Salima laughed.

"I love it. And the music is gorgeous. I keep humming it when I get home."

"Only you," Blaise said, smiling. Salima loved to sing and could sing almost anything. She had a beautiful voice, and an incredible memory for music. It was a gift she'd had even as a child.

They chatted for half an hour, about the school shooting, her other classes, some gossip she'd heard about two of the teachers at her school having an affair. She didn't know who, and there were rumors like it from time to time, but it was always intriguing to hear. Her source had been vague. Salima was easy to talk to, and it made Blaise feel guilty again, talking to her, thinking she should call her more often. But Salima was busy with her own life, and always in good spirits. She was very independent and didn't sit around waiting to hear from her mother. And Blaise had always been busy. Salima was used to it.

"I'll call you as soon as I get back," Blaise promised. "I'll try to come up this weekend."

"I'm fine, Mom," she told her again. "Don't come up if you're too tired after the trip."

"We'll see." She loved visiting her at that time of year anyway. The turning of the leaves in New England always thrilled her. But it was a bigger thrill to see her daughter. Even though she didn't see enough of her, Blaise loved her. And Salima understood the priorities that governed her mother's life.

"Fly safe," Salima said as they hung up, and Blaise sat thinking of her for a minute, and then went to get dressed. She had just enough time to grab something out of the fridge and make her flight.

Tully was waiting for her when she got downstairs. He looked a lot more tired than Blaise, whose day had been just as long, and she had been busier. And she was quiet on the way to the airport, thinking of Salima again. She was determined to go to Massachusetts now on the weekend. She hadn't seen her in a month, since Labor Day weekend, right before school started. It was time for a visit. She tried to get up to see her once a month, or if she was traveling a lot, every six or eight weeks. Sometimes it was the best she could do. It was always fine with Salima, she made that clear to her mother. She was nineteen now after all, not a baby. But even when she had first gone away to school, she had been very brave about it, and never begged her mother to visit or take her out of school. She was just happy when Blaise came to see her. She was completely undemanding. It would have been easier for Blaise if Harry visited her occasionally too, but he rarely did. Only Blaise. He was a good man, but a lousy father. Once Salima went away to school at eight, he hardly saw her, and they had no relationship to speak of now, and never had.

Two officials from British Air met Blaise at the airport and escorted her to a private VIP room, where they let her relax until it was time to board the flight. According to her preference, she was the last one to get on the plane, in first class, and there was a small stir as she walked down the aisle and people recognized her. There was almost no one in the world who didn't know who Blaise McCarthy was, and she was easy to spot with her distinctive looks and bright red hair.

The two airline officials left her at her seat, and the purser on the flight took over, offering her magazines, newspapers, and champagne, and she declined all of it politely, and took out her research, to prepare for the interview the next day. She had brought her own cashmere blanket and a small pillow and continued reading after they took off. She declined the meal, but asked for a cup of tea. She didn't like eating on late-night flights, and never understood how people could, but she supposed that people felt they had paid for it and wanted their money's worth. Blaise preferred sleep to indigestion. And when she finished reading, she turned off her light, had the steward turn her seat into a bed, which was why she traveled first class, put on a sleep mask, and was asleep in five minutes, with her cashmere blanket around her. She had asked them to wake her up, half an hour before they landed, so she could brush her teeth and comb her hair and have a cup of tea before the descent. She was being met by a VIP escort from British Air and airport security to get her through customs quickly. She had no time to waste, and the driver from Claridge's would be at the airport. She glanced out at the British countryside as she drank her tea. And it all went like clockwork when they landed.

She was in the car from Claridge's within twenty minutes, and at the hotel forty-five minutes later. She had an hour to bathe and dress, send e-mails, make some notes, and get to Downing Street for the interview. The cameraman was meeting her there. And as soon as she checked into the hotel, they took her to the familiar suite she always requested. It had pale yellow walls and flowered chintz furniture, and looked like a guest room in an English country home to Blaise, and she loved it. She ate a quick breakfast, although it was lunchtime in London by then, but she never suffered from jet lag, which made traveling easy for her. She looked fresh as the proverbial daisy when she arrived at Downing Street, where the cameraman and crew were waiting in a van with all their equipment. He had identified himself to the guards outside, and they were expecting Blaise.

Three secretaries helped them set up in a pretty

sitting room, and by the time the prime minister joined them, promptly and on schedule, they were ready, and Blaise glided into the interview with ease. She found the prime minister extremely astute and charming and very witty. He fielded her questions nicely with a twinkle in his eye, and answered fully those he liked better. It was an excellent game of verbal Ping-Pong, and they were evenly matched. He liked her, had been looking forward to meeting her, and he had been told she was a very clever woman, and he wasn't disappointed. But he answered enough questions in depth, and with seeming sincerity and candor, that the interview was a success for her. She had gotten what she came for, a glimpse behind the mask of the new prime minister. The interview felt warm and personal, and she had put him at ease. And he enjoyed her enough, and admired her, to answer questions he might not have otherwise, which was what always happened with her subjects. And when he asked her what she was doing next, when the camera was no longer rolling, she told him about the interview in Dubai the next day, and he grinned broadly.

"Now that's an interview I'd like to see. He's a much more interesting subject."

"More controversial perhaps," Blaise said with a gleam in her own eye, "but surely not as interesting, or charming." She thanked him for the interview then, wished him luck in his endeavors, and they both walked away feeling they had made a friend, which happened to her often. Blaise was very good at what she did, and all her subjects, the men anyway, fell just a little bit in love with her. She came to life on camera as she did nowhere else. And she went back to the hotel, pleased with the interview, and knowing Charlie would be delighted. The prime minister had been an excellent subject.

She had just enough time at the hotel to change her clothes again, put on something more comfortable, relax for a few hours, take a walk down New Bond Street in the crisp October air, order a quick meal when she got back to the hotel, and leave for the airport again, for the flight to Dubai. It was almost the same length as the flight the night before from New York to London, about forty-five minutes shorter, and she was planning to sleep so she'd be fresh when she arrived. She couldn't afford to be slow or sluggish or dull-witted for the Saudi prince. He was known to be sly and adept at avoiding key questions. She knew she'd have to be at her best for him, and she went to sleep the moment she got on the plane. And as she requested, they woke her up right before they landed.

There was VIP escort service for her again, a Rolls-Royce Phantom limousine with a liveried driver, and she was taken to the Burj al Arab Hotel. She only stayed at the best hotels when she traveled, particularly in foreign cities, which was in her contract. And they had to provide her limousines everywhere. She had been doing this for twenty-five years, and she had earned it. She took it for granted now, as part of the landscape for her.

She had been to Dubai before, and she was impressed to see that they had put up even more modern structures since the last time she'd been there, and the hotel where she was staying looked palatial. The suite they gave her was one of the largest and most opulent she'd ever seen, and she had her own butler. There was a helipad for arriving guests. Her interview was scheduled for nine o'clock that night, and she took the opportunity to take a drive around the city with her driver in the Rolls, while he pointed out the sights to her, and it was very impressive, although it was a place she wouldn't have chosen to come to on her own. But in the context she was seeing it, as a location for an interview, she found it fascinating. And when she got back to her hotel, she had new questions in mind to ask him. She knew that her subject normally lived in Riyadh, but due to the restrictions on women in his city, he had agreed to meet her in Dubai, when he had to go there on business. It was the most liberal of the Arab cities.

She wore a long sleeved, high-necked, somber but chic black dress as she waited for him to come to her suite, in the living room, where the cameras had been set up. And she looked respectful and subdued, as was fitting. He was actually younger than she was, and she knew he had a somewhat racy reputation when he traveled, with a keen eye for young women, but she had a feeling that he would be more circumspect here, and with her.

Blaise wasn't disappointed when she met Mohamed bin Sabur. He came to her suite in an exquisitely cut

English suit, made by his tailor in London, and impeccably shined John Lobb shoes from Paris. He was dark and had jet-black hair and a mustache, and he was one of the handsomest men she had ever seen. He was thirty-five years old and looked younger, and if she had been less serious about her work, she would have been tempted to flirt with him. Instead they sparred for two hours in the interview. He was clever and amusing and had a great sense of humor. He had been schooled in England.

For the first hour he dodged most of her questions, but she had anticipated that and had saved the important ones for later, hoping to wear him down and surprise him. And she even dared to ask him about his brother, the alleged terrorist, and he laughed out loud when she asked the question.

"What an interesting reputation my brother has," he said easily, without embarrassment. "The only one he terrorizes is me. He beat me up regularly when we were boys, quite mercilessly. And now he charms away all my women. He's a devilishly handsome man." He had slipped right through her question with ease.

"So are you," Blaise said with the smile that she had been famous for since her youth in television. She was an even match for him.

"Thank you, Miss McCarthy." She asked him several more pointed questions then, about oil in the Middle East, and his business in the United States. He answered cautiously but seemed to be sincere, to a point. He was no fool, and he told her nothing he didn't want said on TV. He was just guarded enough, and just open enough, to make the interview fascinating to their viewers. And he was an incredibly seductive man, with an air of mystery about him. And from his playful answer, she surmised that his brother probably was exactly what was said about him, a terrorist of some kind, but she knew enough not to press the point. And she drew the interview to an elegant close. He bowed when it was over, and thanked her, and then surprised her totally by pulling a small box out of his pocket and handing her a gift. She was stunned. No interview subject had ever done that before, although a few had sent presents to her afterward, but it was rare, except when they established genuine friendships. This, she knew, was just part of his charm. She opened it while he watched her, and found a gold bangle bracelet from Cartier with small diamond studs on it. It was an extremely generous gift from a very handsome man, and she was touched and flattered.

"Thank you for a most enjoyable evening," he said to her. "I was wondering if you would be kind enough to join me for dinner?" She hadn't expected that either, but Blaise had always been adventuresome, and she accepted without hesitation, and he was pleased. It was nearly midnight, but they were both exhilarated by the interview and wide awake.

He took her to one of the finest restaurants in Dubai, Pierre Gagnair's Riflets, in his Ferrari, and she felt totally at ease with him. Whatever his reputation with women, he was also very much a gentleman, and extremely sophisticated and civilized. He spent considerable time in Paris and London every month, with frequent trips to New York on business. She had fun with him. He seemed very taken with her, and she was intrigued by him. She had a strong sense that whatever she was seeing was what he wanted to show her, and who he really was remained well hidden. But what she did see was entirely likable. She wore his bracelet on her wrist all evening, and when she thanked him sincerely for both the gift and the evening, he thanked her for the interview again. She promised to send it to him on a DVD after it ran, and she hoped he'd be pleased.

"May I call you when I'm next in New York?" he asked politely, and she smiled at him.

"I'd like that very much," she said warmly, but she was sure he never would. She wasn't nearly racy enough for him, and it was unlikely that they'd become friends. But he had made her brief stay in Dubai a lot more fun, and she had a sense of adventure as she went back to her suite, and looked at the bracelet again. She wrote him a note of heartfelt thanks to send the next morning before she left. He had been generous and cooperative and kind, as well as interesting as a subject. Her trip to Dubai to interview him had been well worth it, and a total success, which wasn't always the case.

She sent what they had to Charlie by computer, and he called her two hours later.

"My God, Blaise, what did you do to the guy? You had him eating out of the palm of your hand." It was even better than he had hoped. Bin Sabur had looked completely smitten with Blaise.

"Not exactly, and I'm not sure how honest he was with me. Like about his brother, and on a number of other subjects, but he gave a great interview."

"You *got* a great interview out of him. He didn't just sit there and spill his guts, you pulled it out of him like silk scarves out of a magician's hat. Lady, you are good."

"Thank you," she said, smiling at the compliment, and even she had to admit it had gone well. She was anxious to see it for herself. "He gave me a diamond bracelet too, from Cartier," she said with a giggle.

"Did you sleep with him?" Charlie sounded shocked, and worried. He didn't want her getting arrested for something she shouldn't do, but Blaise was too smart for that.

"Of course not. It was a gift to thank me for the interview, when it was over. He's actually a nice guy, and very flirtatious. I let him take me to dinner. And after that I came back to my room."

"Well, lock your door in case he shows up tonight. He looked like he wanted more on the feed I just saw. Guys don't give diamond bracelets for nothing."

"Guys in the States expect to get laid if they feed you dinner. At least here they hand out diamond bracelets. It's a better deal," she teased, but she was in good spirits. She had had fun with him, and he made her feel young and sexy again. Not having a man in her life for four years since Andrew made her feel as though she were no longer a woman at times, and wonder if she ever would be again.

"Just be careful until you leave. I don't want to have to get you out of jail, if you break any laws. Or look for you in Riyadh if he kidnaps you."

"He won't. He admitted on camera tonight that he has three wives, and I'm older than he is, by about ten years."

"So? That didn't seem to be slowing him down, neither your age nor his wives. Besides, I think they're allowed three or four, or five."

"Don't worry, Charlie, I'll be home tomorrow. And this was good for him too. It gives him great PR in the States. It was a win-win for us both, and I got a diamond bracelet on top of it. I'd say Dubai was a success."

"Just get your ass home. I'll feel better when you're back in New York." She would too, but she had enjoyed it and was pleased it had gone well. As it often was in the life she led, interviewing fascinating subjects, it was more than just work. Sometimes it was magic, when it clicked. And it had. Perfectly.

She didn't hear from Mohamed bin Sabur again before she left, and she left her thank you note to him at the front desk to be delivered to his hotel, and she caught her flight back to New York. She felt a little bit like Cinderella after the ball. But instead of losing a slipper, she had a beautiful Cartier bracelet on her wrist and smiled every time she looked at it on the way home. She arrived in New York after the fourteen-and-a-half-hour flight, and she was back in her apartment three days after she had left. And both interviews looked fantastic when she saw them at work the next day. All of her producers were thrilled. It had gone particularly well. And Charlie made sure he checked out the bracelet when he saw her and looked impressed.

"I'll bet you hear from him when he's in New York."

"I doubt it. Saudi men just give very generous gifts. Believe me, it doesn't mean a thing."

"I gave my wife a Cuisinart for our tenth anniversary," Charlie said, looking at her. "I didn't give her a bracelet like that." She laughed.

"That's why I'm not married anymore. I'd rather buy my own Cuisinart. You're not supposed to give household appliances, Charlie, after ten years."

"She likes to cook," he said, looking miffed.

Blaise's first day back went well, but the time differences caught up with her that night. She went to bed at eight o'clock and fell asleep in five minutes, and she was up at five the next morning, in time to see the sun rise, as she went over some research for interviews she was doing the following week. She was still thinking about going to California to cover the UCLA shooting, but the story seemed a little cold now. Pat Olden was still in a coma, and the doctors were no longer sure he'd come out of it, nor what his brain function would be if he did. It was tragic but not necessarily newsworthy anymore, it was just sad.

And as she sat in her kitchen reading the newspaper online at seven, she thought of visiting Salima at school. She had said she might, and she wanted to see her.

She had no plans for the weekend and she had the time. She looked at her watch and decided to do it. She was wide awake for the three-hour drive to Springfield, Massachusetts. She could be there by ten o'clock that morning, spend the day with Salima, and come home that night, which was what she usually did. There was a bed and breakfast near the school, where Blaise occasionally spent the night, but she preferred coming home to her own bed, and Salima didn't mind. They packed so much talking and hugging into a day's time that one day together seemed like enough to sustain both of them until Blaise came up again.

She showered and dressed, got her car keys out of her desk, and called the garage to get her car ready. She only used it occasionally on weekends, and to go out to the Hamptons in the summer. Mostly she used it to visit Salima. She was smiling as she left the building. It was a beautiful sunny day, and it had been warm when she got back to New York the day before, in typical Indian summer fashion. She loved this time of year in New York. She could hardly wait to see her, and it was always a pretty trip. She was feeling happy all the way to the garage, and as she started her car, she noticed the diamond bangle on her wrist again from the handsome Saudi man she had met in Dubai. She remembered what they said about her then, that she led a perfect life. And for once, she had to agree. It really was.

Chapter 3

The drive to Springfield was peaceful and beautiful, and by the time she took the turnoff, three hours after she'd left New York, she felt happy and relaxed. Coming here was like going on vacation. It was another world, far from the stresses of New York. And when she came to visit her, she focused on Salima and nothing else.

She saw the familiar landmarks on the road to Caldwell School, where Salima had spent the last eleven years, and she noticed a new house that had been built, and a church that had been restored. But essentially, nothing ever changed here. Most of the houses had been built a century before. And Blaise turned into the driveway with a sigh, anxious to see Salima. The students lived in cottages of three or four, with a monitor living with them, since they were younger than Salima. The seniors were in two-person cottages. And Salima had the only single small house on the grounds. Blaise had encouraged her to stay on after she graduated. She went to a community college nearby and was driven there every day. Salima came home for vacations, but Blaise felt it was a better life for her here, and Salima agreed. She didn't want to live in New York anymore. She wanted to stay in the quiet rural community that had been home to her for eleven years. Blaise was hoping she'd stay through college. She was a sophomore now, and the community college she attended was small. It wasn't challenging enough for her, but it was easy for her to manage. She had considered going to Dartmouth, but didn't want to live in the dorms. And going to a community college, she could stay at Caldwell. She liked having her own cottage here, and she was getting straight A's at school, which looked good if she ever transferred. She had gotten great grades and was a diligent student at every age.

Blaise drove straight to Salima's house, at the back of the property with beautiful trees all around it, that were all turning scarlet. In summer, everything was a lush green. And Blaise had made a contribution that had allowed them to build an Olympic-size swimming pool years before. Salima was an outstanding swimmer, and had been on the swimming team all through high school, although she couldn't compete anymore now that she was in college. But she was greatly loved at the school where she had been for so long. The younger students looked up to her, and the teachers were very kind to her. Abby, the monitor who lived with her, had been assigned to Salima for five years, now they were best friends. Abby was thirty-six years old, but living in the protected environment of the womblike school, she still acted and looked like a young girl. She wore pigtails most of the time, and she adored Salima.

Blaise stopped her car in the little parking area nearby, and walked down the well-tended path to the cottage. She could hear Salima's voice when she reached the door. She was singing, and the door was open, as Blaise quietly walked in, and saw Salima with her back to her in the living room. She and Abby were laughing at something while Salima tried to sing and finally collapsed, laughing, on the couch. She still hadn't heard anyone come in, and Blaise took three steps across the old beams of the floor in the front hall, and the moment she did, Salima's head turned.

"Mom?" She knew her step anywhere, and always recognized it the moment Blaise walked in. "Mom!" she said then, sure of it, and dashed across the living room to the hall, as Blaise smiled widely at her and held out her arms, knowing Salima would be in them in seconds.

"I missed you too much. I had to come up today," Blaise said, as Salima threw herself into her mother's arms and nearly knocked her down, and then spun her around. Abby watched them with a warm smile, and Blaise waved at her with a free hand. Salima looked as beautiful as ever, with features identical to her mother's, down to the cleft chin. The only difference was her dark brown hair, which she wore long. She turned her face toward her mother's, and felt her face. She felt the tears Blaise always shed when she first saw her. "You're crying! Have I gotten uglier since last time?" Salima teased.

"Totally. It makes me cry just looking at you," Blaise said with a smile.

"Then I'm glad I don't have to see it," Salima said, joking with her, as they walked into the living room together, with Blaise's arm around her waist as Salima leaned close to her, and then flopped down on the couch. She knew exactly where things were. Everything in the cottage was familiar to her, and she had no trouble getting around. She was blind.

She had been diagnosed with type 1 diabetes when she was three years old, which had been the heartbreak of Blaise's life. Her perfect baby had a severe case of juvenile diabetes, which could only be treated with insulin. And at first Salima had cried at every shot, and prick of her finger to check her insulin levels. They had eventually gotten her a pump, but she still had to be closely monitored. The pump kept her insulin levels at safe ranges for her, delivering the insulin over twenty-four hours through a catheter under the skin. And they clipped the pump itself to the waistband of her skirt or jeans. It had always worked well for her.

Her eyes had been affected by the time she was six, which they had been told was unusually early. She was too young to lose her sight, the doctors had assured Harry and Blaise. When she was seven, she could still see partially, when her retinas detached, and by eight she was fully blind. They had tried to keep her at home, but Harry lived in Los Angeles, and Blaise traveled all the time. She didn't trust the caretakers they had with her, she was never sure they were monitoring her properly. And Blaise had had to face the decision of giving up her career to take care of Salima full time, or place her in a school for the blind where they were better equipped to supervise her, monitor her medically, and keep her safe. Her diabetes had to be carefully managed. There was a full medical staff at her school. And they had decided to try it for six months. Salima had loved it from the moment she got there and felt at home with other children like her. She didn't feel different anymore, she had friends to play with all the time, and Blaise could relax, knowing that she was impeccably cared for.

Blaise had continued working, and at the end of six months, it was clear that Caldwell was better for Salima, so much so that eleven years later, she had made the decision to stay on after graduation. She couldn't imagine living anywhere else anymore. Sometimes Blaise felt guilty knowing what a secluded life she led, and wondering if she needed more, but Salima was so happy here that Blaise didn't have the heart to bring her back to live in New York, with all the risks it presented for her. And Abby wouldn't have come with her. She had a mother who had been in poor health for years, and she wanted to stay nearby. So Salima had stayed on, and Abby went to the community college with her every day. Blaise had given her a car, and Salima was free to come and go. She had resident status now, and was no longer subject to all the rules that applied to the younger children there. And most of the teachers were her friends, but Abby was more like an older sister to her, or a mother. Thinking that always hurt Blaise a little, but Abby was so much better for her, and did everything Salima needed, at all times. Blaise knew only too well that she couldn't have done it, even if she didn't work. The responsibility of handling Salima's illness on her own had always made her anxious and frightened her.

"So what have you two been up to?" Blaise asked, as she sprawled on the couch next to her daughter. The two young women were like Siamese twins, always together, inseparable at all times.

"I was trying to teach Abby to sing scales." Salima laughed at her. Abby was plain looking but had a sweet face and was wearing jeans and a white fisherman sweater Blaise had brought her back from Ireland. And Salima was wearing the designer jeans and a pink sweater her mother had recently sent her. They both looked like kids, far younger than either of them were. Salima looked about fifteen, and Abby scarcely older. "She's hopeless," Salima added about her caretaker's singing skills. "She can't carry a tune to save her life. She can't even sing scales. I played some of the music for her that we've been studying at school, Renaissance music, and she hates it." Salima had sung in the school choir all through high school. And in a local church choir on Sunday.

"That music is so depressing," Abby said with a wry smile, looking apologetic.

"I think so too," Blaise admitted. "Can't you study something more cheerful? Christmas carols maybe? Then we could all sing along, or at least I could. I don't know where your musical gift came from, but it sure isn't from me," Blaise said with a grin.

"I'm going to take Gregorian chants next semester," she said, enjoying torturing both of them. She had been gifted with an exquisite voice. And she leaped at every chance to sing. She had the best voice in the entire school, and the purest. She could hit the high notes every time.

"I'm moving out if you start chanting," Abby threatened, trying to sound menacing, but convinced no one.

"No, you won't. I'm the only one who knows how to braid your hair. You'll look a mess if you move out," Salima warned, and they all laughed. Salima managed extremely well, especially on familiar turf. And she knew every inch of Caldwell and the grounds like the back of her hand. She was even able to get from one building to another sometimes without Abby, although Abby usually went with her. Salima particularly hated using a white cane and wouldn't use one. She just relied on Abby. And she had refused to have a seeing-eye dog ever since she'd gone blind. She hated dogs and didn't want one. Abby met all her needs to perfection. And in the cottage, Salima almost appeared sighted, she knew the placement of everything so well.

"Do you want to go out for brunch?" Blaise offered, but Salima usually didn't. She was happiest on the familiar school grounds, except for her classes at college, where she had no choice. It was why she had decided not to go to Dartmouth, despite her excellent grades. She thought it would be too hard to get around, and Abby couldn't go with her. And Salima couldn't manage without her. She was totally dependent on her, which was both good and bad. Blaise was well aware that if Abby ever left for any reason, Salima would be lost without her.

"Abby promised to make her special waffles," Salima said, looking like a child again.

"It would be fun to eat at Peterson's," Blaise suggested. She always thought it would do her good to get out, but Salima seemed to have no need or desire to venture into the world. She was happy in her cottage.

"I'd rather eat here," Salima said bluntly. She lived in a cocoon that Blaise had provided for her, and Abby was happy in it with her. She was a local girl who had never ventured far from home. She had gone to New York for the first time with Salima, and looked terrified the whole time she was there when they came home for school vacations. It was Salima who had reassured her. Abby was used to it now, but it had taken several years. And while Salima was at home, they rarely left the apartment. They watched movies on Blaise's big movie screen, which Salima could listen to and follow, with tapes recorded by a "movie describer" to describe the action for the vision impaired. Salima loved movies. They ordered meals from restaurants to be delivered to the apartment. Blaise always had a tough time getting them out, even here. But Abby took exquisite care of her. She monitored her blood counts and checked her pump scrupulously, and did everything for Salima. And Salima looked immaculate, beautifully groomed, and perfectly put together. The only thing Abby couldn't do was braids, and sing, and Salima teased her mercilessly about both.

Abby went out to the kitchen a few minutes later, set the table, and served them freshly made waffles.

"I forgive you for not being able to sing," Salima announced with a mouthful of waffles and diabetic maple syrup. "Your waffles are fantastic!" Abby loved to spoil her in countless small ways. It made Blaise's heart ache. Abby was the mother that she knew she could never be. She didn't have the time or the patience. Abby did. Blaise lived in a much bigger world, which she had shielded Salima from religiously. Salima was not a secret, but Blaise never talked about her diabetes or her blindness. And she had kept her away from the press all her life. Blaise was intensely private and protective of Salima.

Her going blind, and being diagnosed with diabetes before that, had broken Blaise's heart, and Harry's. He had never been able to adjust to it. And rather than accepting that he had a blind daughter and dealing with it, he ran away from it and hardly ever saw her. It was too painful for him. He sent her birthday cards, and had Blaise buy her Christmas and birthday gifts. He didn't know what she wanted, even as a young child, and her blindness confused him, so he didn't bother getting her anything, and asked Blaise to do it, which she did, and always credited him with fabulous gifts, beautiful dolls when she was younger, which she enjoyed even if she couldn't see them. She was like any other child. She loved music as she got older, leather jackets, a fur parka when she turned eighteen that Salima had worn ever since. But her father hardly ever coming to see her had been a disappointment to her all her life. He never called her either. She rarely spoke about it and had made her peace with it, but sometimes when his name came up, Blaise could see how much it had hurt her. Blaise tried to explain it to Harry, to no avail. He just said he couldn't. He found parenting any child hard enough, but doing so for a blind one was too much for him. It was easier for him to ignore her.

"What do you want to do after lunch?" Blaise asked her, as Abby put the dishes in the dishwasher Blaise had bought them.

"How about a movie? I just got two new ones." She particularly loved musicals. She had "watched" *Annie* and *Mamma Mia!* and *Mary Poppins* and *The Sound of Music* hundreds of times and sung along.

"Why don't we get some air?" Blaise suggested.

"You can watch a movie anytime. It's a beautiful day outside." It was the one problem Blaise always had with her. It was hard to get her out of her comfort zone, even to go for a walk on the grounds. She didn't like to go out unless she had to, and Abby didn't push her. She hated making Salima unhappy, and Salima liked to stay home in the cozy cottage. The only time she left it now was to go to school.

"Tell me about your trip," Salima said, trying to distract her from insisting on a walk, but genuinely interested too. Blaise told her about both interviews, and how fascinating both subjects had been. She told her all about Dubai, or what she'd seen of it, and the diamond bangle from Cartier. She had Salima feel it on her wrist.

"It feels expensive," Salima said with a grin. "He must have liked you a lot."

"No, he was just generous. Saudis are. And how would you know it's expensive?" Blaise was intrigued.

"It's heavy, and I can feel the diamonds all around it. It wasn't cheap."

"No, it wasn't," Blaise agreed with a smile.

"Was he handsome?" She loved hearing about her mother's trips, and listening to her interviews. She was Blaise's biggest fan. And her mother was hers. Salima was a remarkable girl, and had been since she was a child. She was sad that Harry hardly knew her, and that she herself didn't have more time to spend with her. The years had flown by.

"He was very handsome, and extremely smart," Blaise said about the Saudi prince.

"Was he hot for you, Mom?" Salima teased her, mostly because of the bracelet. But she knew her mother was beautiful. Everyone said so.

"No. I'm about ten or twelve years older than he is, so that rules me out. And he already has three wives. That's three too many for me."

Salima knew all about her mother's romance with Andrew, and how it had turned out and why. She had met him and liked him, and he had made an effort with her, but she didn't like how it had ended, or how dishonest he had been with her mother. Salima had been fourteen at the time, and her mother's voice had sounded so sad afterward, for months, maybe a year. It made Salima's heart ache to hear her. Salima herself had had a couple of romances at the school, but all the boys there were too young for her now, and she hadn't met anyone at college. She was always with Abby, and they came and went for her classes and never stuck around. And Salima was shy. With sighted people, she was self-conscious about being blind. And the only sighted people she knew were teachers, not kids. It was the downside of living at a school for the blind. She had no idea how to behave around people who could see. All her peers were blind, and had been for the past eleven years, since she was eight years old. But Blaise was still convinced that she was better off here. But as the years went by, Salima was less and less familiar with the outside world. New York would have been a jungle for her now, and far more dangerous than Blaise was willing to deal with. At Caldwell, Blaise knew she was safe. And Salima never asked to come home. She only did so when she had no other choice, when school was closed for vacations.

It took some doing, but Blaise finally convinced her to go for a walk. She described the trees to her, turning orange and scarlet, and Salima tucked her hand into her mother's arm as they walked, while Abby walked right behind them and said nothing. She was there if they needed her, but she didn't want to intrude. She was always very discreet, and Blaise liked her nearby. She was never alone with her daughter, and preferred it that way. She didn't feel competent to meet Salima's needs if something unexpected happened, and she knew Abby could. All Blaise could do, as far as she was concerned, was tell her stories of her work and travels and make her laugh. They always had fun together, which was something, but Salima needed so much more than that.

Abby made them hot tea when they got back to the cottage, and Blaise sat with them until late afternoon, when it started to get dark. And at six o'clock, with a tone of regret, she said she should leave. She had a long drive back to the city.

"Would you like a sandwich before you go?" Abby offered with her gentle smile.

"No, I'm fine. I should get on the road." She hated to leave. She always did. "I'll come back soon," she said, as she hugged Salima, who clung to her mother for a minute, savoring the feel and smell of her. She always loved the scent of her perfume, and her shampoo. Sometimes she could smell her in a room. Salima's senses other than her sight were acute, especially hearing and smell. "I'll call you this week," Blaise promised, vowing to herself that she would. She loved being with her, and hated how life got away from them, and interfered. Salima was the greatest gift of her life, no matter how infrequently she saw her.

"Thanks for coming up, Mom," Salima said with a smile, as she walked her mother to the door. "It was fun. It always is when you're here." She thought her mother was exciting.

"I can't wait till you come home for Thanksgiving," Blaise said, and meant it. "I'll get tickets to a Broadway musical. That would be fun," and she knew Salima would love it. They tried to see a musical whenever Salima came to town.

"The opera would be nice too . . . or a concert. Beethoven, if there is one." She looked excited at the prospect. The one way to spark her interest and get her out was always music.

"I'll see what's playing that weekend," Blaise promised.

"Drive safely," Salima admonished her as Blaise hugged her for a last time.

"I will."

Salima waved and then closed the door, and as Blaise left, she could hear Salima put music on, and the two girls laughing again. They had a good time together, and as she walked to her car, Blaise felt strangely left out, and she realized how lucky Abby was. She had so much time with Salima, and Salima loved her so much. At times, Blaise wished that she had made different choices, but she knew that the choices she had made were right for both of them. Blaise needed her work, as part of who she was, and Salima was happy at the school. It was just the way things were. And as she got on the road and headed south, she wiped a stray tear from her cheek.

Chapter 4

The week after Blaise's visit to Salima was typical of life at the network. She planned her show, covered a variety of stories, did several editorials, and was working on two specials, when she heard a rumor, and at first wondered if it was true. It was the kind of thing one heard frequently, that someone was being hired or fired, or shifted around, that management was making changes, and often it was only gossip. She had learned over the years not to panic or react too quickly. The network was a rumor mill.

The first she heard of it was from Charlie, who told her simply that there was a new girl in town. She had been brought in from an affiliate in Miami, she had been a model before that, and he said she was a knockout, and twenty-nine years old. And the next day Blaise heard it from Mark. The new girl was going to be doing weekend news for a while, which was where new faces often started, to try them out. And when

Blaise was introduced to her at a meeting, she was as beautiful as Charlie had said. She was a tall, statuesque blonde, with astounding breast implants and a tiny waist, and she had a lovely face. And Blaise thought she seemed enthusiastic and smart. Susie Quentin had gone to Brown and had a master's in journalism from Columbia.

As they left the meeting, the new girl in town walked over with an awestruck look as she spoke to Blaise.

"I've always wanted to meet you," she said in a breathy tone that Blaise couldn't envision on the news. Her voice was unfortunate and made her sound less bright than she was. But her looks more than compensated for it. And her eyes observed everything, and Blaise had the distinct impression that Susie Quentin was gunning for her. Blaise could smell it, and she had been there for too long not to know how it worked. It was how she had come in, twenty-five years earlier. She had arrived from San Francisco to replace someone else, whom the world had forgotten long since, and Blaise had too. She couldn't even remember her name, and she'd only been there for a few years before Blaise. But with Blaise they had gotten a lot more than they'd ever expected. She had become a major star at the network, there wasn't a house in the entire country where they didn't know her name, and everyone working at a network, an affiliate, in any city wanted to be her. And Susie Quentin had come from Miami to do just that. She wanted to be the new Blaise McCarthy, and as their eyes met, Blaise knew she was in trouble again. It had happened before, they had brought in others over the years, to warm them up, and get them ready to take her place. It had always backfired, but she knew that one day someone would come along, smarter or better, more exciting, and prettier to look at, and young above all, and she'd be gone. She just wasn't ready for it to happen yet. Blaise was at the top of her game. Her specials were getting better and better, her editorials more astute, and her ratings were solid. And now they had brought this girl in, and just looking at her, Blaise could feel management breathing down her neck.

"You were my idol and role model all through school," Susie said to Blaise, as Blaise felt her blood run cold. Susie Q, as people were calling her behind her back, made Blaise feel about ninety years old.

"That's nice to hear. Welcome to New York," Blaise said, trying not to look upset. She was a big network star after all and tried to tell herself that she had nothing to fear. But Blaise knew better. There was always something to fear at the network.

"I just got here last week," Susie explained. "Everyone's been terrific. They're letting me use a corporate apartment, till I find a place." More bad news. They never let anyone use those apartments unless they expected them to go far, or were planning to see that they did. They were obviously investing in Susie Quentin and expected to get their money's worth. When she went back to her office, Blaise's heart was in her feet, and her stomach between her ears. Mark said nothing to her about it, until the next day. He knew he had to tell her, before she heard it from someone else.

"They're giving Susie Q a special on the homeless to do," he said in an undertone. It was an important story and a major piece, and the kind of thing they would have normally asked Blaise to do.

"Thanks for the tip," Blaise said without further comment, and went back to work at her desk. She knew what this meant for her. She would have to work even harder and better and longer hours, be more innovative and creative, and keep her ratings up in the stratosphere somewhere. They were already great, but there was no room now for any slips. The pressure was on.

Blaise was panicked, even if she didn't show it, and she started going to the gym in the afternoon after work, to stay calm. She called her trainer and a masseuse and made a date with both for the weekend. And she worked late every night developing new ideas. She wondered briefly if they had only brought Susie in to push Blaise harder and make her produce, but looking at Susie, Blaise knew that wasn't true. They were grooming her for something big. And it didn't get bigger than Blaise. It might take her a year to get there, but she was on her way, like a heat-seeking missile headed for Blaise's seat. Blaise hadn't been this stressed in years. And for the next two weeks, she concentrated on her work to the exclusion of all else. There was no margin for error now.

In spite of the pressure and distractions at work, she called Salima several times, just to check in. She didn't tell her what was going on at the network. But Andrew Weyland called her from L.A. a week after Susie had arrived. He had heard the rumors too. In true passive-aggressive style, he told Blaise he was worried about her and the strain it would put on her, but in truth he had just called to gloat. He was still angry that she had ended their affair when she found out his divorce was a lie. His career in L.A. wasn't going well, and his ratings had slipped severely.

"You don't need to worry about a thing," he reassured her, sounding loving, but fake to Blaise. She knew him well. "She could never handle your job. There will never be another you." But she wasn't so sure. One day there would be, and maybe that time was now. His sympathy sounded insincere.

"You never know," she said calmly, sounding noncommittal. "So how's life in L.A.? Do you get to the beach every day?" He had moved to Malibu, in a spectacular house she had seen in a magazine, while he and his wife posed by the pool. The wife he had supposedly still been planning to divorce, even after Blaise left him. Another lie until it became obvious it wasn't true. They looked like the perfect couple in matching white shirts and jeans, with his arm around her, and California smiles, in the magazine spread she'd seen. Even after leaving him, seeing the article had upset her, and hearing from him only made it worse. But she always took his calls and was never sure why. Probably because there was no one else to talk to about her life. They knew each other so well, and familiarity counted for something. It was a poor excuse, but the only one that made sense to her. But he always managed to hurt her feelings, even when he appeared to be nice. Sometimes it was even worse when he was. It made her miss him, and the good times they'd had before she learned the truth. He had been so convincing. And now she no longer believed a word he said.

"We ought to have dinner sometime, for old times' sake. I'm coming to New York in a few weeks," he said in a smooth voice. Like the snake in the Garden of Eden.

"Yeah, maybe," she said vaguely, although she knew she wouldn't. She had no desire to torture herself to that extent. All she did now was take his calls and listen to him, but never see him. She hadn't seen him in over a year and didn't want to again. Her ultimate goal was to stop talking to him entirely, by phone, text, or e-mail, but she hadn't achieved it yet. "I'd better get back to work. Thanks for the call." Why was she thanking him? she asked herself as she hung up. For what? Upsetting her again? Scaring her about Susie? Making her doubt herself? Reminding her of what a liar he'd been and how badly she'd been hurt? She had felt like roadkill for a year after they broke up, and now she was numb. She couldn't listen to any man now without wondering if he was lying to her. Andrew's legacy lived on and maybe always would.

Blaise could no longer imagine believing a man again, and didn't want to. There was no room for romance in her life anymore. And with Susie Q in her face, romance was the last thing on her mind. All she wanted was to save her skin. And the rumors about Susie were rampant. She was management's new Golden Child, and they thought she could do no wrong, although she had yet to prove herself. And they loved her youth and her look.

Two weeks after Susie arrived at the network, Blaise was working on a story, when the phone rang and Mark was out to lunch. She picked it up herself. All she could hear at the other end was incoherent sobbing, and she had no idea who it was, or if the call was even for her.

"Hello? . . . Who is this?" Blaise asked the unknown caller from a blocked number, sounding confused. "I'm sorry. . . . Are you there?" And then she heard a familiar scream. It was a sound she hadn't heard in years. Salima. She had screamed that way as a baby, and when she started to go blind and was scared. Blaise's heart started to race. "Salima? . . . Talk to me. . . . Is that you?" And then the voice broke down in sobs, she was talking incoherently and saying something about Abby, but Blaise still couldn't understand what it was. "Baby, come on. . . . Slow down. . . . What happened?" With a feeling of panic, she wondered if Abby had quit, or been fired. It was the only reason Blaise could think of for Salima to fall apart. And if she'd been fired, Blaise would force Caldwell to bring her back.

There was nothing they couldn't fix. "Where are you?" Blaise asked her, wondering if Abby was there. Had they had an argument? Was Abby hurt?

"At the cottage," she said in a tone of anguish. It was the first thing she had said that Blaise could understand.

"Where's Abby?"

In answer to the question, Salima broke down in sobs again. It was several very long minutes before she could speak again, while her mother told her to breathe.

"She got sick. . . . She woke up this morning with a fever. . . . I called Mrs. Garner and asked her to send the nurse. She called the doctor and they took her away. They took her to the hospital, and they wouldn't let me go with her."

"Baby, she'll be all right," Blaise said in a soothing tone, but Salima only cried harder. "It's probably just a really bad flu, and they don't want you to catch it."

"They said she had meningitis. I called the hospital, and they wouldn't let me talk to her. They said she was sleeping. I never got to say goodbye to her, Mom." Her voice was raw, and a chill ran down Blaise's spine.

"Why would you say goodbye to her?" her mother asked her, sounding frightened.

"She's dead," Salima said, and then dissolved in sobs again as Blaise sat clutching the phone in disbelief. She had died within hours, which Blaise was aware happened with meningitis, but it was impossible to believe. She looked at her watch and knew what she had to do.

"I'll be there as fast as I can. I'll leave the office in a few minutes. Hang in, baby. I'm on my way. I know this is awful, beyond awful, it's unthinkable. I'll be there in three hours." It took a few minutes, but she got Salima off the phone and called Charlie. She told him she had a family emergency and had to leave immediately. And with a lump in her throat, she told him she couldn't do her broadcast the next day. "I know this is short notice, and I'm sorry, but I have no choice."

"What happened? Is your daughter okay?" He sounded concerned. Blaise never left the office without plenty of warning, nor missed her broadcasts, ever.

"The woman who takes care of her just died. She's hysterical. She loved her more than she loves me." She said it without rancor, and he was one of the few people at the network, other than Mark, who knew Salima was blind and diabetic.

"Just go," he said kindly. "Call me tonight and let me know when you're coming back."

"It might be a few days," she said honestly. "This is going to be really hard for my kid. And Charlie," she said as an afterthought, "please don't give Susie Q my morning spot to fill in." Blaise knew better than anyone that this was no time for her to disappear, and she had never done that before. It might give Susie her big break. But she couldn't face that now too. Not yet.

"Don't worry. It won't happen." Charlie loved

working with Blaise. They were a great team. "Just relax, and go take care of your kid."

"Thank you," she said, and hung up, and then dialed the school. She asked for the headmaster to make sure that they had someone with Salima who would be able to comfort her until Blaise arrived. He explained to Blaise what had happened.

"We still can't believe it. She was dead in four hours. She was fine yesterday. They said meningitis is like that. Now we're worried about an epidemic." He sounded panicked, and so was Blaise, for Salima.

"What are you going to do?" Blaise asked in a strained voice. She was worried about Salima now, living so closely with her. What if she had been exposed and died too? Blaise felt sick thinking about it. Salima was the only person in the world she loved. And she knew enough about bacterial meningitis, which Abby had died of, to know that you could get it from an infected person coughing or sneezing.

"I don't know yet. We'll talk about it when you get here. I'm meeting with someone from the board of health in an hour." He had just come from telling Abby's mother that her daughter died. It had been a nightmarish day for the entire school, but for Salima most of all, they both knew.

"I'll be there as fast as I can." She told him what she had said to Salima, and then she flew out the door. She passed Mark in the hall and told him where she was going and why.

"Oh my God" was all he could think of to say, looking shocked. "Is there anything I can do?" She shook her head and raced past him. She was in the elevator within seconds and across the lobby. She found Tully outside and had him drive her home, where she threw some clothes into a bag, and then he took her to her garage and helped her get her bag in the car.

"You need to calm down before you start driving," he told her sternly. "You'll kill yourself getting there if you don't."

"I'll be fine," she said, but didn't look it. And three minutes later she was on the road, weaving through traffic toward the East River to drive north.

She drove as fast as she could all the way. She fully expected to be stopped by the police, but she wasn't. And she was at Caldwell two and a half hours later. She went straight to the cottage, where Salima was crying uncontrollably, and Blaise took her in her arms and held her while she sobbed. All she could do was hug her and make soothing sounds. There was nothing to say, no way to make it better, and worst of all, no way to bring Abby back. Salima sounded as though her heart were broken. And eventually Blaise put her to bed. One of the school monitors Blaise knew only slightly was with her, and Blaise sat on her bed and held her hand until Salima fell asleep. And as soon as she did, Blaise went to find Eric, the headmaster, in the main building where he lived. He looked devastated when he greeted Blaise, and she could see that he had been crying too.

"We're closing the school. Tomorrow," he said with

an ominous look, as Blaise stared at him, in shock yet again.

"Forever?" He shook his head in answer. He was running out of words.

"The board of health recommends that we close for sixty to ninety days, depending on whether or not we get any new cases. We have to send everyone home. It's dangerous for any of us to be here. We were all exposed to Abby. We notified everyone an hour ago. Several of the parents have already picked their children up. I'm expecting a dozen more tonight. The rest are leaving in the morning. Above all, we want to avoid an epidemic."

"What will happen to the kids?" Blaise asked in a shaking voice.

"We're going to send as many monitors home with them as we can. But I have a problem, Blaise," he said, eyeing her squarely. He had always been honest with her, for the past eleven years, and she considered him a friend. "None of the monitors who'd be suitable for Salima can leave here. None of the female ones, that is. They're all married and have kids, and live nearby, and they won't go to New York. I've talked to them all."

"What about Lara, the girl who's with her now?"

"She has a husband and two kids. She won't go. She had a hell of a time even finding someone for them for tonight. She doesn't usually live in," which was why Blaise had hardly ever seen her and didn't recognize her at first. And she didn't work weekends. "I have someone terrific for you. But not a woman. He's a great guy." Blaise looked horrified by what he said.

"I can't take a guy with me. I travel all the time. He can't get Salima dressed or in and out of the bathtub. What am I supposed to do with that?"

"Make it work. It's all I can do," he said honestly. "He's the best teacher I've got. I would have sent him home with Timmie Jenkins, but they're putting Timmie in another school now in Chicago, closer to home. They've been wanting to for a while. So that frees up Simon. I asked him, and he's willing to go to New York."

"I can't take a man," Blaise said stubbornly. "You have to get me someone else. A man won't work." She was desperate. He had to help her.

"He's all I've got." Eric looked at her unhappily, and Blaise looked panicked. "It's him or no one. Don't you have a woman who can help you out? A housekeeper of some kind?"

"I have a housekeeper, but she only works days. She doesn't live in. And I travel for work, at least half the time. This will be very hard on her."

"It's hard on us having to close the school. We all have to make the best of it. When are you taking Salima out? You can leave tonight if you like."

"She's asleep. We'll leave in the morning. When is Abby's funeral?" Blaise asked. She had never met Abby's mother and knew it must have been devastating for her to lose her daughter.

"It's the day after tomorrow," he said grimly. It had been the worst day in the history of the school.

"I'd like to stay till then, for Salima's sake," Blaise said quietly. "She'll want to go. I guess we can stay at the bed and breakfast till then."

"I'll tell Simon to be ready in the morning," Eric said, looking harried. He had fifty students to send home, with monitors to go with them, and a school to close.

"Can I at least meet him?" Blaise asked, sounding skeptical.

"Of course. I'll have him in my office at nine o'clock tomorrow morning. I think he'd be great for Salima. In a way, better than Abby, although I loved her too. But Simon has excellent training, and his skills are very strong. He went to Harvard. He has a master's in special ed, and another one in psychology. He's been here as long as Abby, and I'd trust him with my life."

"He's a guy," Blaise said, looking unhappy. She left Eric then and went back to the cottage. Salima was still asleep, and Lara had gone to sleep on the couch in a sleeping bag. She didn't want to use Abby's bedroom and was nervous about even being there. Blaise was planning to sleep with her daughter.

Blaise called Charlie on her cell phone while standing in the kitchen, and lowered her voice so she didn't wake anyone up. The last thing she wanted was Salima awake and crying all night.

"How's it going?" he asked her.

"It's a mess. The only monitor they can give me for

her is a man. I don't know how we're going to work that."

"You'll figure out something. Maybe you can find someone here."

"Yeah, maybe. But I'd rather have someone from the school. I just don't know what to do with a guy. I'm not set up for that." She was convinced it wouldn't work.

"Do you know when you're coming back yet?" Charlie sounded worried.

"The funeral is the day after tomorrow. We'll stay at the bed and breakfast till then. Salima will want to go. I need to be off tomorrow and the day after, and then I'll come back to work."

"That's fine. Don't worry about it. You're entitled to three days off." Not with Susie Quentin on deck, Blaise thought to herself, and competing with her, with the management guys snowed by her. The timing was terrible on this. And now Salima would be at home for two or three months, and Blaise would be pulled in all directions with a male caretaker for her, who would be more of a headache than a help. "Stay in touch," Charlie told her, "and let me know if I can do anything to help."

"Thanks, Charlie," Blaise said, and hung up. She put on her nightgown after that and slipped into bed with Salima, who was sound asleep.

Salima started crying again the next morning as soon as she woke up. Blaise made her breakfast, which she wouldn't eat, and then went to shower and dress.

And she was at Eric's office at nine o'clock, to meet Simon, and left Salima at the cottage with Lara. She hadn't told Salima yet that Simon was coming to New York. And as soon as Blaise saw him, her heart sank. Simon Ward looked proper and respectable and was wearing a blazer and jeans. His hair was trimmed, and he was wearing a clean well-ironed shirt, but he was tall and well built and good looking, and was about thirty-five years old, with dark hair and eyes. Everything about him said male, and all she needed was for him to fall for Salima, who was a beautiful girl. This was a headache she just didn't need, especially now. Eric invited them all to sit down in his office, and Simon looked a lot more relaxed than Blaise. He was deeply sympathetic to her loss and said he knew how attached Salima had been to Abby, and he was prepared to do everything he could to help both mother and daughter at this trying time.

"I don't think this will work," Blaise said honestly to Simon. "We're just not set up to have a man in the house. And who will dress her? I leave for work at six A.M., and I travel most of the time."

"If I lay out her clothes for her, she can dress herself," he said calmly. He didn't add that at nineteen she should have been doing that herself for years. But he knew Abby had babied her and did everything for her. He and Abby had argued about it at staff meetings, when they discussed their caseloads and theories about them. He had said that she wasn't doing Salima any favors by treating her like a child. "I think we'll do fine," he said in a gentle voice. But Blaise wasn't convinced. She could think of a thousand things that could go wrong. She looked deeply worried. "We'll do the best we can. Is there anything you'd like to ask me?" he asked Blaise, looking her in the eye.

"How long have you been doing this kind of work?" she asked, but it didn't make a difference. She didn't want a man.

"For eight years, since I left graduate school. I'm thirty-two. I graduated from Harvard. My master's degrees are in special ed and psych. And my brother went blind at eighteen. He was a downhill racer, training for the Olympics. He got a head injury and lost his sight. He gave up on everything at first. He's two years older than I am, and I just wouldn't let him give up. I hounded him till he went back to school and got back on track, so I've been doing this kind of work for a long time," he said with a small smile.

"And where is your brother now?" Blaise asked, curious about him. Simon was at least well spoken and seemed like a nice man. He would have been fine at a dinner party, but not to take care of her daughter. What would he do when she needed to take a bath, and there was no one to help?

"My brother teaches French literature at Harvard. My father is the head of the physics department, and kind of a mad scientist and inventor. My brother is much more down to earth. He's married and has four kids. So I guess the badgering worked." Simon smiled, and Blaise didn't.

"And your mother?" It was an irrelevant question, but Blaise's interest was piqued by his history, and the brother he had helped, and the mad scientist father. They sounded like an intriguing group.

"My mother is a poet. She's French. She publishes every five or ten years with obscure publishers who do poetry that no one wants to read. She's from Bordeaux, and she was a student of my father's. He's twenty-two years older than she is. He was a confirmed bachelor when they met and fell in love. They married a year later, and they're very happy together. They're both fairly eccentric, but it seems to work. Or at least it has for the past thirty-five years. So that's my background. What do you think, Miss McCarthy? Would you like me to come to New York? I think I can be helpful to you and Salima while the school is closed. And I'm a fairly decent cook." In fact, he had studied at Cordon Bleu in Paris and spent two college summers as a *sous chef,* but he didn't tell her that. "I'll do my very best."

"We don't have much choice," she said with a bleak look. She couldn't take care of Salima alone.

"I think with a little guidance, Salima will need a lot less assistance than you think." His goal, if he went with them, was to make Salima as independent as he could. It would be his gift to her. Unlike Abby, who had kept her in a cocoon.

Blaise was no more convinced when she left Eric's office, but they really had no other choice. And as Eric walked her back toward the cottage, he told her that

Simon's mother was not just French, she was a Rothschild, and his grandfather was a baron. And as she walked the rest of the way to the cottage, Blaise thought about him again. He was obviously intelligent and good looking and everything she didn't want in her home. They were two women. She didn't want a man taking care of Salima, or even around her, no matter who his grandparents were.

As soon as Simon left Eric's office, he took his bicycle and rode into town. He stopped at a house with a dilapidated front porch, and hurried inside. He had told Megan he would meet her there. She was also a teacher at Caldwell and had left the school the night before. And there were toys everywhere. She lived there with her husband and three sons.

"Are you going?" she asked him, looking anxious. He had called her the night before to tell her of Eric's offer, to send him to New York with Blaise.

"Yes, I am," he said quietly, standing in her kitchen, which was a mess. She hadn't cleared the breakfast dishes away yet. And in spite of the fact that she was married, he'd been in love with her for three years. "I have no other choice. I need the job, and she needs the help." He looked at Megan with despair. "We're going nowhere, Meg. You said you were getting divorced. That's the only reason I got into this. If I thought you'd stay with him, I never would have."

"I was going to, then his brother died, he lost his

job, and his mother got sick. What do you expect me to do?" There were tears running down her cheeks. "I don't like this either, but I can't just kill the guy on the way out."

"You're killing me. I never wanted to be in a situation like this. It's dishonest. I'm tired of sneaking around, while you tell me how miserable you are with him and don't leave. And one of these days, he'll figure it out and kill us both. Or just me. Or you, which would be worse. I love you, Meg. But I'm not trying to steal you from him. You told me before we started that you were leaving him. You never did. It turned into a huge mess with us sneaking around and lying to him while you drag your feet. That's not how it was supposed to be. If you want us, you have to get out of this mess on your own so we can start clean." It had gone on for three years. "Maybe three months away from each other will do us both good. It's too depressing this way." He couldn't call her at night, or on weekends. Either her husband was around or the kids were, and they had been meeting in motels in the next town for a few hours. It was tawdry and their affair had started when Megan got a job at the school three years before and had told him she was getting divorced. She put her arms around him and sobbed.

"I don't want you to go. Don't leave me here, Simon. It'll kill me if I lose you now."

"No, it won't. Or then do something about it. I can't stand listening to how much he drinks and slaps you around. Meg, you're driving me insane."

"Are you in love with Blaise McCarthy?" she asked, looking up at him with frightened eyes, and he shook his head.

"No, I'm not. I barely know her. She's a huge star, Meg. She doesn't even want me there. She wants a woman, but I'm the only monitor who'll go. I feel sorry for her, and I'd like to help get Salima out of the cocoon Abby built for her that's strangling her." But Abby wasn't the issue now, nor was Blaise. Meg was, and the illicit affair they'd been having for three years. She was still tangled up in her marriage and couldn't seem to cut loose. And if she didn't, he would. He had been saying it to her for months. And the school closing had turned out to be providential. He needed time away now to breathe. He felt suffocated by the situation they were in. "I have to go, Meg. They're waiting for me. I think we're staying at the bed and breakfast tonight. We're leaving for New York after the funeral tomorrow. If you go, I'll see you there."

"I can't go," she said miserably. "I have to take my mother-in-law to chemo." He didn't say it, but he thought it was just as well, and he wanted to say goodbye to her now. For the next few months, at least, until she decided what she wanted. He was no longer willing to continue the affair if she stayed married. "And he'll be home tonight, so I can't get out. Will you call me from New York?" she asked, sounding desperate again. She hadn't expected this to happen, or that he'd leave so soon. But he had been warning her of this for a while. And the school closing was giving them the break he needed. He loved her but he felt like a scumbag sneaking around with her, and meeting in motels. Three years had been way too long.

"I don't know," Simon said honestly, about calling her. "I'm not sure I should. And when am I supposed to call? He's home at night, and the kids are here the rest of the time." Everything was wrong with their situation, and they both knew it. Simon had never been in a relationship like this in his life, and never wanted to be again. And loving her just made it worse for him.

"You can call when they're in school," she pleaded with him.

"I'll be with Salima," he said, walking to the door, with a last look at her, not sure if he'd ever see her again, and there were tears in his eyes too. "I love you, Meg. I'm sorry," he said, and then he was gone. He hurried down the steps, got on his bike, and rode back to Caldwell, where he knew Blaise and Salima were waiting for him. And he felt as though his heart were breaking as he pedaled up the road as fast as he could.

Chapter 5

When Simon got back to the cottage, Blaise and Salima were waiting for him. Blaise was slightly annoyed that Simon had disappeared for half an hour, but she didn't say anything as he loaded the heaviest bags into the car. Salima normally kept all of her favorite clothes there, but it was impossible to know what Salima would want in the city, so Blaise thought it best to take everything with them. And Blaise's car was loaded to the gills. There was hardly room for them, and it would be a tight fit. Blaise thanked Lara for everything as she left.

While Simon was out, Blaise had explained to Salima that Simon was going to New York with them, and that Eric had no one else to send. Salima had tried to object, and sensing it was hopeless, she sobbed in despair. Her life had turned into a nightmare overnight.

Parents had been arriving at the school all morning

to pick up their children. Blaise was one of the last to drive off the grounds, and Eric showed up at the cottage just before they did to wish them luck, and promise to keep them informed. Everyone was concerned about other kids getting sick, and Eric promised to advise them of the exact date they'd reopen. He didn't know it yet, other than that it would be sometime in January after the holidays, which made the most sense and worked with the quarantine. It seemed like a lifetime to Blaise. All three of them were silent as they drove the short distance to the bed and breakfast where Blaise had reserved two rooms for the night. She and Salima were going to share a room with a large bed, and Simon had a similar room to himself. They were the two best rooms in the house. When they reached the bed and breakfast, Blaise led Salima inside and upstairs to their rooms. They were small but pretty, and Salima said she wanted to stay there all day and not go out.

"We have to leave the inn to eat," her mother said gently, as Salima found the bed, sat down on it, and shook her head.

"I'm not hungry," she said, as she started to cry again. It was going to be a long day in the tiny room. Simon showed up a short time later, and suggested they go to Peterson's for lunch. Salima just listened and shook her head. He and Blaise exchanged a look, and he nodded and left.

He was back half an hour later with delicious sandwiches on fresh bread, a bag of fruit, and some cheese he had bought at a deli nearby. He was very aware of Salima's calories and carbohydrates, and only used sugar substitutes, as Salima had to be careful with carbs and anything sweet because of her diabetes. And she tried to be conscious of her weight. But Salima hardly touched any of it, and Simon and Blaise took their sandwiches outside.

"She has to eat," Blaise said, looking worried. The sandwiches were delicious, and they devoured them while they talked. She was grateful that he'd brought the food back. Salima had eaten very little breakfast that morning and she had to be responsible about what she ate, and not skip meals. She had only eaten the bare minimum required for her since the day before, when her mother arrived, she was too sad.

"She'll eat more when she's hungry," he said calmly. "There's too much going on. It will do her good to get home tomorrow. The funeral will be rough." He quietly brought meals to her for the rest of the day. Salima ate them but never said a word to him.

The funeral the next day was worse than rough. When the three of them went to the tiny church just outside town, all the teachers from Caldwell were there, and Abby's childhood friends, and her mother was pushed into the church in a wheelchair, sobbing uncontrollably, as Abby's casket sat in front of the altar, and the church was filled with flowers. Blaise led Salima into a pew, and they sat down. The priest spoke glowingly of Abby, he had known her since she was a child, and you could hear people crying all over the church. Salima sobbed throughout, until the moment came when Salima had agreed to sing the Ave Maria, and Blaise led her to the organ. She stood pale and shaking and tore everyone's heart out with her incredibly pure voice.

With Blaise's help, she stopped to speak to Abby's mother on the way out. Salima hugged her when she thanked her tearfully for singing, and all the two women could do was hold each other and cry. And then Blaise led her back to the car. She had to sit in the backseat amid her clothes and bags of belongings piled everywhere. Simon slid into the passenger seat but offered to drive.

"It's okay. I'm fine," Blaise said quietly. It was noon when they set off for New York, after the funeral for the young woman Salima had loved so much. The silence in the car was deafening, all you could hear was Salima crying as they got onto the highway and headed south. It was going to be a very long three hours, and a much longer three months.

Simon was silent, as he stared out the window at the scarlet trees, thinking of Megan, and Blaise turned on the radio to drown out the sound of Salima's sobs. She paid no attention to what station she put on, she was vaguely aware that it was some kind of gospel music, and they drove on, all three of them lost in thought. Blaise was panicking over the next few months. So far Simon had done nothing but stand discreetly aside, while Salima clung to her mother's arm. She wanted no one else.

As she was driving, Blaise was thinking about the work she had to do when she got back, when there was a soft sound from the backseat. Salima had recognized one of the gospel songs, and was singing softly. Her voice grew as the choir joined the soloist, and Salima hit all the high notes with ease as Simon turned in his seat and stared at her. He had never heard a voice like hers in his life. Her rendition of the Ave Maria at Abby's funeral had been touching and beautiful but more subdued, but in the car with Simon and her mother, she let her voice soar as a form of release. She sang the next two songs with the radio as well. She liked listening to gospel music sometimes, and she and Abby had kidded around as Salima let her voice fly to the rafters, just as she did now. It was a relief of sorts from the sadness she felt, and then she fell silent again. Simon was in awe of what he had just heard.

"I didn't know you can sing like that," he said in amazement. And then he vaguely remembered that she had been in the choir and dropped out when she started college.

"I used to be in the choir," she confirmed his recollection. "Miss Mayberry is tone deaf," she said wryly, and he laughed.

"That explains some of the performances we've had at school. Have you ever taken lessons?" She shook her head in answer. "Maybe you should." At Eric's request, he had called the community college for her that morning, and informed them of what had happened at the school and that they were closing for three months.

They had agreed to let her follow a course of independent study for credit while she was in New York. "That might be a fun way to pick up credit for college. It would be a lot more fun than a math class."

"I don't want to go to school," she said, and Blaise could sense that she didn't like him. She wasn't sure about him herself. He seemed very confident and self-assured. He was polite, but he was a big presence, and because he was a man and sure of himself, Blaise felt like he was in her face, and she guessed that Salima did too.

He had opinions about everything and he wasn't afraid to voice them. And he had already said to Blaise in Eric's office that he thought Salima should become more independent, now that Abby was gone. Blaise didn't want him pushing her too far, particularly now. And she suspected that Salima would be mourning the gentle young teacher for a long time. Simon was already trying to draw her out. No one in the car said a word for the next three hours. Blaise felt as if it were the longest drive of her life, and she was relieved when she turned to glance at Salima and saw that she had fallen asleep. She was exhausted from the emotions of the past two days, and constant crying.

"She'll be all right," Simon said softly, trying to reassure her, and Blaise looked as if she didn't believe him.

"It's going to take a long time," Blaise said sadly, wondering if they would ever find someone like Abby. Simon was not what she had in mind, as a teacher maybe, but not as the kind of caretaker Abby had been, nurturing and loving, and protecting Salima from everything. Simon was very much a man, and seemed like a bull in a china shop to her. She wasn't looking forward to living with him for the next three months, and hoped that Eric would find someone else. She had asked him to continue looking for a woman.

"We need to keep her busy," Simon responded, looking out the window as they crossed the bridge into upper Manhattan. He hadn't been there in a year, and hadn't realized how much he'd missed it. He had grown up in Boston, while his father taught at Harvard, but he didn't get there often either. He hardly ever left the school, and for the past three years, he'd been spending all his free time with Megan, lately in cheap motels. It depressed him to think about it. He suddenly realized the seamy life he had been living with her, while he waited for her to leave her husband. And he strongly suspected now that she never would. He was grateful for the opportunity to come to New York, and take a break. He was still thinking about her and how much he already missed her, while Blaise pulled up in front of their building. Simon was staring out the window, with a blank look, still thinking of Meg.

"We're here," Blaise said firmly, to catch his attention, and Salima stirred in the backseat, as the doorman began unloading their bags. He recognized Salima immediately but had never seen the man before. They looked like a motley crew, entering the building a few minutes later with all of Salima's things, as she held on to her mother's arm for guidance, after Blaise asked the doorman to take the car to the garage. And without prodding, Blaise saw Simon tip the doorman, who tipped his hat to him. She was pleased he had thought of it himself. "Thank you," she said to him, and Simon looked startled. To him, it had been the obvious thing to do. To Blaise, it was evidence that he had been well brought up and did the right thing. At least he knew how to tip. It was one thing less for her to think about, and he made himself useful. He carried all the bags into the apartment for them as Salima felt her way around, getting acclimated again. She was far less familiar and at ease here than she was at school—she didn't come home often.

Blaise showed Simon to Salima's room, so he could bring her bags in. There was hardly space for all of them in the small sunny room that was empty most of the time.

She pointed out her own suite then so he could carry her suitcase, and then she walked him into the kitchen and escorted him to one of the two tiny rooms behind it, the maids' rooms they never used. Looking at his size, with his long legs, and the narrow bed, she suddenly realized how inadequate it was for him, but she had nothing else, except her own room and Salima's.

"I'm sorry. I know this room is really small for you. We're just not set up for guests." And even less so for men, she almost added, but didn't. But he looked perfectly content as he set down his two small bags and tossed his laptop case onto the bed. He never went anywhere without it.

"I must have been a monk in a past life. I don't mind small spaces. My room at Caldwell isn't much bigger than this," he said with an easy smile, and she was relieved. At least he wasn't demanding. She had expected him to have a fit when he saw the room. And now her housekeeper would have to sleep in the other room whenever Blaise went away, so there would be a woman in the house to help Salima bathe and dress.

"Thank you for being nice about it," Blaise said quietly as they went back into the kitchen.

"Do you mind if I cook once in a while?" he asked as he looked around the fabulous kitchen. It was his dream come true.

"You don't need to," Blaise said, looking distracted. "My housekeeper leaves things we can heat up. I come home from work pretty late, and I don't have time to cook. I usually just eat a salad when I'm alone, or don't bother at all. And we can order in." She wasn't interested in his cooking. He was here to help Salima and nothing else. And he didn't comment on what she said. He just nodded and followed her back to Salima's room.

"Do you need some help hanging things up?" he asked her. Salima was sitting on her bed, looking glum. "We can put them in your closet by type and color. I can put Braille labels on the hangers for you. I brought my machine. Then you can pull them out on your own and dress yourself," he said helpfully. Both women looked shocked.

"She doesn't need to dress herself," Blaise said with a look of disapproval. "My housekeeper will help her with that. And I'll do it on the weekends." They were already off to a bad start, but Simon looked undisturbed.

"Let's label your toiletries at least, so you don't get them mixed up and brush your teeth with the wrong stuff." He sounded firm about that, and it made sense to Blaise, but Salima snapped at him immediately.

"Abby puts my toothpaste on the brush for me." She didn't tell him that sometimes Abby even brushed her teeth for her. She knew that would sound lame.

"I think you can do that yourself," Simon said quietly, gently pushing her with his suggestion, and Salima didn't like it, and neither did Blaise. The last thing she wanted was for him to upset Salima, and spark a war between the two of them.

Later, Blaise led him into her office off her bedroom, so he would know where to find her, since it was the room where she spent most of her time when she was home. And she looked him squarely in the eye the moment they were alone. "I think we need to get one thing clear right away. You're not here to rock the boat. All we want to do is get Salima through this incredibly difficult time in her life, without the woman she loved and relied on, until she goes back to school. We're not planning to reinvent the wheel."

"I don't think the wheel has been invented yet,"

Simon said just as firmly, meeting her gaze. "Abby and I had very different views about things. Maybe it's the difference between men and women, but I think being self-sufficient is key. Salima is nineteen years old, not two, and she needs to know how to take care of herself. What if she wants to live alone one day? She can't stay at Caldwell forever. She needs to get ready for that day. And with Abby gone, this seems like the right time."

"She's never going to live alone," Blaise said in an even stronger tone. She had already provided for that. Salima would have a caretaker forever.

"You never know," Simon said. "My brother said the same thing. He lived at home after his accident, for several years. My mother babied him, just as Abby did with Salima. Now he has a job, a wife, four children, and he takes care of them. Whatever she does, or however you provide for her, Salima still needs skills. And it will make her feel better about herself," he insisted.

"She feels fine about herself. What she feels like shit about is losing Abby. Let's try not to make it any worse." Simon didn't answer her, but he nodded, in order to keep the peace. And Blaise could tell that she hadn't convinced him, which unnerved her. She felt as if she were swimming upstream in her own home, fighting the currents, and she didn't like the feeling. He wasn't at Caldwell anymore, he was in her apartment, and she expected her word to be law. And she was getting the strong feeling that Simon didn't live by other people's rules. He was courteous and considerate, but he definitely had his own ideas, and they weren't hers.

He went to check on Salima then, and after a few minutes, she let him unpack for her, and she told him where she wanted her things. He noticed that her closets here at home were almost empty, and he realized how seldom she was there. Caldwell had become her home, and he wondered if Blaise was going to try to keep her there, or at a similar place once she got older. Simon thought that would be a tragedy for Salima, and a terrible waste. She had a bright mind, and was capable of far more than anyone expected of her, particularly Abby. He didn't want to speak ill of the dead, and he had liked her, but he thought now that with time, she would have crippled Salima. He was beginning to think that it was a blessing Abby was out of her life. And undeniably, everything he had in mind for her would be very different, and even painful at times to make the change from total dependency to freedom. And it was easy to see that Blaise wasn't on board either. He would have to pull it off on his own. And he intended to try in the next three months. He wasn't afraid to make waves. It would be for Salima's good in the end, even if neither she nor her mother understood that.

He put Salima's voice-activated computer on the desk and plugged it in. She could give it voice commands, and a mechanical voice would respond and read her any material she wanted. Blaise had always gotten her the most up-to-date aids available to assist her, and was constantly searching for new ones. Salima used a software program called OpenBook, with a scanner that read her mail and textbooks to her. And she had something called Oratio that allowed her to use a BlackBerry. Everything Salima had was state of the art, thanks to her mother, and she knew it. And Simon also noticed that she had an excellent stereo in her room. She had all the most expensive devices and aids, and advanced technology, but she still couldn't brush her teeth alone. And Simon wanted to change that as soon as he could, for her sake.

When he left her room, it was in good order. She was putting on some music, and she wanted to e-mail some of her friends from school to see how they were. She loved her mother, but she hated being home. And she was beginning to hate Simon even more. He didn't understand anything.

He went back to his own room then, and put away his things, and then appeared unexpectedly in the door to Blaise's office. She looked up in surprise. It was strange to see a man in her house. She always wondered now how she had lived with Harry, or thought she would marry Andrew and live with him. The idea no longer appealed to her at all, and the reality of Simon in her home even less. He felt like an intruder to her, and to Salima.

"Would you like a cup of tea?" Simon asked her, and she shook her head, wanting to tell him that he didn't need to come to her office unless she called for him or there was a problem. No one had offered her a cup of tea in her own home in years. Not since she'd been married to Harry and they had help, more than ten years before. The housekeeper she had now only did laundry and cleaned, and left simple food in the fridge for her. She never offered her tea, or would even have thought of it. If Blaise wanted tea, she made her own. And she didn't expect Simon to wait on her, any more than she expected him to cook for them, although he had offered. All she wanted was for him to keep Salima happy, whatever it took, and stay out of her way. With Salima's arrival, her unavoidable needs no matter how much she loved her, and Simon in their midst, Blaise felt invaded in her own home, and they hadn't been there for two hours. And at the look on her face, he withdrew immediately.

Blaise went to check on Salima an hour later. She was listening to music and lying on her bed, thinking of Abby, and there were tears rolling down her cheeks. Blaise sat down next to her on the bed and stroked her hair, and then kissed her.

"How's it going?" Blaise asked, but she could see, not well.

"Horribly. I miss her so much." And Blaise knew she always would. A bond like theirs was irreplaceable, even if they found another competent caretaker in time. She had genuinely loved Abby.

"I know you do, sweetheart. Let's try to do some fun things while you're here. I'll try to get some concert tickets tomorrow."

"I don't want to do anything," Salima said sadly. "And I hate Simon. He's a pain."

"Yeah. Maybe. He seems a little pushy to me too,

but this is all new to him, the apartment, us, that ridiculous little room we have for him. I think he's just trying to be helpful. And he's a guy. We're not used to guys here." Blaise smiled at her. There was no point in either of them getting wound up about him, although he annoyed her too. She enjoyed her peaceful home, and even having Salima there was a huge change for her. Having Simon put it out in the stratosphere somewhere.

"Why can't we just have no one?" Salima said mournfully, sounding five and not nineteen. "You can take care of me," she said hopefully, and Blaise felt instantly guilty.

"Remember me? I work. Or had you forgotten? And I travel all the time. What would you do if I got sent away on a story? You need someone here with you." And Blaise couldn't see herself putting toothpaste on Salima's brush. She could learn to do that herself now, like a big girl, blind or not. It was the only thing he'd said so far that Blaise agreed with. Salima was used to having everything done for her. Abby had done it all.

Blaise wandered back into the kitchen around eight o'clock that night. None of them had eaten dinner, and she wasn't hungry. Simon was sitting at the kitchen table with his computer, and looked up when she walked in. Megan had just sent him an e-mail, telling him how much she missed him and how sad she was. He was too, but he had decided not to answer, and he turned off his computer and looked at Blaise.

"Can I make you guys dinner?" he offered, standing

up. He felt as though he should be doing something for her, and Salima had made it clear she didn't want him in her room, so he had nowhere to go, except the tiny maid's room, and there was nowhere to sit there. So he had set up his computer at the kitchen table.

"I think I'll order pizza," Blaise said vaguely. At least Salima liked that, and might eat. "Or sushi."

"Does an omelet appeal? Or pasta? I can whip that up pretty quickly." The omelet sounded good, but she didn't want to admit it, so she shook her head.

"We're fine," she insisted. She called for pizza, and he didn't interfere. She asked him what he wanted, and he said a large with everything on it except anchovies, which sounded good to her too. And she ordered a small pizza margherita for Salima, and she called her when they arrived. Salima came out of her bedroom and sat down at the kitchen table. Simon watched her mother serve her a slice on a plate and set it in front of her, and the three of them ate their pizza and said not a word.

After dinner, Salima went back to her room, and to bed a little while later. Blaise had told him she'd check Salima's insulin pump herself, so he didn't go in to see her. And Simon could see the light on in Blaise's office for a long time, but he didn't disturb her. He stayed on his computer for a while, read two more e-mails from Megan that sounded increasingly desperate, didn't answer her, and finally went to bed. It had been a long, stressful day. And he was well aware of just how unwelcome he was in their home.

* * *

When the alarm went off at four o'clock the next morning, Blaise felt like she'd been beaten with a stick. The past few days had taken their toll. The shocking news of Abby's death, her funeral, the school closing, Simon in the house. And Salima to take care of for the next few months. It was overwhelming. The one thing she was grateful for was that Simon knew all the protocols for Salima's blood tests, monitoring her insulin pump, checking it at night, and dealing with her diabetes. He knew exactly what he was doing, which was a relief. But everything else he did unnerved her. His very presence in her home felt like an intrusion and rubbed her the wrong way. She was trying not to let it upset her, but it did. And she didn't want to let Salima know how much. Salima disliked him enough already, and it would only make matters worse. Salima had objected strenuously to Simon moving in with them. And Blaise had told her they had no other option and she had to make her peace with it. She had to please her mother, but grudgingly. And Blaise couldn't deal with a war in her home and didn't want to. They were stuck with Simon, for now anyway, and had to make it work, like it or not. And Salima didn't love it.

Blaise got out of bed slowly, not quite ready to face the day and all the stress she knew was waiting for her at work: Susie Q, and all the projects Blaise was working on and hadn't finished when she left in a rush three days earlier. She would have to deal with all of it today. She took a shower instead of a bath, trying to wake up, even though she wet her hair. The hairdresser on the set could deal with it when she got there. And her shoulder-length red hair was still wet when she walked into the kitchen half an hour later in a crisp white shirt and gray slacks, and no makeup. She needed a cup of coffee desperately, and had the newspapers in her hand when she walked in, and nearly screamed as she saw Simon at the kitchen table. He stood up and handed her a cup of steaming-hot coffee, just the way she liked it. He had noticed the way she took it the day before. Two sugars, no cream. She wanted to thank him, but she couldn't as she took the cup from him. She didn't want to talk to anyone at that hour, and he could see it instantly on her face.

"Sorry," he said apologetically. "I couldn't sleep, and Salima said you have breakfast at five o'clock every day. I figured I'd make myself useful." He didn't tell her that the bed was much too small and his legs hung off the end. He didn't want to complain. It was hard enough having him there, and he knew it. Whatever he did, right or wrong, he wasn't Abby. For Salima, it was a felony. For her mother, an unwelcome invasion. The barbarians were not just at the gate, they were in her home, and her kitchen. He could read it in her eyes.

"I like making my own," she said simply, as she sat down at the kitchen table, opened the papers, and didn't say another word. He felt as though he had committed a crime making her coffee. She never thanked him, she didn't want to encourage him to do it again, and he had gotten the message, he wouldn't. He planned to stay out of the kitchen in the morning from now on. He had read her loud and clear, and he had to admit it was early. And he was a creature of habit too, so he respected that in her.

He heard the front door close when she left for work, and the apartment was silent. Salima was still asleep. The housekeeper didn't come till ten. And Eric called him at eight.

"How's it going?" He sounded optimistic but concerned. He was checking on all his teachers who had gone home with kids. So far, everyone was happy, and the parents were grateful and relieved to have help at home.

"A little rugged," Simon admitted. "Salima is heartbroken over Abby. And I think her mother hates men, in her house anyway. She's not used to having Salima here either. It's a little dicey. We're all adjusting. And Abby must have treated her like a five-year-old, more than any of us knew. She did everything for her except chew her food. She infantilized her completely. We have a long way to go here, just to get her up to speed. And no one is enthused about that project. Salima's mother keeps telling me not to rock the boat." Simon sounded exasperated as he explained the situation to him. He was trying to be zen about it, but it was a challenge.

"I'm sorry, Simon," Eric said sincerely. "I know she babied her, and they had a very close relationship, so it's hard to make changes. And it's very soon. And I think that her mother liked Abby's style. She never objected to how cocooned she was when Salima went home. I think it assuages some of her guilt for not having her at home, and having a demanding career."

"Maybe," Simon said thoughtfully. He was trying to figure it out and be patient. "The apartment really isn't big enough for me. Or even for Salima. It's set up very nicely for a single woman. Salima is in Siberia, at the end of a long hall, and pretty isolated, and I'm in a maid's room behind the kitchen, which is fine, but there's nowhere for me to sit without annoying someone. I made a major faux pas this morning, and made her coffee at five A.M. before she left for work. She looked pissed. I guess she doesn't like talking to anyone before she goes to work." He was walking on eggshells, and Eric could hear it and felt bad for him. He was such a decent, capable guy, he hated to have them make him so uncomfortable, but he'd had no one else to send home with Salima, or he would have. And Blaise was right, a woman would have been easier, in close quarters with Salima and her mother.

"See how it goes and keep me posted," Eric said, sounding concerned. He was wondering if he should say something to Blaise. He didn't want Simon to quit, or just walk off the job, but he knew Simon wouldn't do that, he was tenacious, and brilliant at what he did. Eric knew that if anyone could turn it around, he could. But they clearly didn't appreciate his skills. He was the best teacher Eric had. He was a natural problem solver and creative thinker.

"Don't worry, we'll make it work," Simon said, trying to sound hopeful, but he wasn't. And the day got off to a bad start when Salima woke up and found her way into the kitchen, and she gave a start when Simon said good morning. She acted as though she didn't expect him to be there.

"Did you sleep okay?" He tried to sound more casual than he felt. She looked ravaged, and was still in deep grief over Abby.

"Yeah, I guess," she said, slumped at the kitchen table.

"What would you like for breakfast?" he asked cheerfully, ready to make her anything she wanted. He was a great short-order chef, but she had no reason to know it.

"Poison," she said glumly, staring into space, and not looking in his direction. With his students, he always made them look in the direction of the person speaking. It was a good habit to get into, even if they couldn't see them. But he said nothing to her. It was too soon.

"Sorry. I'm fresh out. No poison today. How about bacon and eggs? Or whole wheat pancakes?"

"Abby always made me special waffles. But we don't have a waffle iron here. My mother doesn't believe in keeping fattening foods in the house, and she always wants me on a diet for my weight and diabetes," Salima said unhappily. Simon was aware that Blaise was very slim, but Salima wasn't much bigger. And he was well aware of the diet Salima needed to follow for her diabetes.

"I can buy a waffle iron today and keep it in my room." Maybe under the bed or in my closet, or on my head, he thought to himself. Salima looked in his direction then and smiled.

"She'll get mad if she finds out," Salima warned him.

"Then don't tell her." He was trying to find a way to ally with Salima, and if a waffle iron would do it, he was willing to risk her mother's ire. "What are we going to do today? After breakfast." He wanted to get some food into her first. She looked depressed, and he thought food might help.

"I just want to stay here." She seemed lifeless as she said it.

"I have some errands to do, and I need your help. I don't know the neighborhood, and I haven't been to New York in a year." She didn't look enthused at the prospect. "Which reminds me, I need a bunch of phone numbers, and things off the Internet. I'd like you to get them for me on your computer." It was a way to get her involved.

"Can't you do that yourself? I'm not your secretary," she said tartly. He didn't respond or react.

"I need some new CDs too. I forgot all of mine at school." It wasn't true, but he wanted to buy music with her and see what she liked.

As he chatted with her, he scrambled some eggs, cooked two slices of bacon, made some toast, and set it down in front of her. She could smell it cooking, and she looked unimpressed when he put a fork in her hand.

"Eat, get dressed. Then we'll go out." She didn't

thank him for breakfast, but as she started to eat, he could see from the look on her face that she liked it. She really was a child.

"The eggs are good," she finally admitted. "What if I won't go out?" He knew she was testing him, and he didn't want to react.

"Let's see, what would be suitable punishment for that?" He took her comment lightly, which seemed to be the best way to handle her. "Set your hair on fire maybe? Steal your favorite CD? Lock you in your room and refuse to feed you? Make you eat brussels sprouts?"

"I like brussels sprouts," she said, smiling again. She almost liked him sometimes, but not quite. He wasn't Abby. But she could tell he was smart. She had hardly ever spoken to him at school. He was in a cottage with younger boys.

"Then that won't work. What food do you hate most?"

"Beans, of any kind."

"Good. Beans. If you won't go out with me, you'll have to eat beans for a week."

"You can't make me," she said, sounding belligerent again.

"Eat beans?"

"No. Go out."

"Yes, I can. I can force you to do all kinds of horrible things with me. Like advise me about what music to buy. Something tells me you know a lot about music."

"I just like to sing." Her face brightened as she said it.

"Like what?"

"Anything. I've always loved to sing. It makes me happy." He was smiling at her as she said it. He had found the key to the secret garden. She had just handed it to him.

"Can you play the piano?" he asked, and she shook her head in answer.

"I never wanted to practice. I'm lazy," she confessed.

"I can. My mother made me practice every day. But it's kind of fun to know how." He didn't offer to play for her, and she didn't ask. And a few minutes later she got up and started to walk out of the kitchen, and left her empty plate on the table. She had eaten everything he'd made her.

"Excuse me," he said, stopping her with his tone of voice, and she looked surprised. "Table service, please. You need to put that plate in the dishwasher." He sounded casual, and she looked stunned. Abby would never have said that to her, and hadn't in five years.

"I don't have to do that," she informed him in a supercilious tone.

"Yes, you do," he said simply. "You're not my secretary. I'm not your maid. That's how it works." He didn't mention cooking as part of the deal, but he wanted to give her good habits, and she had very few. She was polite but used to Abby waiting on her hand and foot. Those days were over, and only for her own good.

"My mother doesn't expect me to bus dishes. We have a maid."

"That's pretty rude, isn't it? Why should you leave

that for her? It takes two seconds to rinse it and put it in the machine." Salima hesitated for a long moment, and then she picked the plate up off the table, walked to the sink, rinsed it, and put it in the dishwasher. She did it perfectly. And then with a haughty look, she walked out of the kitchen and back to her room. Round one, Simon thought to himself. And she hadn't had the guts to defy him completely, which was good. She was back in the kitchen half an hour later. She could hear him in the room, and he was pleased to see that she was dressed to go out, in jeans and a red leather jacket. She was a very pretty girl, with her long dark hair, and she had on dark glasses, which she wore when she went out.

"You look nice," he said admiringly. "I like your jacket."

"Me too. It's red," she said, as though he didn't know. She was proud that she did. Abby had put a little slip of paper in Braille in the pocket, which told her the color.

"I know. And I like your Ray-Bans. Are you ready to go out?"

"I guess so," she said, sounding cautious. "Where are we going?"

"Music store first. Did you look it up?"

"I know where the closest one is. I always stock up there. I download music, but I like buying CDs too."

"Close enough to walk?" She nodded, and he got up, pleased that she was willing to go out. And he glanced at her as they were about to leave. "Do you have your stick?" He meant a white one with a red tip, to identify her as blind and guide her while they walked.

"I don't use one." He looked surprised by her response.

"Why not?"

"I don't need it. I just hang on to Abby when we go out."

"Wouldn't you rather have a little more mobility than just hanging on to me?"

"No, that's fine." She didn't want to identify herself as blind, but he thought she should use a stick, since she didn't have a dog. He wondered about that and asked her about it as they set out down the street toward the music store.

"Why no dog?" She had her hand tucked into his arm as they walked.

"I hate dogs. I got bitten once by a German shepherd when I was a little kid. All guide dogs are German shepherds."

"That's not true. Some are Labs. They're nice, and they don't bite. That might give you more freedom."

"I don't need freedom, or a dog," she said, shutting down again, but she opened up the minute they got to the music store and spent two hours picking CDs. She introduced him to some bands and singers that he didn't know, and gave him good advice. And she picked out twenty new CDs for herself, some of them old groups, and others new ones. She had very eclectic taste in music, which Simon found interesting. She had fun and so did Simon. He was getting to know her through music. Whatever worked.

And after the music store, he took her to a lively place for lunch. She said she wasn't hungry, but he insisted he was starving, which wasn't true. But she went to be polite, and they talked all through lunch about what interested her, her values, her philosophies, how she felt about her father hardly ever seeing her, her mother's career. She began to lay the keys to the kingdom at his feet.

For Blaise, the day had gotten off to a bad start. First, she found herself face to face with Simon before she even had a cup of coffee. He was in the kitchen before she'd fully woken up. She hated talking to anyone in the morning, even if she'd slept with them the night before. Early morning was a sacred time to her. And she felt as though her life had been invaded from the moment he handed her the cup of coffee until she left for work.

Then her usual hairdresser didn't show up for work. Blaise was unhappy with what the replacement girl did to her hair, and she thought she looked a mess when she went on the air.

To make matters worse, after finishing her morning segment, she saw Susie Q sucking up to one of the network executives who was on the set. Watching her made Blaise feel sick. She was so obvious it turned her stomach.

And the rest of the day was a series of annoyances and aggravations. Tully was on vacation so she had a driver she didn't like. By the time she got home that night, an hour later than usual, due to traffic, all she wanted was to take a bath and go to bed. Instead there was music blaring in the house, on the stereo system she never used. She could tell that it was Salima's music. She could hear her singing. And Blaise could hear voices in the kitchen. She walked in with a scowl on her face.

"What are you doing?" she said to Simon in a harsh voice. The day was ending as it had started, with Simon in her space.

"Cooking dinner," he said calmly. He was wearing an apron, and he had Salima handing him ingredients. Their day had gone very well. She was teaching him the difference between reggae and ska. And she also loved jazz and blues, just as he did. They had bought a lot of CDs. However, the one on the stereo just then was not one that her mother loved. "It will be ready in ten minutes," Simon warned her, "or longer if you need more time."

"I told you not to cook dinner," she snapped at him. "And I'm not hungry," she said rudely.

"We are," he said simply. "You don't have to join us if you don't want." She stalked off to her room then, and Simon put a soufflé in the oven, as Salima sat nearby.

"What are you making?" She sounded curious, and the smells in the kitchen were delicious.

"You'll see. I hope you like it. It's an old family recipe I learned from a chef in Paris. Just not my family. No one in my family can cook. My mother's cooking would kill you, except for blood sausage, which I love."

"Yerghk." Salima made a face. They had gone to the butcher after the music store, and he was making leg of lamb, "*gigot,*" with lots of garlic. Blaise could smell it in her room and was annoyed, but she washed her face and hands and walked back to the kitchen, just as he took the soufflé out of the oven. She looked surprised. And the table was set for all three of them. He had Salima do it. She said she hadn't done that since she was a child. Probably before she went blind, he guessed. For the past eleven years she had done no chores at all. That was clear.

"You made soufflé?" Blaise was stunned, and warmed up a little as they sat down at the table together. And she had to admit, the cheese soufflé was superb. They all had second helpings. And the *gigot* was just as good, maybe better. He had made mashed potatoes to go with it, and tossed a salad. It was a spectacular meal, with fresh fruit for dessert. "This is like eating in a four-star restaurant," Blaise complimented him. It was an absolutely delicious dinner, which put all of them in a good mood. They sat around the table afterward, looking relaxed. And he made an infusion of fresh mint for Blaise. "Where did you learn to cook like that?" She was intrigued. He was a man of many faces, talents, and skills, and all of them pleasant so far. She knew she had been less than nice to him. And she noticed that Salima seemed to have eased up on him that day. She hoped she wasn't falling for him. But at least she couldn't see his good looks. Blaise was grateful for that. He was a very handsome man.

"I went to cooking school in Paris," he told her, "after college and before I went to grad school. It's something I always wanted to do. Cooking is fun."

"Where did you do it?"

"Cordon Bleu," he said shamelessly, and she laughed.

"No wonder. You should be opening a restaurant, not teaching at a school."

"I like both," he said easily. "I like cooking for my friends. It relaxes me."

"Well, it certainly was a spectacular meal." She stood up, as Salima helped him clear the table, and her mother looked surprised. She suspected that was Simon's doing too, and she didn't comment. It wouldn't hurt her to put the dishes in the sink, and she looked happier than she had the day before. Blaise was sure she still missed Abby terribly, but at least she wasn't fighting Simon, for now.

Blaise was about to leave the kitchen, when he turned from the sink to ask her something. "I see that you have a piano. Do you mind if I play?" She looked surprised again.

"No, that's fine. As long as you don't play too late, or my neighbors will have a fit."

"I won't." He finished loading the dishwasher with

Salima, and she thanked him for dinner and went to her room, while Simon quietly walked into the living room and sat down at the piano, opened it, and began to play. He didn't play anything in particular, he started with show tunes, and played some of his favorites from the sixties, including a number of Beatles songs, and by the time he got to them, he saw Salima appear like a ghost. Blaise was listening in her room too. You could hear his playing throughout the apartment, and he was good. Maybe not as good as he was a chef, but it was close. And before she had reached the piano, Salima was singing to what he played. She knew all the songs, which was what he had hoped. He didn't know her favorites yet. But once she heard the music, she couldn't stay away. And Blaise could hear her too, and realized how clever he was. He was using the things Salima loved to establish a rapport with her.

They sat together for an hour while she sang and he played, and then with regret he closed the piano, and said they'd better not play too late or they'd get in trouble with the neighbors and her mom would be mad. Salima was sad to see their musical alliance end.

"Have you ever thought of taking singing lessons?" he asked her as they left the room.

"No. I used to want to be a singer when I was a kid. But I don't want to be Ray Charles or Stevie Wonder when I grow up. And I don't write music. You kind of have to if you want to be special." She looked disappointed as she said it.

"You don't have to be a pro. Why not just do it for

fun?" he suggested. "That's why I cook. Because I enjoy it."

"Maybe." Salima thought about it, and then said goodnight. She stopped in at her mother's room on the way back to her own. Blaise was at her desk, writing an editorial for the next day, with a stack of research beside her.

"You and Simon sounded great. He certainly has a lot of talents. Music, cooking." And he was handling Salima well.

"Could I ever take singing lessons?" Salima asked her, and Blaise looked surprised again. It was the first time Salima had ever inquired about it, although she'd had a singing talent all her life.

"I don't see why not. I'll see what I can find. Someone who can come to the house." Salima nodded. It sounded good to her. She kissed her mother goodnight then, and drifted back to her own room. She listened to several of the CDs they'd bought that afternoon, and sang along with them.

And in the kitchen, Simon was at his computer, checking Facebook, which gave him something to do. He saw then that Megan had sent him another e-mail. He read it, deleted it, closed his computer, and went back to his room. The one thing he knew was that their desperate, dishonest, twisted illicit affair had to end. But as he lay down on his bed and thought about her, he was sad. At least work was going well.

Chapter 6

The next day got off to a better start for Blaise. She walked into the kitchen just before five A.M. and fully expected to see Simon there again, handing her a cup of coffee. But he tried not to make the same mistakes twice. Her coffee was hot and waiting, but he was nowhere to be seen, and his door was closed. He had set the table for her, and put the newspapers next to where she sat. Her coffee was ready, and she didn't have to see him. It was perfect, and she left for work in a much better mood.

Her morning segment went smoothly, and when she got to her office, she asked Mark to find her a music teacher, and he looked at her in amazement.

"You want to take singing lessons? Tap too? Does this have anything to do with Susie Q? You're adding vaudeville to your segment?" She laughed at his response, and it was certainly a thought.

"It's for Salima. She has a beautiful voice, and her

new caretaker must have suggested singing lessons to her. It's not a bad idea, especially since she'll be home for a few months. It will keep her busy." Blaise liked the idea too.

"Who do I call?" He looked blank. It was an unusual request for him.

"That's up to you. Juilliard maybe? Or maybe they can steer you in the right direction. Maybe some of the students give lessons. I think there's a high school for arts and music too. See what turns up."

"Will do," he said, and he called Juilliard a little later and was given several names. He left voicemail messages for each one and reported back to Blaise. "How's the new guy working out by the way?"

"I'm not sure. Yesterday morning I was ready to kill him when he got in my face at five A.M. Last night, he made a meal worthy of La Grenouille, and he played the piano while Salima sang, and now he has her wanting to take singing lessons. He certainly opens up the world to her. Abby was more of a homebody, and a cozy person. This one opens up all the windows and gets air into the house. He even has her doing dishes. I don't know, maybe it will work. At least until she goes back. It's different anyway. But he keeps her busy. And whatever else he is, he's a very bright guy."

"Do you think he's got the hots for her, with the piano playing and all of that?"

"No, I don't. I just think he's trying to figure out what interests her, and trying to relate to her through that. He's a very proper guy. He's got nice manners, and he's well brought up, and he's not inappropriate with either of us. It's just weird having a man in the house. I'm not used to it anymore."

"Maybe it will do you both good," Mark said with a knowing look. He worried about her being alone all the time, and he was sad for her that at forty-seven, she hadn't had a date in four years. It didn't seem right to him, and she was beautiful and a good person, talented and smart. But he knew the story of Andrew Weyland and how badly she'd been hurt. He had seen her look devastated afterward for nearly a year. And now it was four, and she had removed herself entirely from the dating scene. She was much too comfortable alone. And he hated to see her stay that way. She deserved so much more. And her career, no matter how satisfying, wasn't enough, even if she thought it was. And in Mark's opinion, success was so ephemeral. Someone like Susie Quentin could come along anytime and maneuver Blaise right out of a job.

Blaise got a hint of the prevailing winds that afternoon. She had lunch at her desk, and glanced up to see an e-mail coming in on her computer. And she sat staring at it after she read it. And then read it again. The president of the news division had resigned and been replaced. He had been lured away by another network. And she knew instantly from experience that everything was about to change. The new president was thirty years old, and she knew him by reputation. Everyone in the business knew him. He was a hotshot, and was considered a renegade, previously at another network, and known to keep the bottom line in his sights at all times. He loved reality shows for that reason. And they were so much cheaper to make. He was also famous for firing people on a whim, with no warning. One slip in the ratings, and you were dead. And he would find someone cheaper to replace talent who he felt made too much money. He was good at what he did, and he would be watching Blaise like a hawk. As if she didn't have enough problems at the moment. She looked panicked when she told Mark about Zack Austin.

"I hear he's a real son of a bitch," Mark said in a whisper, as though the walls had ears now. "No one is safe with him running things." He had come from the entertainment division and Blaise was afraid he'd be looking to jazz things up, possibly with talent closer to his age. Blaise looked nervous. Even in her position, no one was ever totally secure at the network. She made more money than any on-air talent, and if he could replace her with someone cheaper, younger, and whom he considered as good, there was no question that he would. She was a big target, and she had the distinct feeling that Zack Austin would be gunning for her. Blaise was a nervous wreck by the time she got home that night, and Simon could see that she looked strained.

He made another delicious dinner, although simpler than the one the night before, since he knew Blaise was careful about what she ate. He made a simple saffron risotto, roast chicken, green beans, and fruit salad. And they ate it all. And she lingered for a moment when he was cleaning up. Salima had gone to her room for something, and wanted to sing with him again. And he had taken her to Ellis Island that day. He thought she should write a paper on it for school, for her American history class.

Blaise was pouring herself a cup of tea from a chamomile infusion he had made, and he glanced over at her. "Are you okay?" he asked her, worried that he was crossing a line. But she looked anxious and distracted all through dinner. She started to nod, and then decided to be honest.

"No, I'm not. They brought in a new head of the news division who doesn't know anything about the news. He's from the entertainment side of the business. We'd all better get out our tap shoes." Simon looked stunned by her answer.

"Are you kidding? You're Blaise McCarthy, you're a legend all over the world. People in the desert on camels know who you are." She shrugged.

"Maybe. But the network's not as impressed as you or the camels are. They always figure we're replaceable, and they're always looking for someone younger and cheaper. I cost them a fortune. And they don't give a damn about 'Blaise McCarthy,' the 'legend.' As long as they sign the checks, they call the shots. As someone once said to me, it's the Golden Rule. He who has the gold rules. And they do. I'm just hired help as far as they're concerned. There's nothing secure in this business, and the longer I'm in it and the older I get, the greater the chance they'll get rid of me sooner or later. In fact, they're grooming someone to knock me out of my spot now. She's just not ready yet, or I'd be collecting unemployment, or doing stories about dog shows for the four A.M. news."

Simon looked horrified. In his mind, she was a star. In hers, she had to fight all the time. And she knew it was true. It had the ring of truth to him too, and opened his eyes to the stress she lived with every day. He had been convinced that being as famous as she was meant that you never had to worry, that she was safe. Instead, she had to worry even more. He wondered if she had to worry about money too, and hoped not for her sake. But it was obvious she depended only on herself. There was no one else around. And somehow, listening to her, he realized that being a star was not enough. It was a lonely, scary life. And he wouldn't have traded places with her for anything in the world. For all the glory and so-called glamour, she still had a kid who needed special attention that nothing would fix and was trying to give her a good life. There was no one there to help her, and she had no partner and was alone, and she lived with constant stress at work. He was glad he didn't have her job, and he had greater respect for her now after what she'd just said. At least he could be there for Salima. He gave Blaise a sympathetic look, and she smiled at him with a weary expression, as Salima walked in and told him to hurry up. She wanted him to play piano for her again. She'd had fun the night before. And she didn't realize that he'd been having a serious conversation with her mother. He left the kitchen with Salima a minute later.

And hearing them from her room a little later, Blaise closed her eyes and listened to her daughter singing in her beautiful pure voice. She was singing old Barbra Streisand songs, and then switched to gospel songs, which Blaise always loved. And all Blaise could hope was that Zack Austin never found a reason to fire her, and no one else would take her place. She wished that Simon was right and she was untouchable because of who she was. But who she was, and how big she was, put her that much more at risk. The top was a lonely place to be, in a life that wasn't perfect at all. And Simon had just gotten a glimpse of that for the first time. Most people never knew.

Not surprisingly, Blaise couldn't sleep that night and decided to work late. Concentrating on her work always calmed her. She was doing early research for several political profiles she wanted to pitch to Charlie. And with Zack Austin watching her now, the heat was on. She had to be even better than she had been, to justify her existence and hold her own, although the ratings still loved her. But with changes in management, you never knew. She finished at two A.M., and was making herself a cup of warm milk, when Simon heard her and walked in. He was still dressed too.

Blaise smiled at him as she poured the milk into a mug. At that hour, tired, she looked vulnerable and younger than she was. And he looked tired too. He had been reading old e-mails from Meg, wondering how he had gotten into such a mess, sacrificed his integrity, and done something he knew was wrong. She was a married woman, and despite her promises that she didn't keep, he had gone on. To him, loving her seemed like a poor excuse. He knew better than to do what he'd done. And this was the first time he had gotten involved with a married woman.

"You and Salima sound great together," she complimented him, as she sat down at the kitchen table, and he smiled. "If all else fails, we can open a restaurant and nightclub. You cook, the two of you sing after dinner, and I can wait on tables," she teased, and he laughed. At least she had a sense of humor about it, but he could see that she was worried and exhausted.

"That'll never happen. They may give you a tough time, but they'd be suicidal to get rid of you. You're an icon."

"Even icons get fired. If my ratings ever slipped, I'd be dead meat in about five minutes."

"That's a hell of a way to live," he commented.

"The fast lane. It comes at a high price."

"Is it worth it?" he asked her honestly, curious about her. He liked how straightforward she was with him, and about everything. He had the feeling that he could ask her anything and she'd tell the truth. He had judged her well. It was why she and Harry were still friends. She was a woman eminently worthy of respect.

"Sometimes it's worth it," she said, looking thoughtful. "I love what I do. It's exciting. I guess it's glamorous, which isn't why I do it. Maybe I love the challenge. I've had fun doing it for a lot of years. I don't like the insecurity anymore, or the pressure. It's like playing Russian roulette every day. But the highs are pretty high. It's addictive."

"I don't think I could do it," he said thoughtfully. "In fact, I know I couldn't. I don't like risk. I'm not a gambler, and I like a quiet life. And I don't like playing by other people's rules. My parents taught me that. My father is an inventor and he taught me to think outside the box. And my mom is pretty out there too. They're both eccentric. But thinking outside the box is why I do what I do. I teach kids not to accept limitations, of any kind. If they can dream it, they can do it. My father taught me that."

"But why at Caldwell?" she asked. She was curious about him too. He was so smart to be buried away in a small school in Massachusetts. She thought he was capable of more.

"I don't know. It's easy, comfortable. I'd like to work at a bigger school, like Perkins in Massachusetts outside Boston, or one of the big schools for the blind here in New York, like the Institute for Special Education. I kind of got stuck at Caldwell. I got involved with someone and didn't want to leave. I haven't started to resolve it until now. I was trapped. I think this break, with Caldwell closing for a while, is what I needed."

"You got involved with someone at the school?"

He nodded. "Another teacher. She's married with three kids. She said she was getting divorced. And instead of waiting for her to do it, I jumped the gun. I knew better, but I was lonely, she was bored. I hadn't been in a relationship for a while, and I fell madly in love with her. Three years later she's still married and has a thousand reasons not to leave him. It goes against everything I believe. I can't do it anymore. I just told her."

"Maybe she'll leave him now," she said, thinking about Andrew. But he hadn't left his wife when she broke it off. She still believed that if he had loved her, he would have. Some people just never leave. They get away with what they can for a while, and then do it again with someone else. "I did something like that myself." She was honest with him, and he looked at her, intrigued. "I knew it was wrong too. Same story. Only he lied to me, and said he was in the process of divorce. He wasn't. He just lied. And I believed him for a year. Then the house of cards came down when I found out he'd lied. I broke it off, and I figured he'd leave her then and clean it up. He never did. He's still with her four years later. He still calls sometimes, and I talk to him. I know I shouldn't, but there's no one else, so I talk to him anyway, and he makes me feel like shit all over again. Some people have a real knack for doing that." She looked at him ruefully, and he smiled.

"I hate the dishonesty," Simon said, looking pained.

"She lies to him, she lies to me. How can you have a relationship built on lies?"

"You can't," she answered for him. "I tried. And I thought he was honest with me, but he wasn't, which is maybe a little worse. But either way, the lies catch up with you in the end. I learned a hell of a lesson, and I haven't dated anyone since. I don't even miss it." And then she corrected herself with a thoughtful look. "That's not true actually. I do miss it, and even him sometimes, but I don't miss the pain of what we had or the price to pay. I wouldn't do something like that again."

"Neither would I," Simon said. "You don't miss having someone in your life?"

"I do, just not him. And I've always been in love with my work, that helps. Probably too much so. Whenever there was a choice to make about priorities, I picked work. I feel guilty about it for Salima, but she's very forgiving and seems to accept me as I am. It's the way it is. When I was married to her father, I was more in love with my career than I was with him, and he knew it. Success is heady stuff. I have no regrets though, and we wound up friends. My only regret is that married asshole who lied to me and I should never have gotten involved with. Probably the only man I've ever really loved is my first husband. I was married to him when I was barely older than Salima, and widowed when I was twenty-three. He was a cameraman for CNN and got killed by a sniper. After that, all I cared about was my career. It didn't hurt as much as loving a person. People die, they cheat, they lie, they disappoint you. And work is just work."

"That's a very solitary way to live," he said, looking sympathetic. "My parents are still in love with each other, and they've been married for thirty-five years. They're kind of cute together, although my mom is pretty nuts, and says whatever comes into her head. It used to embarrass the hell out of me when I was a kid. She's outrageous, but he loves it. It was a little dicier as their kid, and not quite as charming." Blaise smiled at his description of his parents. They sounded interesting to her.

"My parents were pretty ordinary. My father was a butcher, my mother was a teacher, they had a strong work ethic and good values. My father always told me work was everything and to do something I loved. I got the message. But they didn't say much about loving people. I was their only child, and they were both killed in a car accident when I was in college. They left me a life insurance policy that got me through school, and after that I was on my own. I grew up in Seattle, and I started in news there, as a weather girl," she said with a grin. "It was a stupid job, but it got me in. And after that it was San Francisco and New York, and now here I am, trying to cover my ass every day. They don't tell you that in the beginning. It must be in the small print in the contract."

"You make me feel like I should be doing more," he said honestly. "I've taken the easy road till now, and took a job I could do without too much challenge. By the time you were my age, you were a big star, had been married twice, and had a kid. Not bad," he said admiringly. She had come a long, long way from being a butcher's daughter in Seattle. And he had had an easier start. His father had a prestigious job in the academic world, his mother had money, and they were still alive and married. He wondered if that was the difference. Maybe he'd had it too easy. His family had always been behind him. Blaise only had herself.

"It's not too late," she reminded him with a wry grin. "You're still a kid."

"Thirty-two is not a kid," he said seriously, but he looked like one to her at times. And she was fifteen years older, and they had been action-packed years. "That's why I got out of it with the married woman. I don't want to waste the next fifteen years waiting for someone else to get their life together, while they screw up mine. I finally had to think of myself."

"So will you stay at Caldwell?" Blaise asked him, curious about him as a person now.

"I don't know. Maybe not. I want to send some applications around to other schools while I'm here, bigger ones, preferably one in a city, where I'll have a fuller life. And I don't want to fall into the same trap again with her, if I go back to Caldwell after this year. I have to go back when they reopen, to honor my contract, but after that I don't know."

"I think you're capable of more," she said, and he was touched that she thought so. He had a lot of respect for her, more so now that he had seen her at home, what she stood for, and what she did, and the toll it took on her. She was the first to admit that she hadn't been present enough for Salima, but she was an honest, honorable person.

"Thank you. At least I'd like to try," Simon said, about doing more with his life. "Otherwise I'll never know. I don't need to be a star, or even want to be. I just need to be the best I can be at what I do." He looked very earnest as he said it.

"From what I can see so far, you are the best. Eric said so. Give yourself a break. What you do is very noble. And if you want to, you'll find a better job. You have everything you need, the credentials, the talent, the motivation, the gift. What you do for others is a gift." Salima had begun to blossom in just two days, and she could see the difference now between Abby protecting her and holding her back, and Simon inspiring her to do more with herself. And he was kind to Blaise too.

They chatted for a few more minutes, and then Blaise stood up and said she had to go to bed. She had to get up in an hour, and he apologized for keeping her up.

"It was worth it," she said in a gentle tone. "Sometimes I get scared at night when I think about my life. All I see are the mistakes in the past, and the dangers up ahead."

"We all do," he said gently. "Don't be so hard on yourself." One of the things she was coming to like about him was that he wasn't impressed by who she was. He respected her and thought she'd had an amazing career, but he wasn't dazzled by the tinsel. He understood who Blaise was, and just like her, he was real. They both knew that was rare. Simon treated her as though she were an ordinary, normal person, not a star. No one had done that in years.

"Goodnight, Simon," she said, and waved from the doorway. "You don't have to get my coffee ready in the morning. Get some sleep." It was more than she would be able to do, having to get up in an hour, but he could sleep in till Salima got up.

"Someone has to take care of you," he said seriously. "From what I can see, no one else does. You take care of everyone else, or at least you're responsible for them." He was the first person who had noticed it in years, maybe ever. And he was right. No one took care of her, and no one ever had. She was a fighter and a survivor, used to doing everything on her own. "At least I can provide hot coffee and some decent dinners while I'm here. It's not much, but it's something."

"It's a lot," she said. "Thank you. Goodnight." She closed the kitchen door, and he went back to his room. And she went back to hers, after she checked on Salima, feeling like she'd found a friend. It was a nice thing to have.

Chapter 7

With all the pressures and tension at the network, finding a music teacher for Salima had slipped Blaise's mind. She and Simon were singing together almost every night, and Salima was having fun, but Mark hadn't dropped the ball on the project, even if Blaise had. A week after she'd made the request, he put a memo on her desk for her to find after her morning segment.

There were three names with phone numbers and e-mails, two women, one man, two from LaGuardia High School of Music & Art and Performing Arts, and one from Juilliard. His memo said he had spoken to all of them, and Blaise wandered out to his desk to discuss it with him.

"So who did you like best?" she asked, impressed with his thorough research. Salima was going to be thrilled.

"The one from Juilliard, hands down. The others

sounded good, but the woman from Juilliard was more appealing. A little wacky maybe, but she was excited to work with Salima even though she's blind. I thought the other two might be more nervous about it, although I could be wrong. And all three come from great schools."

"Follow your gut," Blaise said without hesitation. "Call her. Ask her to come to the house, so Salima can check her out. She has to like her too."

"No problem." And half an hour later, there was a follow-up note on her desk with the teacher's name, and a time for an appointment the next day with Salima at the apartment, and of course Simon would be there too. It was set for the time Blaise usually came home from work.

The following day Blaise had only just come through the door five minutes before and was talking to Salima when the doorman called to announce their "guest." It was the Juilliard teacher, Lucianna Goldstein. Mark had already told her that she was an Italian woman, married to an American, hence the name. And when she came through the door five minutes later, while Blaise was still taking off her coat, the woman was as incongruous as her name. She had a wide, welcoming smile, bright blue eyes, and a mellifluous voice, and a head full of shining gold curls. She had a large, generous body, an enormous bosom, and tiny spindly legs. She wore lots of bangle bracelets, too much perfume, dangling hoop earrings, and enormously high stiletto heels. And to top it all off, a hat with flowers on it that moved, which she carefully removed as soon as she entered the apartment and set down on the hall table as Blaise stared at it in fascination. It looked like a garden with tiny living things on it. There were so many different component parts to her outfit that Blaise didn't know where to look, and she was sorry that Salima wouldn't be able to share this vision. But the most noticeable thing about Lucianna was her voice. It was smooth as silk. And her eyes were the most brilliant blue she had ever seen, as she looked at Blaise warmly.

"Oh my," Lucianna said with a smile that showed off perfect teeth, "you're older than I thought you would be." She looked straight at Blaise. "But that's all right, it's never too late to learn to sing." She had a lovely accent, and Simon was grinning. The teacher thought Blaise was Salima, and she was quick to explain, as Salima arrived in the front hall, having heard the doorbell. She was listening intently and wrinkled her nose at the perfume that assaulted her as soon as she joined them.

"This is Salima, your prospective student," Blaise explained. "Won't you come in?" She offered Lucianna a cup of tea as they walked into the living room, but she declined, then she noticed the grand piano. It was a Steinway, and she approved. She seemed a little nervous with Salima, and even more so around Blaise. She knew exactly who they were and had told Mark she didn't know that Blaise McCarthy had a blind daughter. And he told her that there would be a confidentiality agreement to sign if she was hired. It was standard fare in Blaise's life. And the teacher had no problem with the agreement. She mentioned that she'd never had a blind student before.

They chatted for a few minutes, as Lucianna perched on the couch, and Salima mostly listened. She could hear that the woman was nervous, and Lucianna told them she had studied opera in Milan. She rattled off the various opera companies she had worked for all over Europe, and now she had been in the States for eighteen years, and with Juilliard for fifteen. She told Salima that if she was serious about a music career, she should apply. But for now, all Salima wanted were some lessons, and after half an hour of introductions, Lucianna asked her to sing. Simon had agreed to accompany her on the piano, and Salima took her place next to him. She was glad that he was there, and she asked Lucianna what she'd like to hear. She said she didn't know any opera, but she knew show tunes, contemporary music, and gospel hymns. Diplomatically, Lucianna suggested one of each. She started with a song from *Mamma Mia!,* went on to *Les Miserables,* and finished with a gospel song that Blaise loved whenever she sang it. Her high notes were so high, they sounded as if they could shatter glass, and she hit them with ease. She went through the three songs easily, and Lucianna stared at her when she was finished.

"Did you warm up before I came?" she asked, looking worried.

"No, I didn't. No one told me what time you'd be here," which was why she was wearing sweatpants and socks, instead of at least jeans and shoes.

"You'll ruin your voice if you do that," the ample Italian woman warned her. "You must never sing without warming up first. And the gospel song—can you always hit those high notes?" Salima said she could, with a grin. Lucianna looked at her then with tears in her eyes. "Do you realize how lucky you are? What a gift you have? People train for years and can't hit notes like that. You just soar right through it like a bird in the sky," she said, and dabbed at her eyes. "What I could have done with a voice like yours." She had explained that she was from Venice originally, although she had lived in Milan while she trained and studied. She asked Salima if she had any interest in opera, and Salima said she didn't. She wanted to enjoy what she sang. It was mostly fun for her. "You should really be in school," she said. "This is very naughty of you, to treat your voice like a toy. It's not a plaything, it's a gift." She was a very funny woman, and Blaise thought she looked like a caricature of herself with her enormous body, skinny legs, and tiny feet in high heels. And she had gentle, loving eyes. Simon was watching her in fascination, and Salima was listening to her raptly.

"Would you be willing to take my daughter on as a student?" Blaise finally asked her bluntly, as everyone else beat around the bush.

"Of course," she said with a wide smile that was

wasted on Salima, but she reached out and touched her hand. "I would love to, it would be an honor. But I will expect you to work very hard," she admonished Salima.

"How many times would you like to meet?" Blaise asked her and was startled when she said three times a week. "Is that too much?" Blaise asked with a look of concern. It seemed like a lot to her.

"Not if she's serious about singing," Lucianna answered. "If she had less of a voice, I'd say once or twice a week. But if we want results, and to train her voice properly, it should be three or even four times a week. We can start with three and see how she does."

"What do you think, Salima?" Blaise didn't want to leave her out of the decision and treat her like a child. "How many times a week would you want singing lessons?"

"Every day," Salima said, grinning, and Lucianna looked thrilled. She looked like she had discovered gold that afternoon, or a diamond on the street.

They set their first meeting for the following afternoon, and Lucianna kissed Salima's cheek and reminded her to keep her neck warm at all times and wear a scarf. She put her hat back on, shook hands with Blaise and Simon, and a moment later she was gone as they all stared at each other and began to laugh. She was a sweet woman even if she looked a little like a clown. That had only occurred to Blaise once they sat down.

"She smells awful, but I like her," Salima was the first to comment.

"You should see what she looks like," Blaise added with a smile, but she liked her too. There was something very warm and lovable about her.

Simon agreed that she was nice, and her credentials were excellent if she taught at Juilliard, and whatever happened, he thought it would be something fun for Salima to do. She was excited and talked about it all through dinner. Simon was cooking for them every night now. He tried to keep it light for Blaise but occasionally showed off with some of his fancier dishes. They were all superb. And it added a festive feeling to the evenings. Blaise found herself looking forward to their dinners together, and it was nice having someone ask her how her day was, and he looked as though he cared. Ever since their conversation about what she dealt with at the network, he had had even more respect for her, and sympathy when she came home.

And Salima was adjusting to Simon too. They had occasional arguments about how to spend their time. He had suggestions for every day, and he thought everything they did should have some educational value. But he also made her negotiate the post office, the pharmacy, the grocery store, the dry cleaner, the bank. And he forced her to take public transportation instead of cabs. She insisted that her mother preferred that she take taxis, but he didn't care. He was trying to teach her everything that he considered useful to her, while he was there. He even made her put the groceries away, and complained when she did it out of order and he found cottage cheese in the cupboard and pasta in the fridge. He expected her to get it right, and occasionally he was a hard taskmaster, but whenever he was and she accomplished the task he had set before her, she felt great about herself. Blaise was watching her grow more self-confident every day. And he still wanted to work on her about getting a seeing-eye dog. He thought that with a dog she could go to school alone. He didn't think she needed a caretaker all the time. And the thought of that panicked Blaise when he talked to her about it, and she told him to slow down.

"I have a fantastic opportunity with her while we're here," he explained. "I want her to gain as much ground as she can before she goes back to Caldwell," he told her mother, and Blaise pointed out to him that he was moving ahead at jet speed, and so was Salima. She loaded and unloaded the dishwasher now with ease, and even helped him with the cooking. He had shown her how to make an omelet on her own, and it was good. She had surprised her mother with one on Sunday morning. They were definitely on a crash course toward success, and once her music lessons started, Salima was ecstatic. Some of what she had to do was boring, like scales, but the rest of the time she had a ball, and Lucianna also let her play with her voice. She loved to hear her sing. And once in a while they sang duets that were exquisite. Lucianna had a beautiful soprano voice, and when their voices blended, it sounded like angels singing. Sometimes it brought Blaise to tears to hear them, and Simon was deeply moved. Salima had a powerful voice, and it was growing stronger with the lessons. He could hear the difference within weeks.

And on the weekends, when she didn't have work to catch up on, Blaise joined Simon and Salima on their outings. Even when she brought work home, she would stop what she was doing and go out with them for a while. They went to movies, stores, museums that had tactile exhibits, and a performance of *La Traviata* at the Met. Simon was using all the wonders of New York to educate and entertain her, and little by little he was making her more independent. He was constantly asking her to help him with chores or on the computer, and he asked her to do her own laundry, and she refused. She said her mother didn't either, and he laughed. She had a point, and maybe Salima would never have to, so he gave up on that.

It was also a huge relief to Blaise that enough time had passed—Salima hadn't come down with meningitis and was healthy. She had discussed it with their doctor, and the incubation period had passed. The school was staying closed for longer, but the risk of illness was at least not still a concern.

All of them were busy: Simon with Salima, Salima with the things he asked her to do, and especially her singing lessons, which were time consuming too, and Lucianna gave her homework. And Blaise was constantly swamped at work and trying to prove something to the boys upstairs. Zack was still breathing down her neck, and Susie Quentin got more ambitious every day. She wanted Charlie to give her more specials, and she was obviously jealous of Blaise. She wanted to show everyone what she could do. Zack played along with her with an idea that was typical of the entertainment division he had come from and unheard of in news. After a long meeting with Susie, he suggested she do a live interview with the first lady in January. It would be a first. He thought it would be a great coup to establish Susie as a valid alternative to Blaise, since all of her specials and interviews were taped. He said a live interview with the first lady would be "fresh and exciting," and Susie came out of the meeting with stars in her eyes. She confided to several people that she was sure she'd be even more important at the network than Blaise after that.

Charlie had a quiet meeting with Zack as soon as he heard about it, trying to explain that a live interview with a first lady was fraught with risk. It was traditional and much safer to have it taped, as Blaise always did. Zack was quick to brush him off.

"We're through with traditions around here," Zack said, looking irritated. "We need new blood, new people, new ideas. We're going live. And Susie's just the one to do it." Charlie hoped he was right and broke the news to Blaise himself, before she heard it from someone else.

"Is he crazy? What if something goes wrong? If the first lady says something she shouldn't?" They both knew that happened. "She'll never do it live." But much to everyone's amazement, her press secretary agreed to it. Susie had won the plum of the year. And Blaise felt like she'd been left in the dust. She would never have dared to suggest a live interview with the wife of a sitting president, or anyone else of that magnitude. Her subjects were far more comfortable knowing they were being taped, in case anything went wrong. It was Zack's idea, but Susie was unlivable, she was so full of herself, after it was announced. Zack had created a monster, and Blaise had to live with it every day.

Mark felt sorry for her, and she talked to Simon about it several times at night.

He was shocked at the abuse she had to take, and the stress she was under, and he admired her immensely for her grace and poise, and strength. Although to him she readily confessed that she had an overwhelming urge to strangle Susie every time she saw her. And he didn't blame her a bit.

In the weeks he'd been in New York with them, Simon had somehow become her confidant. He was smart, interested, and there every night. Blaise was surprised at the things she told him, how much she trusted him, and valued his opinions and advice about her life. And he was equally open with her about his own. He confessed the secrets of his childhood, his fears about his life and if he'd ever make something of himself, his regrets about Megan and the unhappy relationship he'd fallen into with her. And they talked about Salima a lot, and Blaise's dreams for her. She wanted her to find a career path that was meaningful to her. It was the same advice her father had given her at the same age. Blaise wanted her to have a job she loved, to give meaning to her life. The rest would fall into place after that.

Simon respected Blaise enormously for the things she said. And despite the times she knew she hadn't been there for her, Simon admired the kind of mother she was. Her heart was in the right place. And living under one roof, Blaise's relationship with Salima was flourishing.

Both Simon and Blaise were surprised by the multitude of subjects they discussed, sometimes until very late at night. And neither of them felt the difference in their ages. They were just two people who had become friends, and respected each other, and liked each other better every day.

Both of them took pride in Salima's progress. Thanks to Simon, she was more independent than she ever had been. She had learned how to do countless new things, and she was much more willing to go out into the world. But she still refused to use a cane, or talk about a dog. She was perfectly happy being with him.

"But what if I'm not here one day? If you're a famous singer on a concert tour? You think I'm going to do that with you?" He teased her to make the point.

"You'd better!" she shouted at him and gave him a playful shove. She was totally comfortable with him now too. He was like the big brother she'd never had. "That's your job!" she reminded him.

"What? Follow some crazy rock star around, while you sign autographs and keep me up all night, fighting off your fans? Hell, no! I'm going back to Massachusetts to live out my life in peace."

"You'd be bored to death now after New York," Salima said to him, and what she said was truer than she knew. He had been thinking that himself. He was having a ball in New York. And he loved spending time with Salima and Blaise. It no longer felt like a job to him after he had been there for a while. It had begun to feel like home, and they had a lot of fun together. His time with them had turned out to be none of what he expected. And when Eric called to check on him again, he told him so.

"Well, don't wind up staying there with them," Eric said mournfully, well aware that Blaise could afford to pay him far more than the school, and might steal him from them. "I'm expecting you back when we reopen in January," Eric reminded him, but it seemed like a long way off. And Simon knew he had a contract with them that he had to honor until May. But in the meantime, he was thoroughly enjoying New York and everything it offered. And their dinners together every night felt like family. He loved his long conversations with Blaise.

Blaise was helping him clear the table one night and loaded the dishwasher with him, while Salima had a lesson with Lucianna later than usual, and Blaise was complaining about the network again. She couldn't stand Zack Austin as her boss, and the trouble and angst he created for her every chance he got. Susie's upcoming live interview still stuck in her throat, and the unpleasant, supercilious way Zack spoke to her sometimes made her want to quit. With his propensity for firing people without warning, she was tired of living with a sword over her head all the time. The tension he created around him was palpable and not the way she wanted to work.

"Sometimes I feel like if I blink for a minute, someone will knife me in the back and I'll be gone. I just don't want to live like that anymore, no matter how much they pay me. I want to be treated like a human being." As she said it, she reached past him to take a plate out of the sink, and brushed very close to him. She could feel his warmth, and without thinking, he gently touched her cheek with his hand. He had never wanted to do that before, and she felt a current of electricity run through her. She looked up at him, and as their eyes met, she completely forgot what she'd been saying and so did he. He had felt it too. He didn't know if he should apologize or ignore it, and Blaise went back to loading the dishwasher as though nothing had happened, so he took his cue from her. But it had been an odd feeling wanting to touch her, and he couldn't stop himself.

Blaise had noticed more and more recently, that the age difference between them didn't seem to exist. She looked up to him as a man, and shared many of his values and opinions, and he thought of her as a woman his own age. It had been so long since she'd had a man to share her thoughts with, and it suddenly seemed normal to talk to him about everything. He made so much sense. And he loved the absence of drama in her life. For three years, every day had been a roller coaster with Megan, as they hid from her abusive alcoholic husband, which had begun to seem normal to Simon. With Blaise he felt sane again. The fifteen years between them didn't matter anymore. It was an odd but endearing friendship for both of them, which crossed the boundaries of her being his employer and the difference in their age.

She never mentioned how much time they spent together to anyone, or how impressed she was with him. All she ever said was what a terrific job he was doing with Salima. And she had said it to Mark several times. She never said anything else about him, and all Mark knew was that Abby's replacement was working out well.

Blaise was on an all-day trip to Washington to interview a freshman senator who was making noise about running for president when she realized she had forgotten some papers at the office that she would need when she got back that night, and she called Mark to have him drop them off at her apartment on his way home.

"I'm sorry to do that to you," she apologized. "I was so tired when I left yesterday, that I didn't even notice they weren't in my briefcase till I got on the plane today."

"Don't worry about it. I'll take a cab and drop them off after work. Can I leave them with the doorman?"

"They're a little sensitive. There's a report on the senator who just got outed for having an affair with a fourteen-year-old. Do you mind leaving them with Simon?"

"Sure, no problem." And it would give him a chance to see Salima, which he hadn't done since she got home. He hadn't seen her in a year. They only talked on the phone, and he was one of her biggest fans.

Mark rang the doorbell when he got there, and he had the cab waiting downstairs. The papers Blaise wanted were in an envelope marked confidential. A man opened the door. Mark found himself looking at a tall handsome man with his shirtsleeves rolled up. He was wearing jeans and cowboy boots and had dark tousled hair. Simon looked at Mark and immediately guessed who he was. He matched Blaise's description of him to perfection. Short, bald, and slight, he looked like a bundle of nerves, and he was wearing a blazer and an Hermès tie. He dressed for work every day. And Mark thought Simon looked like a movie star. He was tall, dark, and sexy, and suddenly Mark wondered if there was more going on with him and Blaise than what she said.

"I'm Simon," he said, holding out a hand to Blaise's assistant with a broad smile. "Come on in. I'm sure Salima would love to see you. She talks about you all the time." Mark could hear her singing in the background. She was having her lesson with Lucianna.

"I don't want to disturb her," Mark said, looking nervous, just as Blaise had said he would. He handed Simon the envelope and quickly moved toward the elevator and rang. Simon looked disappointed and as though he were afraid he had said something to offend him. He hadn't, but Mark had been so totally unprepared for his looks and the aura about him, and the ease Simon obviously felt in her home, that he was embarrassed to come in. The elevator was there in an instant, and with a wave and a smile he was gone. "Faster than the speed of sound," Simon said to himself, closed the front door, and went to put the envelope on Blaise's desk. She found it there when she got home. And she asked Simon about it when she had a cup of tea with him in the kitchen. Salima had already gone to bed, after a long, exhausting lesson. Lucianna was demanding a lot from her, but she loved it.

"Did you meet Mark today? He's such a nice guy. He's the best assistant I've ever had. I hope he stays forever."

"I did meet him," Simon confirmed with a puzzled look. "For about fourteen seconds. I was afraid I did something to upset him. I shook his hand, he looked panicked, and then he rang for the elevator and left."

"He's like a hummingbird," she said, the perfect description of the man he had met. "He's always in motion, and I told you, he's very nervous. But he gets everything I need done." Simon already knew how much she relied on him, and had been looking forward to meeting him. They had spoken many times on the phone.

"I hope I didn't insult him in some way."

"That's just him," she said, looking unconcerned, and then told Simon about the meeting in Washington that day. With her open, winning way, she had gotten the senator to admit he wanted to be president before he was thirty-nine years old, which was a major coup. It was going to shoot the ratings through the roof.

"Just as you always do," Simon said, proud of her, as Blaise thought how nice it was to have someone to talk to about her day.

Mark mentioned the meeting with Simon the next day too, and he looked awkward when he spoke of it to Blaise. "You should have said something to me and warned me," Mark chided her. "The door opened, and this hunk stood there smiling at me and held out his hand."

"What was he supposed to do?" Blaise laughed at him. "Grab the envelope and slam the door in your face?"

"I had no idea he looked like that, Blaise. He looks like a movie star." And then he couldn't resist asking her the question that had been on his mind all night. They had a good relationship and she was always honest with him, unless it was something confidential she couldn't tell him, or didn't want him to know. He wondered if this might be one of those. "Are you in love with him?" She looked shocked when he asked the question, that he could have thought that, and she shook her head with a baffled look.

"Why would you think that? Did Simon say something inappropriate?" If so, she was going to talk to him about it, but it didn't sound like Simon. He was polite and discreet and always very correct with her, even though they had become friends. Their developing friendship had been unexpected, but went no further than that. He had never been presumptuous or out of line with her. There had been that odd moment once at the kitchen sink, but they had both brushed it aside, and it hadn't happened again.

"It wasn't anything he said," Mark corrected the impression immediately, to justifiably absolve Simon. "It's what he looks like, and how comfortable he seems in your space. He's right at home."

"Obviously. He's living there with us. You get pretty friendly when you see each other over breakfast and dinner every day, and run into each other in the kitchen at midnight over a cup of hot milk. If anything, we're becoming friends. But I'm certainly not in love with him, and besides, he's fifteen years younger than I am. He's much more likely to fall for Salima than me. And there's no sign of that either." She sounded relieved.

"Well, if you're not in love with him, you should be," Mark said ruefully. "He's the best-looking guy I've ever seen. And he doesn't look his age. He looks older, and you seem like a kid. You two probably look good together. You don't look a day older than he does."

"Are you angling for a raise?" she teased him, but she was surprised by what he'd said. There had been no hint of romance between them, nor would there be. They would never be more than friends.

"I'm sorry. I just had to ask the question. Maybe it was wishful thinking. I was a little shocked at first. But when I think of the raw deal you got from Andrew Weyland, I wish you'd end up with a guy like Simon. You say he's a great guy, and smart, and he's fabulous looking. You deserve a prize after all the shit you've been through. And look at your ex-husband. Harry goes out with girls nearly fifty years younger than he is. What's a mere fifteen?"

"That's different. He's a man. It's acceptable when men go out with young girls. If women do it, people call them names."

"They're just jealous. If the opportunity arises, go for it. That's all I have to say." She was totally amazed by everything he'd said, and she said nothing about it to Simon that night. It would have been too embarrassing, and he probably would have thought she was crazy and trying to put a move on him. Besides, she could tell he was still suffering over Megan. For a thousand reasons, Mark's fantasy was never going to happen, but it was interesting to hear.

In the avalanche of stresses and challenges she dealt with every day, thanks to Zack, Susie, and a host of others, she forgot all about Mark's comments, until the following weekend, when Simon was helping her clean out a closet to make more room for Salima's things. Blaise still had all the toys she used to play with, and she wanted to get rid of them now to give her more space. She was on top of a ladder and teetering dangerously when she stretched too far in one direction, and Simon reached out to grab her and steady her, with a firm grasp around her waist. And he kept it there until she stepped down. As she came down the ladder, she stopped when she was eye to eye with him, and the world seemed to stand still around them. Neither of them said a word, but Blaise felt the same electric current run through her that had happened once before at the sink. She tried to tell herself it was her imagination, but this time she knew it wasn't. And Simon didn't take his eyes off hers, nor his hands from around her waist. She could feel him there, and for an instant she felt herself moving closer to him, and then he shifted his gaze, and helped her the rest of the way down the ladder. She had no idea what had just happened, and she was afraid to ask him. Maybe nothing had, and as she put all the old toys in boxes, she told herself she had imagined it. It was nothing. But a little voice inside her said something different. And when she looked at Simon, his eyes were guarded and he was busy.

They both pretended not to notice. And everything was back to normal when he cooked dinner that night. Salima had requested homemade pizza, and the ones he made were delicious, with a huge salad. He had baked apple crumble for dessert, made with sugar substitutes for Salima's diet. He served it with homemade dietetic vanilla ice cream. He was a genius at making the foods she could eat and making them taste great. And as they chatted and joked after dinner, Blaise realized again how close they'd gotten, and how at ease they were with each other, and she remembered the moment in the closet that afternoon, and the question Mark had asked her earlier in the week, about being in love with him. She didn't think she was, but maybe those two moments that felt like an electric current running through her had been some kind of fantasy of her own. And if that was true, it made her feel like an old fool, and maybe she was. Mark was right, he was very handsome. But she saw much more than that in Simon now. She saw the person he was, the kind heart, the good values, the honesty. It was his qualities she liked so much, not his looks. That was just icing on the cake. And it was a cake she didn't plan to eat anyway.

As though to remind her of it, Megan called him when he was sitting in the kitchen with her that night, after Salima went to her room to use her computer and write to a friend from school. They communicated through Facebook, and Salima had a lot of fun with it. Thanks to the programs on her computer, she could do Facebook like anyone else, and she loved it.

Blaise could tell instantly from the look on Simon's face who the call was from. He hadn't been answering Megan's e-mails, but he had told Blaise that once in a while he took her calls, usually late at night when he was in bed, and thinking about her anyway. He admitted that he missed her, and what he said about her sometimes reminded Blaise of how she had felt about Andrew Weyland at first, when she missed him so terribly, but knew she had done the right thing to break up with him. She had never doubted it, but she missed him anyway, and her illusions about him.

Simon looked pained the moment he took the call, and disappeared to his room with his cell phone in his hand, while Blaise sat quietly in the kitchen, thinking about that afternoon and what it meant. She was sure it was nothing, just a moment between two people who were alone. But they weren't going to wind up with each other because of it. And Blaise wondered if he'd go back to Megan when they both went back to school. The pull between them seemed to be strong.

He came back five minutes later with an apologetic look. "Sorry. I told her she has to stop calling me. She calls every time he slaps her around. It drives me nuts. It's why she wanted to leave him in the first place. I told her to go to Al-Anon and she won't."

"It's okay," Blaise said reassuringly. "You don't owe me any explanations." She could see how upset he was by the call. She wasn't sure if that meant he still loved her, or was trying to escape and having a hard time. And Megan didn't make it any easier by calling him all the time, just as Andrew had done. Megan was hanging on to him for dear life. But not dear enough to leave her husband.

"I won't take her calls anymore," he said as much to himself as to her.

"Don't feel bad," she said with a sympathetic look. "I still take Andrew's calls sometimes, four years later, although I'm always sorry when I do. It's just an echo of old times, and not a good one for me." But she knew it was different for him with Megan. Their relationship was more recent and the pain still very fresh.

"I think she loves me, or she says she does," Simon said, with a troubled look. "The problem is she loves him too, even if she won't admit it to me. If she didn't, she wouldn't still be with him, after three years with me. Maybe she loves him more." He was still trying to sort it out, although he felt better since he'd come to New York and had some distance from her and her troubled life.

"Or history and kids," Blaise said sensibly. "It's hard to know why people stay together. Andrew has cheated on his wife for years, and probably always will. And she puts up with it. And I'm sure they'll never leave each other. They like the fantasy of their marriage, but there's not much there. Some people are willing to settle for that."

"That's not enough for me," Simon said, looking anguished. "I want the real deal or I'd rather be alone."

"Yeah, beware of what you wish for. That's what I said, and now look at me. I'm alone, and probably always will be. At your age, you have lots of relationships ahead of you." It made her sad to think about it, that her romantic life might well be over. It certainly looked that way. And in a lot of ways, she had made her peace with it, and told herself she didn't have time anyway. Who could handle a relationship when you had a career like hers? She had neither the time, nor the energy. Her life with the network was all consuming, just as Harry had said. And nothing had changed. For one shining moment, she had believed in what she shared with Andrew. And he had made a mockery of it. It didn't make her want to try again.

"I told Megan I was happy here," Simon interrupted her train of thought. "It's true. I'd really like to find a job in New York for next year." He sounded hopeful as he said it.

"Then start looking," Blaise encouraged him. "There are some excellent schools for the blind here. You should fill out some applications, and take a look at the schools while you're in New York. You can even take Salima with you." Blaise had no intention of keeping her in New York, once Caldwell opened again, and Salima had never asked to stay at home. She knew it wasn't an option. But it was clear that Simon wanted a chance at something new, and Blaise thought it would be good for him.

They spent an easy quiet weekend. And on Sunday night she flew to L.A. Pat Olden, the congressman who'd been shot at UCLA, had died without regaining consciousness. Blaise wanted to attend his funeral, and pay her respects, and then she was interviewing the head of the university on Monday afternoon. Afterward, she was filming a special with a hot new movie star on Tuesday, and returning Tuesday night.

Simon had promised her he'd take care of everything. And she kissed them both goodbye when she left.

"Call me if anything comes up," she said to Simon, as he carried her bag to the elevator for her.

"You know I will. We'll be fine." He smiled at her. And in the flash of an instant, she thought she saw something in his eyes that she had seen twice before, and then it was gone. And there was no doubt in her mind. She had imagined it. Mark was crazy. She was sure of it. She and Simon were just friends, and it was enough for both of them.

Chapter 8

Pat Olden's funeral was as heart-wrenching as Blaise had expected it to be. He had been shot down in the prime of life, at forty-three, with a wife who loved him, a great career, and four terrific kids. Who knew? He might have been president one day. It was all so unfair, Blaise thought to herself. The first lady had spoken, and the president had sent a message to Pat's family because he couldn't be there. And Pat's wife and children were devastated. The death toll from that day had reached eighteen, including the shooter. It was tragic.

Her interview with the president of the university that afternoon went extremely well. It was a serious conversation about the dangers to young people today, and a certain hopelessness in youth around the world, due to the economy, the environment, and the opportunities that had dwindled for them in recent years. It was a strong message to parents everywhere to pay attention to their kids.

And the next day she spent with the young movie star, which was a welcome counterpoint to her serious interview the day before. The star was outrageous, sexy, and full of fun, and had just won a Golden Globe at twenty-one. Blaise had asked her every question she'd dared, and the girl had answered them all and had volunteered some shocking information of her own. It was the kind of interview Blaise loved to do sometimes, to break the monotony of the more sober ones. And she had nailed this one easily. It was light-hearted, sexy, and the subject was outspoken and in-genuous. Blaise was pleased when she flew back to New York on the red-eye and fell asleep on the plane.

Tully was there to meet her, and she went straight to work from the airport, just in time to do her seg-ment. And as soon as she got to her office afterward, Simon called her to tell her everything was fine, and had gone smoothly while she was away. She hadn't had time to call them while she was rushing for the red-eye the night before.

"Are you exhausted?" He sounded concerned. The schedule she lived would have killed anyone. But she seemed to thrive on it. And she sounded happy about the interviews she'd taped in L.A.

"No, I'm fine. I slept on the plane. Although that L.A. red-eye is always just a little too short. It's better going to Europe." That was a seven-hour flight, com-pared to five and a half from the West Coast, which was cutting it a little close for a good night's rest, even for her, and the first class seats didn't turn into beds. She knew the configuration of every plane that flew.

And to make matters worse, she had to stay late at work that night, for a meeting. But for once, there were no bad surprises, although it annoyed her to see Susie Quentin at the meeting. She was on top of the world. And they were sending her to Paris, to do a special on French fashion, attend the haute couture shows, and interview the French president's wife. All plums, although the fashion shows would have been a little lightweight for Blaise.

She didn't get home until eight o'clock. Salima was in her room on the phone, having already eaten, Simon had dinner waiting for her, and he gave her a hug when she walked in. It was nice to see his smiling face, and know that someone was happy to see her. It was new for her, and he held her close to him for a minute and looked at her.

"I'm glad you're back," he said in a gruff voice. "I worry about you." He was still holding her and hadn't let go.

"It's nice to know that someone does. I worry about you too," she said, and realized it was true. And she always worried about Salima. So much could go wrong with her health. But Simon had everything in good control. And she felt confident knowing Salima was with him. And Teresa, the housekeeper, had stayed there too while she was gone, but had left that afternoon.

She told Simon all about what she'd done in L.A. over dinner, Patrick Olden's funeral, the interview with the university president, and the one with the young movie star. The diversity of subjects was typical of her life and what made it fun for her. He could see she'd enjoyed the day with the young actress. He liked learning about it, and seeing the excitement in her eyes. Even after sharing her life and hearing her stories for a while, he was fascinated by it. She talked about people he had only read about before, and they were commonplace to her. The exceptional was part of her routine.

"I love knowing about what you do," he said, smiling at her. But he knew the flip side of the coin now too, all the rigors that went with it. It was far from easy, but she loved the challenge, and rose to it every time.

They chatted for a while, and Blaise finally got up from the table, and said she wanted to take a bath and go to bed. She was tired. She stopped in to say goodnight to Salima, gave her a kiss, and went to her own room. It felt good to be home, particularly with someone to talk to at the end of the day, or when she came home from a trip. With Simon and Salima there, dinner together every night, and all their comings and goings, the apartment felt like a home, for the first time since she had moved in. It was a different world, with Salima singing with Lucianna, and wandering around the apartment, and Simon cooking dinner every night. She was enjoying it so much that for the first time ever, she hated to leave home and go to work. Whether he had intended to or not, Simon had given new meaning to their life.

The following week Blaise asked Simon what his plans were for Thanksgiving, and if he needed to go home to Boston. He didn't hesitate before he answered. He had already decided to stay in New York. He knew she needed him there, and his taking time off would have been a hardship for her.

"Who's going to cook your turkey, if I go to Boston? I don't trust you in the kitchen. In fact, I ordered the bird from our butcher last week. I actually had Salima do it. She was very pleased with herself. Do you invite anyone over for Thanksgiving?" Blaise shook her head. She either went to Caldwell to see Salima, or was on a trip. She hadn't been home for Thanksgiving in eleven years. And this year she had a trip to Israel planned after the holiday. But she was going to be home all this weekend. It was a great weekend for watching football and hanging around the house. And she had tickets to a Rangers game for all three of them. She loved hockey, and so did he.

"By the way," Simon said, looking nervous, "my parents are coming to town that weekend, to see friends. Do you think there's any chance we could have them to tea? My mother is a huge fan, and my father would enjoy meeting you as well. If it's not a good idea, don't worry about it, I'll meet them out somewhere."

"It sounds like fun," Blaise said easily. She was intrigued to meet them both. They sounded like characters to her, from everything Simon had described.

Blaise was fiercely busy for the next two weeks, and the night before Thanksgiving, she and Salima went to church and lit a candle for Abby, who had always spent Thanksgiving with them in the cottage. It was strange to have a holiday without her. They were so used to having her with them. And when they got home, feeling melancholy, Simon was busy in the kitchen baking pies for the next day, all according to the recipes that worked for Salima's diet. Blaise tried to steal a little piece of crust, and he pushed her hand away.

"I don't care how famous you are, do NOT screw up my pies. Or I'll send you to your room for a time-out." But when he was finished, he took an apple pie out of the oven and cut them each a slice as a surprise, with his delicious homemade dietetic ice cream that tasted like the real thing. He had made a serious project of collecting recipes for diabetics, for Salima. The apple pie was fantastic, and he had baked a pumpkin pie too for the next day.

"When are your parents coming, by the way?" Blaise suddenly remembered the conversation they'd had weeks before. He'd never mentioned it again, and she wondered if their plans had changed.

"Friday," he said, finishing the last of his ice cream.

"If that's still okay with you. I promise I'll only let them stay an hour, and then I'll throw them out."

"That's a nice way to treat your parents. I can't wait to meet them."

"I want them to meet Salima too, if she won't be too bored."

"They don't sound boring to me," she said with a smile.

"I guess boring isn't the right word. Exasperating maybe. Annoying. Eccentric. Crazy. My mother gets a little hyper at times. And my father just tunes her out and thinks of something else. It seems to work for them."

"What time are they coming?"

"I told them four o'clock, if that's good for you. I didn't want to bother you with their plans."

"That's perfect. We'll have them for tea." He didn't want to tell her that his mother preferred wine or champagne. But he had already told his mother to behave. She swore she would, which he knew meant nothing. He was hoping for the best, and prayed it was one of their better days, when his father tuned in to planet Earth, and his mother didn't lecture them all on some obscure subject no one cared about, like the importance of hydrangeas in a garden, or the beauty of white lilac, or offer to read them her latest poem, which would put them all to sleep. He had had some exotic social experiences with them over the years, but he was willing to risk it again. They were dying to meet Blaise. Even his father knew who she was, and thought Simon was very fortunate to be working for her, even for a short time. He had told Simon that he hoped she would offer him a job, since she could probably afford to pay him more than the school. Simon was sure she could, but the subject had never come up, since she wanted to send Salima back to Caldwell.

Their Thanksgiving the next day was perfect, thanks to Simon, who prepared a delicious meal. He made chestnut stuffing, cooked the turkey to a flawless golden brown, and made tiny vegetables. And his pies were an impeccable end to the meal. He had pecan pie, pumpkin, and the apple pie they had sampled on Wednesday night. And he and Blaise watched football in the afternoon, and screamed every time their team made a touchdown. She was an ardent fan, which amused him. And after dinner, he played the piano and Salima sang, and at the end, they all joined in. They all agreed that it was the best Thanksgiving they'd had in years.

"My mother has always been very dismissive about Thanksgiving," he said to Blaise when they cleaned up. She had set a lovely table in the dining room they rarely used, with her best crystal and china, and a lace tablecloth that had been her mother's from her trousseau. She only brought it out for holidays and special events.

"Thanksgiving isn't important to her because she's French. So she condescends to celebrate it every year, but she always got creative with the food. She doesn't like turkey. So we had ortolans one year, tiny little birds you serve with the heads, and the eyes looking at you. My brother and I hated them. So she served lobster the next year. I think it's her rebellious spirit. I don't think I had a turkey for Thanksgiving until I was at college and went home with a friend, and they had a 'real' Thanksgiving, instead of the crazy ones my mother dreamed up. One year she served trout," he said, reminiscing as they did the dishes, and Blaise laughed as he rolled his eyes. "You'll see when you meet her. She's one of a kind."

"Our Thanksgivings were very traditional," Blaise remembered. "My father always brought the turkey home from the butcher shop where he worked. It was always the best one, and way too big for our family of three. We ate turkey everything for a week." She smiled, thinking about it. Once in a while she missed her parents—they had been dead for almost thirty years. Her life as it had evolved and was now would have been completely foreign to them. But she thought they would have been proud of her.

They sat in the living room and talked for a long time that night. Simon didn't feel like an employee anymore. He felt like a friend, or a guest. And anytime they got together, they seemed to talk for hours. It was midnight when they said goodnight and went to bed. And Blaise was up early the next day. She was already in the kitchen, drinking coffee, when Simon got up. He always came to the kitchen dressed, even when he looked half asleep. He was respectful of her home. She had never seen him in pajamas or a bathrobe, even when she ran into him in the kitchen late at night. With Simon there, the kitchen had turned out to be the hub of the house. He was always cooking something, working on his computer, or Salima was hanging out. She enjoyed talking to Simon for hours too.

He poured himself a cup of coffee and sat down, looking worried, and she could see that something was wrong. She wondered if it was Megan, but it wasn't. "I wonder if I made a mistake inviting my parents. They can be so nuts. And if they're having a bad day, you'll hate them. I do regularly. I was always afraid to introduce them to my friends, for fear of what they'd do or say. And they haven't improved with age. If anything, they're worse, and think that age gives them the right to do and say anything they want, especially my mother. And now I'm nervous introducing them to you. I feel like a kid again. I called my father and told him yesterday, and he thinks I'm nuts. Maybe I am."

"Don't worry about it. They sound like fun. And parents are never embarrassing if they're someone else's. They're not mine, so I'm sure I'll enjoy them. Hell, look at the people I've interviewed in my life. Do you think they were all normal and polite? Some of them were really rude. A couple of them threatened to hit me. Some Mafioso pulled a gun on me once when he thought I had insulted his wife and insinuated she had an affair. I didn't. I said he did. But whatever your parents do, it will be nothing compared to the people I've met. In fact, I can hardly wait."

Blaise debated at length what to wear for them. In the end, she wore a plain white cashmere sweater, a short black leather skirt that showed off her legs, high heels, and a string of pearls. It seemed the right combination of respectful and a little kicky, since Simon said they were odd and he didn't think they'd dress up. He said his mother was partial to hand-woven things she bought in Mexico, made by the Indians in bright colors, or ponchos, or vintage clothes she found at auctions or garage sales. He had no idea what they'd wear to meet Blaise, but probably nothing normal. That would be too simple, and too unlike them.

But they surprised him, when he opened the door to them promptly at four o'clock. They had never been on time in their life, and Simon was shocked. His father was wearing a tie, although it was slightly askew and one point of his collar was bent and pointing up, and the shirtsleeves peeking out of his jacket were too long, which gave him a slightly goofy look. He had hair like Einstein, and a warm smile that reached his eyes as he shook hands with Blaise and Salima, and Blaise fell in love with him immediately. He looked like someone you wanted to hug. He was as tall as Simon, but stooped over, and despite the slightly cockeyed tie and collar, he looked like a very distinguished man. Simon looked a lot like him, but he had his mother's eyes, which were dark. His father's eyes were blue, and he had white hair, and looked a little like

Pinocchio's father in the fairy tale. And his mother was still beautiful with dark eyes and a wild mane of salt-and-pepper hair that had once been jet black like her son's. She had worn a plain dark blue dress and flat shoes and was carrying a dark blue Hermès Kelly bag. Simon had never seen her look so respectable in her entire life. No poncho, no cowboy hat, no sparkling red shoes like in *The Wizard of Oz,* all of which she was capable of. And she was wearing an armload of bangle bracelets that she never took off. She had slept with them for thirty years and collected them one by one. It made Blaise think of the Cartier bracelet she'd been given in Dubai. She never took that off now either. It was beautiful and simple and had been a fabulous gift.

"You have a very pretty apartment," Isabelle Ward said primly as she sat down, with slightly pursed lips. She had a beautiful full mouth and perfect teeth. It was easy to see why Simon's father had fallen in love with her when she was an eighteen-year-old girl and his student. She must have been a knockout. And Blaise said as much to Simon as they brought the tea tray in together while Salima entertained them and told them all the things that she and Simon had done recently, on their many adventures.

"Can't you take her someplace more fun than a hardware store?" his mother scolded him with a disapproving look. "And the post office?" She looked around the room again then, as his father's head bobbed and he smiled benignly at all of them. He looked like he was enjoying himself as Simon handed him a cup of tea. It was his favorite kind, and then his mother spotted an object in a far corner that caught her eye. It was a silver-plated skull that Blaise had brought back from one of her trips, in this case from Nepal. "Doesn't it upset you having something like that here? Think of what they did to the person they took it from. It's such a violent object to show off." She looked disgusted as she said it and examined Blaise more closely. She was trying to decide if her hair was its natural color or she dyed it. She couldn't figure it out, so she asked.

"No, it's my natural color," Blaise said with a warm smile, and Salima laughed, as Simon tried not to groan and gave his mother a quelling look, which she ignored.

"You must have gray in it at your age. Mine went gray at twenty-five. Do you use a rinse for that?" It was the kind of conversation women normally had at the hairdresser, or with close friends. But his mother was never afraid to barge right in. Boundaries had never existed for her. And she came across them like hurdles at a track meet.

"Yes, actually, I use a rinse. But I'm lucky. I don't have a lot of gray."

"Have you had your eyes done? They look very good."

"No, I haven't," Blaise said, and laughed. "Maybe I'm not as old as you think."

"I read somewhere that you're fifty-two."

"I'm forty-seven. That's bad enough," Blaise said without artifice, as his mother sat admiring the drapes.

"Beautiful fabric," she said, as Simon prayed she would have nothing more to say about Blaise's looks or her age. She was his employer, after all. "Strange color, though. I imagine if people sit too close to them, they look sick." They were a slightly odd shade of yellow that Blaise had fallen in love with and still liked and thought was very chic. Simon's mother did not agree. And Blaise laughed as she listened to her. She had no filter and said whatever went through her head. She stared at Blaise's skirt after that, and Blaise felt suddenly self-conscious, more so than about her drapes. "Your skirt is very short, but you have fabulous legs. By the way, I loved your interview with the French president last year. Is he as handsome as he looks on TV?" It was a topic that interested her since she was French.

"More so," Blaise said with a winning smile, as Simon's father engaged Salima in conversation and was very sweet to her. "Your son is a fabulous chef," Blaise complimented him, hoping to distract his mother for a while, and she smiled the moment Blaise said it.

"Yes, he is, isn't he?" she said in a matter-of-fact way, as she continued to comment on the furniture, the surroundings, her children, and whatever else came to mind, and she said Salima was a very pretty girl. Simon looked like he was dying, and his father was good-natured through it all. He was used to the sensation she made everywhere she went, and had for thirty-five years. She had been just like that when she was young. It was part of what he loved about her, her openness, and indifference to what anyone else thought. She was her own person, and had never been afraid to be. And he had been totally enchanted with her since the day they met and still was. He looked like a happy man. And Isabelle Ward commented on him too. She called his inventions "ridiculous," but said they had been very lucrative, which had allowed them to buy a very nice house, far nicer than any of the other professors, or even the president of the university. She seemed pleased about it.

She asked Blaise then what interviews she was planning to do next, and Blaise said she was going to Israel before Christmas, to interview the prime minister.

"What an interesting job you have. I'm a poet, you know. I'm sure Simon told you. Actually, I brought you my new book," she said, opening her purse and handing it to Blaise. She had autographed it and opened it and then offered to read one of the poems, which she promptly did, while Salima tried to keep a straight face. She was the most eccentric, outrageous woman Blaise had ever met, and she could see why Simon was embarrassed by her, but Blaise liked her anyway. In a funny way, she was refreshing. There was no artifice about her. You knew exactly what she was thinking at all times.

Simon looked as though he'd been released from prison when they finally stood up to leave. Salima said goodbye and disappeared while Blaise went to get their coats, and as soon as she left the room, his mother turned to him with a worried expression.

"You're sleeping with her, aren't you? She's much too old for you."

"In the first place, she's not old. And in the second, I'm not sleeping with her. She's an extremely famous woman, and an icon all over the world. The last thing she'd want is a little schoolteacher like me," he said humbly, discounting his extreme intelligence, and unaware of how he looked.

"That's ridiculous. You're much better than she is. And your grandfather has a title, for heaven's sake." His mother looked disapproving, as Simon prayed that Blaise would come back with their coats quickly, so they could leave. He was already past his limit for what he could tolerate. "I'm sure she's in love with you," his mother said loudly, just as Blaise came back in the room and pretended not to hear. She thanked them profusely for coming, and they thanked her for the tea.

"Good luck in Israel. I hope nobody throws a bomb at you. That would be very unfortunate. Simon really likes his job," his mother said to Blaise.

"I'm sure I'll be fine, I've been there before." Isabelle Ward kissed her on both cheeks then. Her French accent and her customs were still noticeable even after many years in the States.

A moment later they left, his father still bobbing and smiling, and his mother looking respectable for once, but still not acting it. And Simon fell to his knees in front of Blaise the moment they were gone.

"I beg your forgiveness. My mother should have been muzzled at birth. My brother and I have volunteered to do it a thousand times, but my father won't let us. He still thinks she's cute, particularly now that he's going deaf so he doesn't have to listen to her. I swear, I will never bring them back. I'm sorry that I invited them, and I will never, ever do it again. I'm sorry about your hair and the curtains, the length of your skirt, and everything else she said. Ohmygod, I need a drink," he said, getting up, as Blaise laughed at him.

"She's very funny, and I like them. Don't apologize. Your father is adorable. And your mother says everything the rest of us wish we could, but we don't have the guts. She is one ballsy woman," Blaise said admiringly. She could only imagine what it must have been like to grow up with a mother like her.

"She thinks we're having an affair," he said, looking miserable. He was mortified by everything his mother said. He always was. He felt fourteen again, but he was relieved to see that Blaise was undisturbed by it and actually amused, which he found hard to believe. She had been an incredibly good sport, in his opinion.

"What makes her think that?" Blaise asked, about the affair.

"I have no idea. She's always announcing who is having affairs with who, particularly among their friends, or movie stars she's never met. She thinks she's psychic, and once in a million times she's right. I told her we weren't." He was afraid Blaise would be offended by what she said.

"Did you tell her your virginity is safe with me? I'm too old to go after you," Blaise said, smiling at him. "I'd get arrested for child molestation," she teased.

"Don't be stupid," he said, looking annoyed. "You're only about ten years older than I am."

"Fifteen," she corrected him, not that she wanted to add more years, but it was the truth. He was thirty-two and she was forty-seven, which they were both aware of.

"That's not a big difference. My father is twenty-two years older than she is. And he married her when she was eighteen and he was forty."

"Men can get away with that. Women can't."

"I don't agree with you. It may cause more comment when the woman is older, but it's no different. And who cares? You look younger than I do, and you have more energy than anyone I know. You don't look your age," he emphasized again.

"Neither does your mother. She looks fabulous."

"Why couldn't I have been born to a deaf-mute? Then she could insult everybody in sign language and most people wouldn't know what she was saying. Thank you for being such a good sport. I feel like a complete idiot for inviting them. I know better. I just wanted them to meet you and Salima, and I guess insanely, I wanted you to meet them. I'm very proud of my father, and mortified by my mother, and always have been, with good reason."

"Part of being an adult, someone told me once, is accepting your parents as they are, with all their failings." She was trying to calm him down, to no avail. He looked totally shaken.

"That's a tall order in my mother's case. I don't think I'm capable of it."

They walked into the kitchen then, and Blaise took out a bottle of wine. She opened it, poured him a glass, and handed it to him. He needed it. And he looked at her with grateful eyes as he took a sip.

"Thank you, for your patience and understanding, and the wine. Do you have a Valium to go with it? I think I need one."

"She was fine," Blaise reassured him again, and as she did, he looked at her with a strange expression. Their eyes met and held as they had before, and suddenly for the first time, she wondered if his mother was right. Maybe she was psychic. All she wanted to do now was put her arms around Simon and comfort him. Maybe she was in love with him. And what if she was? How disastrous would that be? His parents would be horrified, and the world would laugh at them, or her at least. She never took her eyes from his as she thought about it, and then rejected the idea. She poured herself a glass of wine then, and tried to think of something else. But suddenly, all she could think of was him. He pulled her into his arms then, and put his arms around her. And as he stood holding her, neither of them moved or said a word.

Chapter 9

It took Simon a whole day to calm down after his parents' visit, which was what his mother always did to him. And Blaise kept telling him that it was fine. She said his mother wasn't a vicious woman, just an outspoken one, and there had been no harm done.

But he made a superb dinner that night to thank her, chateaubriand and asparagus with hollandaise. And after Salima went to her room, he talked about his mother again.

"She actually asked me if I was gay when I was in college, because I'd never introduced her to a girlfriend, but she's so outrageous, I was afraid to," he said, sipping the wine he had bought to go with the dinner, to atone for his mother's sins. He had been apologizing for her all his life, and should have been used to it by then, but he wasn't. He still looked embarrassed and contrite.

"What convinced her otherwise?" Blaise asked with a look of amusement.

"I slept with the daughters of all her friends to reassure her," he said, and Blaise laughed.

"I guess that would do it," she said, with no need to be convinced.

"I was thinking about what my mother said today, about our having an affair."

"She would kill you if we did." Blaise was clear on that concept also. And his mother had made it clear the night before. She thought Blaise was too old for him, and Blaise thought so too.

"I told you, your age is irrelevant. But what could I ever give you, what could I add to your life? You have everything, a fabulous career, every material thing you've ever wanted. I couldn't support you on what I make. You have Salima. And what do I have? Nothing." He sounded sad as he said it. He had thought about it all day, and the night before.

"You have *you,*" Blaise said simply. "That's all I've ever wanted from anyone. I've never been dependent on any man in my life. All I've ever wanted from a man is for him to love me. I don't need anything else. You've already improved my life immeasurably. You worry about me, take care of me, feed me. You're wonderful to Salima. You care how my day was, you ask me how I am and want to know. That's more than I've ever had from any man, even the ones I was married to. I'm not worried about what you can give me. Everything you are is a gift, and you already are just as a friend. And I'm not suggesting we have an affair. But if we did, the real problem is what I can't give you. Or probably not at this point. I have Salima, as you just said. And I'm sure you want children. I'm too old to have another one. Technically, I could, but probably not without some assistance. But I'm too old to do that again. And going through Salima being diagnosed with juvenile diabetes was so traumatic that I'd never want to try again. And no one should deprive you of that. You need to be with a woman who'll give you babies. That rules me out as an option, no matter what your mother thinks we're doing."

"I've always wanted one or two," he admitted. "Not four like my brother, which seems like too many for me. But two would be nice. Or one great one. But I have to admit, I'd be sad not to have any at all." He was being honest with her, but she already knew it.

"That's my point. I may be crazy, but I've been feeling some weird stuff between us lately. Some kind of electrical current. But I'm not an option in a real sense. You need someone to give you kids. That's not me." He nodded sadly as she said it. He had suspected that was how she felt about it, especially after Salima. That whole experience had been too scary. And she never wanted to go through it again.

"Why are we talking about this?" he asked, looking at her. "And by the way, I've felt that same current you have. A couple of times, I've almost said something, but I was afraid you'd say that I'm crazy. Something's been happening between us, Blaise. I know it and so do you. We can't ignore it forever. Maybe my mother isn't as crazy as she looks. I want to put my arms around you now every time I see you." He was keeping his voice down so Salima didn't hear him, and so was she. What they were talking about had been building for weeks. And Simon wanted to get it on the table. Blaise knew it was hopeless between them because of his wanting kids, and that seemed fair to her. He deserved to have them. But not with her.

"So that's it?" Simon looked at her, upset. "There's no chance for us because you don't want kids? How dumb is that?"

"It's not dumb. You want kids," she insisted. "I don't. I have the only one I want."

"Is that nonnegotiable?" he asked her, as though they were making a deal. But there was no deal to be made with her.

"Yes, it is nonnegotiable. I'm sure." She was quiet but firm about it. "We shouldn't even be talking about this," Blaise said softly. But suddenly it was all out in the open, and part of her was glad it was. She had been beginning to think she was crazy. Suddenly, she was feeling attracted to him. But she knew him so well now that it had evolved from the friendship they'd been building since they met. "All we can ever be is friends. Or you'll break my heart when you go off with someone young to have babies. It's better to stop it now, whatever the underlying feelings are, and just be friends."

"Are you sure that's a decision? Don't these things just happen?"

"No, they don't." Blaise's eyes flashed at him. "That's how we both got hurt before. You make decisions in life. You stay away from something that's wrong, or isn't what you want. I'm a forty-seven-year-old woman who doesn't want kids. You want them, and should have them. I don't even know if I'd get pregnant again, without a lot of help, or at all. And you'd always be disappointed not to have children. Simon, I can't do that to you."

"Stop talking," he said to her angrily. "You're not negotiating a contract with the network. And I don't give a damn how old you are, or if you want kids or not. I love you. I love your mind, your heart, your values, the way you think. I love how kind you are, your integrity. You're everything I want, and all that I believe in. I don't care if you get pregnant or not. Blaise . . . I love you." And without saying another word, he took her in his arms and kissed her and the roof fell in and then exploded outward and all she saw was sky as he held her in his arms. She kissed him for what felt like an eternity, and when she looked at him, she knew that everything she'd been saying didn't matter, what he had to offer, the babies he wouldn't have with her. They loved each other, and there was nothing else to say. He held her face in his hands and looked at her after he kissed her, and then he kissed her again. And when he stopped, they were both smiling. And Blaise knew that what his mother had said was true. She was in love with him. And he was in love with her too, no matter how impossible it was, or how old she was, or how young he was. They loved each other. It was all they knew. And the rest remained to be seen.

Chapter 10

Once acknowledged, the attraction between Simon and Blaise was so powerful that it was like a genie let out of a bottle, impossible to put back. The electricity between them got stronger, the looks they exchanged across a room or at dinner, which Salima couldn't see, were so breathtaking that they stopped talking, which Salima did notice. It was heady stuff, and both of them were trying to resist it without success. Bumping into each other, hands touching accidentally, shoulders brushing, it all fanned the embers of what had been growing all along, into a mighty blaze. It wasn't destructive, but it warmed them both. And even not talking about it, which they tried not to, it was there.

When Blaise came home from the office now, she found him waiting for her, and it had new meaning. He asked her how her day had gone, and wanted to hear about it. He searched her face to see how stressful the day had been, or if there had been new confrontations. He smiled at the victories, and laughed at her irritated descriptions of Susie Quentin. Unlike anyone in years, he cared about her life, and shared it in a gentle, solid way.

And at night, after Salima went to bed, they sat for hours in the kitchen, talking about life, the blind schools he had contacted, asking for job applications, or Blaise's concerns about Salima. They talked about everything that affected them both, without entering a relationship, but being in one nonetheless, whatever they chose to call it. It was love of the purest kind, which had started on its own, born of everything they shared and had in common, and their bond only drew them closer to each other while they tried to resist it. And Simon was possessive of her, without wanting to admit it.

For the first time in a long time, Andrew called her on her cell phone one night, as they were just finishing dinner. Salima was at the table with them, and Blaise took her cell phone back to her office to talk to him. He said he had been thinking of her and wondered how she was. He was in San Francisco on business, which she knew meant he wasn't with his wife, and could talk freely, hence the call. She was startled to hear from him again.

"How are things with you?" Andrew asked in a jovial mood. It was early for him, and Blaise assumed he had just finished the day's meetings. And he had that boyish, sexy tone in his voice that always used to seduce her. "I hear Susie Quentin is giving you a run for your money." She couldn't believe he had said it, it was so Andrew, a little passive-aggressive jab to keep her on her toes.

"You called to tell me that? What are you hoping, that she gets my job?"

"Of course not. You know I worry about you." In fact, she knew he didn't. And never had. Or he wouldn't have lied to her. "It must be tough for you, though."

"Not really," Blaise said, trying to sound more cavalier than she felt, and wanting to prove to him that she was fine. He always pulled at the loose threads in her life, in the hope that she'd unravel. And even if she did, she wouldn't tell him. "She'll trip herself up sooner or later, they all do. Or they have so far. What are you doing in San Francisco?" And why are you calling me? she asked herself. Just to annoy me about Susie? It seemed so petty.

"Meetings. Nothing special. We're going to Mexico for Christmas. What are you doing?"

"I'm staying here, with Salima. She's been home from school since October. They had a meningitis outbreak and had to close the school for three months."

"I suppose you have Abby with you." He knew all the familiar pieces of her life.

"No, she died." He was quiet for a moment, not sure what to say, and he didn't ask who had replaced her.

"I miss you, Blaise." He said it in a soft, husky voice, filled with emotion. But he had the inflections of an actor from reading the news, and she didn't believe him.

"That's nice to know." It was all she could muster, and she wanted to get off the phone. He just made her unhappy.

"What about you? Happy?" He thought she sounded different, but he wasn't sure.

"I'm fine. I'd better get back to dinner. Thank you for calling." She didn't mean it, but didn't know what else to say. Thank you for reminding me of how sad you made me, for disappointing me, and lying. Thank you for breaking my heart, and staying in touch with me, to remind me, and torture me, whenever you get bored. She knew that all she had to do was stop taking his calls, but somehow she never did. At least not yet.

"You sound so formal," he reproached her. "I still love you," he whispered, and she wanted to scream, "No, you don't! You never did," but she didn't. Instead she didn't respond, just said goodbye and hung up. He was a relic from the past, the ancient debris of her love life. He was dead to her but not buried yet.

She went back to dinner, looking subdued, annoyed at herself, as she always was, that she'd taken the call. He always unnerved her, and talking to him was so pointless. She took his calls out of habit, more than any desire to talk to him.

Salima had left the table when she went back, and Simon finished loading the dishwasher and turned toward her with a grim look, and then sat down with a cup of tea. He hadn't made one for her, which was unusual for him.

"Why do you still talk to him?" He knew exactly who it was, just from her tone of voice and the fact that she left the room. She took all her other calls in front of him. But it was embarrassing to talk to Andrew with Simon in the room. There was something humiliating about it. Andrew was a symbol of loss and defeat.

"I almost never do anymore," she defended herself. "And to be honest, I don't know why. Maybe because it's familiar, or there's been no one else since, or because I want to prove he doesn't upset me."

"But he does. I can see it in your face and in your eyes. He makes you feel like shit about yourself." She couldn't deny it, it was true. "It's masochistic," Simon accused her, and he was angry, at Andrew and at her.

"Maybe. It's human. I'm not perfect. I've been trying to work my way out of that maze since he left. It takes time."

"Four years? That's crazy." He was being hard on her, and he looked hurt.

"I'm sorry. I'm sorry if it upset you. I'm not involved with him. And he hardly calls anymore. Sometimes I don't even take the calls."

"Then why did you tonight? Do you still miss him?" He was searching her eyes for the answers.

"Not really. Not at all, in fact. And surely not since you've been here. For the past two months, I never thought about him. Before that, I did. It's lonely here, Simon. I've been alone for a long time."

"You're better off by yourself than with a guy like him."

"I know that," she said softly, and then Simon looked at her strangely.

"Would you take him back if he came back to you now?"

"No, I wouldn't." She looked and sounded certain. She was sure.

"Then why talk to him?"

"Old times' sake. I'm still friends with Harry. I talk to him."

"You're not friends with Andrew. He's a jerk. And Harry's different. You have a kid." But Harry never called about Salima, just to say hi to Blaise. Most of the time, he didn't even ask about his daughter.

"I didn't mean to upset you," she said gently, and then smiled at him. He sounded jealous. But in truth, Andrew was no threat to what she felt for Simon. And that was very new. She still needed to make shifts. And they weren't in a relationship anyway. "And you talk to Megan. You said so."

"I try not to," he said, looking defensive and suddenly very young. "Besides, it's only been two months."

"And you don't even know for sure yet if you'll get back together with her or not. You won't know that till you go back to Caldwell and see her again," Blaise reminded him. "That's a lot more scary for me than a guy I broke up with four years ago should be for you."

And they had no claims on each other, which they both knew and were acutely aware of. All they had were attraction and feelings, and the life they shared every day. “For all I know, you’ll go back to her like a boomerang the minute you get back to school,” she said softly. She thought about it a lot, and it was one of the reasons she hadn’t allowed her heart to rule her head with him. She was convinced he would. She could sense that his affair with Megan wasn’t over yet. And she didn’t want her heart broken again, or a brief affair. There were plenty of reasons for them not to get involved with each other. And Blaise was trying very hard not to, for both their sakes. She desperately wanted to be reasonable. And Simon had been sensible too.

“I’m not going back to her,” he said, sounding sullen, as he finished his tea. “I never should have gotten involved with her in the first place, while she was still married.”

“And if she gets divorced?”

“She won’t.” As he said it, their eyes connected again, and he leaned over and kissed her and held her close to him, and all thoughts of Andrew flew out of her mind. She was trying so hard not to give in to desire and passion, and do the right thing, but it was almost impossible to resist. What they felt for each other seemed huge, and in many ways it made sense. And without the issue of his wanting children, she might have given in. She didn’t want to deprive him of something so important to him, particularly not at his age.

Neither of them mentioned Andrew again, nor Megan, and Blaise was swamped at work. Simon took Salima Christmas shopping, and she had very definite ideas about what she wanted to buy. She bought a beautiful bag for Lucianna to carry her sheet music in, because Salima said she always had things in paper bags and dog-eared folders. Even Salima had noticed it. And she got her a bottle of Chanel No. 5, hoping she would change perfume, which made Simon laugh. And she used her allowance to buy a bracelet for her mother at Barneys. It was a wide ivory bangle, which Salima thought she'd love when Simon described it to her. And she wrapped all the packages herself, and did it impeccably, at Simon's suggestion. She and her mother had gotten a cashmere scarf for Simon, and warm leather gloves.

Simon brought Salima with him when he shopped for his parents, and asked her advice. She chose a cashmere sweater for his mother, because it felt so nice when she held it close to her face. Simon said it was white. And they bought a Christmas tree and surprised her mother with it, two weeks before Christmas. They bought it on Friday, and Simon and Blaise were decorating it on Saturday afternoon, while Salima had her lesson with Lucianna. Simon had strung the lights the night before, and he had brought the boxes of decorations down from the top of a closet, and he and Salima had bought a few new ones. The tree was almost finished, when they went to the kitchen for hot chocolate, and didn't want to disturb Salima during her lesson.

It had been fun decorating the tree together, and they were both in good spirits as they chatted. She was wearing an old flannel shirt and jeans, and Simon an old Harvard sweatshirt he wore sometimes on weekends. He had just set their hot chocolate down on the kitchen table, when he turned around and bumped into Blaise, with a package of marshmallows in her hands, which she was intending to put in their hot chocolate, and she popped one into his mouth instead, and as he laughed, his arms went around her and he held her close to him, and looked into her eyes. They could hear Salima singing in the living room and knew she wouldn't walk in on them. And she would be with Lucianna for two hours. He kissed her then, after eating the marshmallow, and she tossed the bag of them on the table and put her arms around his neck as she kissed him in earnest. And suddenly they couldn't stop themselves and hold back the tidal wave any longer. They were starving for each other, as his hands went under the old flannel shirt, and hers under his sweatshirt. Their bodies felt smooth, and their hands explored every inch they could as they seemed to kiss forever and finally came up for air. And this time they knew there was no stopping their passion. Silently, they went to Blaise's suite and she locked the door without a sound, and Simon followed her to her bedroom. She gently kicked the door closed with her foot, as they peeled off each other's clothes and dove into her bed and under the covers and began making love in the twilight of the December afternoon as snow started to fall outside her windows. They could barely breathe, their passion was so overwhelming, and it was over within minutes. They lay looking at each other in her big comfortable bed that had suddenly become theirs.

"Oh my God, what did we do?" Blaise whispered to him. She had been swept away by all that she felt for him, and she still couldn't catch her breath, and she lay looking at him with infinite tenderness.

"I'm not sorry, Blaise," he said, still gasping, his beautiful body lying next to hers, "I hope you're not either. I wanted you so badly, and I love you so much." It had all happened so quickly that they hadn't used a condom, and she wasn't on the Pill, but she knew how unlikely it was that she'd get pregnant, and he had been in a serious relationship for three years.

"I love you too," she said, slipping her arms around his neck again and pulling him closer, so she could kiss him. The scent of their lovemaking was heavy in the air, and she closed her eyes as he held her. She felt totally safe with him.

"I know this is right, Blaise," he said gently, "for both of us. Maybe it won't make sense to other people, but it does to me. You're all I want." She prayed that what he said would prove to be true, and they would be good to each other, as good as they wanted to be now. She didn't want to disappoint him, or have him disappoint her.

"You're all I've ever wanted," she said softly to him,

as they lay and looked at the snow falling outside. It was a magical moment Blaise knew she would never forget.

They lay there for a little while, savoring their closeness, and then they got up, before Salima finished her lesson. They took a shower in Blaise's bathroom, dressed, and were about to leave her bedroom, after she made the bed, and Simon laughed.

"What's funny?" She looked at him with surprise.

"Your shirt is inside out. You'd better fix it. Salima feels those things." They both knew they had to be careful now. They wanted to protect this from everyone for a while, until it felt solid to both of them. It was all so new, and for now only theirs.

Blaise took her shirt off and put it on the right side, while he admired her. They both felt luckier than they ever had in their lives, and for now Blaise had decided to stop worrying about the children he wanted. Or Megan. They had each other, and it felt like that was enough.

He went back to the kitchen first, and she followed him a few minutes later. He threw away the hot chocolate they hadn't had time to drink before passion overwhelmed them, and he opened a bottle of wine. He handed her a glass as she walked in, and Blaise smiled.

"Are we celebrating?" she whispered, and he nodded with a long slow smile. They had much to celebrate. The shared life that had suddenly become theirs.

* * *

After the first time they made love, everything changed subtly. They were more intimate without meaning to be, more was unspoken. They looked at each other and knew what the other meant. They stood closer together, and kissed or touched an arm or a face or squeezed a hand whenever they could. And at night, once Blaise knew Salima was asleep after she'd checked on her for the last time, Simon came to her room and stayed in her bed with her until she got up at four A.M. Then he went back to his own room after he made her coffee and let her read the newspapers. They settled into a delicious routine of making love and sleeping in each other's arms every night. And they were careful to be discreet around Salima. They both wanted to keep this quiet for a while.

"I'm not planning to keep this a secret forever," Blaise reassured him, "but we both need time to adjust before we get hit with everyone's opinions, Salima's reaction, and whatever the press decides to say once they find out. We don't need the headache yet." And he completely agreed. Being involved with Blaise was going to mean more attention from the world than either of them wanted to deal with. They didn't want anything to spoil it for them. It was perfect for now.

And in spite of the deep currents of love and passion running between them, Salima suspected nothing. Once or twice when they were looking at each other and not talking, Salima asked what was happening, everything was so quiet, but she had no sense that they were involved with each other. Only his mother, with her unfailing French sixth sense, seemed to know. He had no idea how she knew, but she accused him again of an affair with Blaise, and he denied it.

"So how is your famous employer?" Isabelle Ward asked with an edge to her voice, literally the day after they had slept together for the first time.

"She's fine," Simon said blithely, trying not to react to her suspicious tone.

"She wants you, you know," his mother said with an aura of doom, which annoyed him even more.

"Mother, please. She's a busy woman, we hardly have time to talk to each other. And I'm sure she has a million men chasing her, a lot more important than I am."

"You're young, that's why she wants you. She wants to have an affair with you, and then she'll throw you away like garbage."

"For God's sake, will you stop? She doesn't want me, she's not sleeping with me, and she's not going to throw me away."

"Aha! You slept with her! I can hear it in your voice!" She was right, but he would have died rather than admit it to her, especially after what she'd said.

"I'm not going to discuss this with you anymore. What are you and Dad doing for Christmas?" he said, changing the subject, but he already knew. They were going to his brother's.

"We're going to David's. And we have tickets to a Beethoven symphony the day after. My favorite, the ninth. You'll be in New York?"

"Of course. I'm working. I can't leave Salima." Or Blaise, but he didn't say it.

"Can't she take care of her own child for five minutes? On Christmas Day at least. It would be nice if you could come to Boston."

"I can't. Salima needs monitoring all the time for her diabetes."

"I don't see why you have to do it." He didn't, Blaise checked her during the night too, but he didn't tell his mother. "I think she's a dangerous woman," his mother warned him in an ominous tone. "She'll devour you, if you let her." She had nothing but disaster to predict for him at Blaise's hands, and it annoyed him so much, he got off the phone, and promised himself he wouldn't call her again till Christmas. There was just no point. She only depressed him.

A few days later Blaise surprised him. She had been to the network Christmas party, which she never enjoyed, and had received a slew of invitations to Christmas parties she said she didn't want to go to. She didn't want to be on display, and she said that many people invited her for that purpose, so they could say they knew her and show her off. She only liked going to the homes and parties of close friends, of which she had few. The network party was a command performance every year. And there was no way she could have taken him.

But after dinner that night, when Salima was with Lucianna, Blaise slid an invitation across the table at him. It was red and gold on Tiffany stationery, it was heavy stock, and Simon recognized the host's name immediately. Adam Lancaster was a very well-known writer Blaise had interviewed that year. He had written countless best-sellers and a long list of films. He was giving a Christmas party the next day at his townhouse, five blocks from Blaise.

"He just got married, and his wife is about your age. I think he's sixty-something, but he hangs out with a lot of young people, and he knows everyone in the world. I thought it might be fun to go." Simon nodded. He was sure it would be interesting, and he was happy for her.

"I'm sure you'll enjoy it," he said generously, and she smiled at him, and realized he hadn't understood.

"Not me, us. You. I'd like to take you. Will you come?"

"As your date?" He looked stunned.

"As whatever they call it. Date. Plus one. Escort. Friend." Eventually boyfriend or lover, but for now just going out together seemed like a good place to start. She had never taken him anywhere socially, and she wanted to. And she wanted him to know that she didn't intend to keep him a dark secret. If they made a go of this, they had to be able to go out together and share a social life. She had no idea how people would react or what they would think, or say about her. But she wanted to take their brand-new relationship out for a spin. She was curious to see if they would be comfortable going out into the world. Simon nodded and looked nervous, but he seemed touched that she had asked.

"Are you sure? You're not embarrassed to be seen with me?"

"Are you crazy? You're ten times the man that anyone there will be, except maybe our host, who is something of a genius. But you're smarter, better looking, more exciting, and a hell of a lot nicer and more fun to be with than anyone who'll be there."

"Then why are we going?" he teased her.

"I want to show you off," she said, and then reminded him not to tell Salima. Lucianna was taking her to an early concert, so she would be out. Simon was beaming when they left the room. He was very flattered that she was going out with him, and it sounded like a very intriguing group.

The following evening Blaise dressed after Salima left with Lucianna, and wore a short sexy red cocktail dress and a black coat when they left the apartment at seven. She had come home in time to dress, and Simon was wearing a dark gray suit, white shirt, and navy blue tie. He looked like a banker or a lawyer, and she knew he would fit in. She was proud to leave the building on his arm, and Tully was waiting to drive them the few blocks to the party. He didn't seem surprised to see Simon with her, even in his dark suit and good-looking navy blue coat. It was bitter cold and there was ice on the ground. She didn't want to walk the five blocks in high heels and arrive with windblown hair and a red nose.

The party was already crowded when they got there, in a spectacular townhouse with a two-floor ceiling in the living room, filled with pre-Columbian and modern art. They both noticed three Picassos on the way in, and a Léger. And Simon looked perfectly at ease. She introduced him to their host's new wife, who was a beautiful young woman, and she and Simon realized almost immediately that they had been at Harvard at the same time although she was two years younger. They didn't know each other but had seen each other and had friends in common, and Simon had a long conversation with her, before moving on to a photographer he had always wanted to meet, while Blaise chatted with the editor of *Vogue*.

It was a lively, eclectic group, and every well-known, accomplished person in New York seemed to be there. Blaise stopped to talk to their host, and introduced him to Simon. And whenever people came by that she knew, she introduced him as "my friend, Simon Ward." No one asked if he was her boyfriend, her best friend, her walker, her son, or her nephew, if she was sleeping with him or he was gay. They didn't care. And no one seemed shocked to see them together. She looked very pretty in her red dress, and Simon was very handsome in his suit. He and the host had quite a long chat, and he and Blaise had a great time together. It was fun to be out in a grown-up world, particularly with the kind of people she had access to. When people asked what he did and he said he was a special ed teacher, no one looked contemptuous or was dismissive, and a few asked what kind of special ed, and he explained that he worked with nonsighted children at a school in Massachusetts, but he was currently on leave in New York. No one knew he worked for her, and Blaise didn't say it, but she liked the reaction people had to them. Everyone was friendly and welcoming, and no one cared about the difference in their age. It was a sophisticated group. She had wanted to prove to both of them that they could actually have a life together in the real world. She had wanted to test it for herself most of all. But they both loved the result when they thanked their hosts and finally went home, as the party began to thin out. Simon wished he could take her out to dinner, but they had to get back to wait for Salima, when Lucianna dropped her off.

"Wow, that was terrific," Simon said as they rode the few blocks home. Blaise was beaming when they got out at her building and they walked across the lobby. It had been even better than she'd hoped. She loved being out with him.

"It was great," she giggled in the elevator as he kissed her. He had been starving for her all night, and they still had to wait until Salima went to bed. "Nobody looked shocked or even interested that we were out together. I was afraid people would stare," she admitted, "or make some rude comment." She was enormously relieved and had had a terrific time with him.

"The only person who makes rude comments is my mother," Simon said, as they got out on her floor and walked into her apartment.

"She's going to go crazy when she finds out about us," Blaise said with a look of concern. Simon looked totally relaxed as he took off his coat and left it on a chair. "What will you do?" Blaise asked him.

"About my mother? Ignore her. She's made a big point all my life about how bohemian she is, and not bourgeois, while my father plays by no one's rules and made a career of thinking outside the box. They have no right to get traditional now. They lost their right to that a long time ago, when they got married, and they've been pretty outrageous ever since. And what we're doing isn't outrageous." They both changed their clothes and were sitting, chatting in the kitchen when Salima came home half an hour later, excited about the concert. She had no idea that Blaise was wearing makeup, but they were both wearing jeans.

"Hi, Simon," she said blithely. "Wow, you smell good, Mom." It never dawned on her that they had been out together. "Did you go somewhere?" Had she been sighted, she would have been able to read everything in her mother's eyes.

"I went to a party at Adam Lancaster's house. It was a nice Christmas party not far from here. He has a beautiful place and incredible art." They chatted about the concert for a few minutes, and then Salima went to her room, Blaise went to do some work before they turned in for the night, and Simon said he had some e-mails to answer. But it was several hours before Simon came into her bedroom, and they curled up for the night and talked about the party again. Blaise lay in his arms and looked up at him. "I have fun with you, Simon." More than she had ever had with any man in her life.

"I think that's the idea." He smiled back at her. "I have fun with you too. Thank you for taking me tonight. I felt so special being there with you." He had been truly touched that she had included him in such an illustrious group.

"I wanted to," she said, as she turned off the light and they cuddled. "I felt special being out with you too. It was nice, and no one looked surprised to see us together."

"Why would they?" he asked, and she didn't answer. They both knew. The fifteen years between them that his mother was so worried about. But no one at Adam Lancaster's had cared. He was older than Blaise by twenty years, and his wife was even younger than Simon. Blaise had gone out to dinner with him once, and she had sensed that he thought she was too old for him. He liked much younger women. And now everything was reversed. It still surprised Blaise, and she was grateful that it didn't seem to bother Simon. The evening had been a hit for both of them.

He fell asleep before she did, and she lay looking at him in the moonlight. She wondered if he'd leave her one day for a younger woman, who would have children with him, or go back to Megan. Anything was possible, but for now he was hers. She smiled thinking of it, and drifted off to sleep.

Chapter 11

Blaise managed to squeeze in her trip to Israel before Christmas, to interview the prime minister, while Simon and Teresa stayed with Salima. Simon called her in Jerusalem constantly, he was so worried about her. There had been a bombing the week before she got there, and he was terrified something would happen to her. She reassured him that she was fine and staying in a beautiful hotel with lots of security. She felt totally safe. And her interview with the prime minister went better than expected. She got back to New York a week before Christmas, in time for Harry's annual visit to his daughter, which was as disappointing as it was every year. Salima deserved so much more.

They sat in the living room of the apartment, while Harry looked uncomfortable as Salima walked in, and when she sat down, she told him about her singing lessons, but he looked at his watch every five minutes as though he were in a hurry to leave. Salima looked beautiful, and she had kissed his cheek before she sat down with him and her mother. But he stiffened when she bent near him, and Salima could feel it. She wanted to tell him that blindness wasn't contagious. Nor was diabetes. Her health issues had always made him acutely ill at ease, and even without seeing him, Salima knew it.

She offered to sing one of the songs she'd been working on, but he said he didn't have time, and had to leave. Blaise was so angry that when he handed her a check at the end of the visit, as she walked him to the door, she handed it back to him.

"Buy her something nice, Blaisie. I never know what to get her." The gift of his time would have been better, and Blaise was furious that he hadn't bothered to listen to her sing.

"I'm not going to this year," Blaise said to him with a grim expression. She was tired from her trip to the Middle East, and she hated the way he treated their daughter, as though she were a total stranger to him, which she was, since he spent no time with her. He wanted no responsibility for her, and was afraid to take her anywhere. And Blaise was tired of covering for him, and trying to make him look better than he was to Salima. "Buy her something yourself. She knows the difference."

"I don't know what she likes, what size she wears. How can I pick something for her, if she can't see it?"

It was the same excuse he used every year to have Blaise do it.

"She loves music. Hell, Harry, buy her CDs. Buy her anything, a piece of jewelry, a fur jacket. She's not an invalid. She's a nineteen-year-old girl who loves clothes and perfume and jewelry, just like every other girl her age. She's no different. And her passion is music. And she's good, really good. She has a teacher from Juilliard who's here four times a week now. She's going to have a recital in May. Not that you care." She hated his disappointing Salima year after year. It upset her even more than it did Salima, who was used to it after years of his indifference and always bounced back quickly. But she always looked sad when her father left after his infrequent brief visits. He was in town for a day on his way to St. Bart's to meet friends on a yacht. And Salima was the duty call he made between meetings.

As Harry was leaving, Simon walked in, and Blaise introduced them. Harry observed him with interest, and then Simon went to find Salima, who had gone to her room. He said goodbye to Harry and disappeared.

"Wow, nice-looking young guy, Blaise. Your new boyfriend?" He smiled at her with a lascivious grin, and she was even more annoyed.

"No, Salima's monitor from school."

"You can have some fun with him," he commented. "I can really see you with a younger guy. You look great for your age, and you have more energy than anyone I know."

"He's here for Salima," she said drily. It was none of his business.

"When is she going back to school?" he asked as they waited for the elevator.

"When they reopen, probably sometime in January." She didn't like thinking about it. She didn't want Simon or Salima to leave, and wished they never would.

"That'll be a lot easier for you," he said sympathetically. "It must be hard having her home."

"It's wonderful. It's not hard at all," she said, as the elevator came and he disappeared into it with a wave, and wished her merry Christmas. And as she watched the doors close, she wondered how she could have been married to him. He was such a lousy father and a total zero as a human being, no matter how intelligent he was. She was still looking unhappy about it when she went back to her office to do some work. Simon stopped by to see her after he left Salima in her room, talking to friends on Facebook, as usual.

Blaise looked up and smiled at him when he walked in. "Nice-looking man," Simon said about Harry. But he hadn't liked him. He knew how little attention he paid to Salima and how sad she was about it. He was successful, handsome, and charming, but to Simon, that wasn't enough. And Simon thought it unforgivable that Harry had detached from Salima at three, when they diagnosed her with diabetes. He had heard it from both her and Blaise.

"He said the same thing about you. He asked if you were my new boyfriend."

"Well, that's direct anyway. Maybe he should talk to my mother. He's so cold, Blaise. I can't see you with a guy like him." He had been puzzled by him, and couldn't imagine him connected to Blaise, or anyone. He was all about himself, and it showed.

"Neither can I. I was impressed by him. He's brilliant. And I was very young. I was twenty-five when we met. And he was the same age I am now. I married him a year later, and a year after that the network moved me to New York, so we only lived together for a year. Our time together was pretty irregular after I moved. We were both married to our careers. We weren't even planning to have kids. Salima was a slip. A fortuitous one, it turns out." She smiled at him. "Harry has no idea what a gift she is." Simon had seen that, and he nodded. "He wouldn't even let her sing for him. Sometimes he really is a shit." She shook her head and went back to work, and she was relieved to see at dinner that Salima didn't look upset. Her father always disappointed her, so she was used to it. She had recovered very quickly. Disappointment was the only relationship she'd ever had with him.

A big box arrived from Chanel that night. It was a Chanel backpack from Harry, with a note.

"Merry Christmas! You can use this when you go back to school." It was beautiful, though not really her style. But at least he had tried.

"I can use it for my music," Salima said happily,

touched by the gift. And she could tell that he had picked it instead of her mom. He had actually called the store, spoken to a salesgirl he knew, and told her to pick something for his daughter and put it on his charge. He had no idea what she'd sent. Salima texted him that night to thank him, but he was on the plane to St. Bart's by then and didn't respond.

They were all tired that night, and Salima went to bed early. Blaise was tired too, and said she felt fluish after the long trip a few days before. For once, she wasn't her usual energetic self. And she was already half asleep when Simon came in later that night. He snuggled up next to her, sleepy too. He had done a lot of errands with Salima that day. She was looking for one last gift for her mother, and had dragged him to every store. And after that they'd gone grocery shopping at the supermarket, and then checked out a new stereo.

They made love even though they were both tired, and Blaise muttered something about getting up to check Salima, as she did every night. She was always fine, but Blaise liked to be sure there was no glitch with her pump, and she just felt better if she saw her one last time before she went to bed. And she had made Simon do it while she was away, which he had. But before she could force herself to get out of bed that night, she was sound asleep, and Simon passed out just as fast. Their lovemaking had put him in a daze. And the following morning, Saturday, they overslept. It was daylight when they woke up, and Blaise was horrified to see that it was ten o'clock. She wanted to get Simon out of her room before Salima found them there. At least Teresa didn't come in on the weekends. And by now, Salima could make her own breakfast. The house was quiet when Blaise peeked out and looked down the hall. Salima's door was closed, which meant she was asleep too, and Simon ran back to his room on silent feet. He could tell when he ran through the kitchen that Salima hadn't gotten up. There was no sign of her having eaten, no cereal boxes on the table or dishes in the sink, and he was relieved. He hoped she hadn't gone looking for him, and wondered where he was. He went to take a shower, and was just drying off, when he heard Blaise calling him from the other end of the apartment. She raced to his room then, still in her nightgown, and told him with a look of panic to call 911.

"Salima's unconscious!" she said breathlessly, and ran back, and they both guessed what it was. She was in a diabetic coma. She hadn't eaten, and Blaise suspected that her pump had somehow failed. She had never woken up. A failure of her pump had never happened before, though Blaise was always afraid it would.

Simon called, and then jumped into his jeans while he was still wet, pulled on a T-shirt, and ran to Salima's room with wet hair and bare feet. Blaise was sitting with her, alternately touching her cheeks and stroking her hair, and shaking her and trying to revive her. Salima was deathly pale, and her lips were blue, as tears ran down Blaise's cheeks and she talked to her. Salima showed no sign of life, but Blaise had made sure that she was breathing. She was wracked with guilt as she looked at her. It was the first time in years that she hadn't checked on her when she was home. And within five minutes, the paramedics were there. They gave her insulin immediately, put her on a stretcher, and rushed her to the ambulance waiting downstairs. Blaise literally tore off her nightgown, hastily put on the slacks and sweater she'd worn the day before, pulled on boots, and was out the door with her handbag and uncombed hair. They were taking her to Columbia Presbyterian, and Simon shouted that he would meet her there, as the door closed. He could hear the siren screaming as the ambulance drove away, and he could just imagine what was going through her mind. It was going through his as well. They had been making love the night before when Salima almost died.

The doorman hailed a cab for him, as soon as Simon got downstairs, and after promising to pay him double, the cab driver got him there in twelve minutes, which was heroic. Simon gave him two twenty-dollar bills and ran into the emergency room and asked for Salima Stern. She used her father's name. He was told she had just been taken to the ICU. He followed the nurse's directions, and looked for Blaise in the maze of hallways and treatment rooms. And he found her finally in a cubicle with two doctors and three nurses. Salima was still unconscious, and Blaise was sobbing in the corner as Simon put an arm around her and she shook him off. There were tears in his eyes too. And a moment later the doctor asked them to wait in the waiting room. Simon followed her in silence, and they were alone in the ICU waiting room. Blaise was grateful that no one else was there when she turned to look at Simon with a combination of guilt, anguish, and hatred. The hatred was for herself.

"Do you realize what we did? We made love last night, and I never got up to check her. I was too goddamn tired from having sex and I went to sleep. Her pump failed, the catheter disconnected under her skin, and she had no insulin all night." They had told her that Salima had diabetic ketoacidosis, which could be fatal, although it was a very rare occurrence. "She could have been dead by the time we found her. And she could still die," Blaise said, sobbing. "She was dying and we were screwing."

"We weren't screwing," he said in an equally anguished tone, and he felt guilty too. "We were making love. Christ, Blaise, we're human. You're allowed to fall asleep once in a while. It could have happened even if we didn't make love. It can happen. I saw it with a kid with a pump at school. You take better care of her than I've ever seen."

"Not last night." She looked daggers at him, and then collapsed onto the couch. He didn't dare approach her, and sat down across the room.

"Do you want me to go?" he asked, gently. "I will if you want me to." She shook her head in answer, and burst into tears again, and Simon went to comfort her, and she melted into his arms in grief.

"Simon, we killed her," she said sobbing. "What if she dies?" He was praying she wouldn't, and he just sat there and held Blaise for the next hour until the chief resident walked in. He took off his mask and peeled off his gloves, and he smiled at them both.

"She's going to be okay. She's conscious. She gave us a hell of a scare, but she's a strong girl. And don't blame yourselves, these things happen. For a kid with type 1, she's in remarkably good health. I can tell you're doing a great job with her. You can't watch everything, or predict this kind of problem, even if you watched her all the time. The catheter just slipped out. Once in a blue moon it happens."

"I always check her at night before I go to bed," Blaise said, sobbing from relief now, and Simon was crying too. It had been a nightmarish morning, and it was only noon.

"Judging from her levels, my guess is that she lost the catheter delivering insulin early this morning, so even if you'd checked her, say, at midnight, it wouldn't have made a difference. But you definitely found her just in time. I wouldn't have liked to see her go without much longer than she did. You did all the right things," he reassured them both, and Simon looked even more relieved than Blaise. He had been feeling terrible about what had happened and his part in it.

"Can we see her?" Simon asked even before Blaise.

"Of course. I'd like to keep her overnight just till we

get all her levels straightened out. She's going to be fine," he said again, and Blaise hurried to see Salima, with Simon right behind her. Salima was pale, and she looked like she'd been hit by a bus, but she was smiling when they entered the cubicle again. The worst was over. But they all knew that slipping into a diabetic coma or winding up in insulin shock were risks she'd have to manage all her life. It was why Blaise had put her at Caldwell, because she couldn't face worrying about her all the time and living at the edge of a cliff, especially if she was away. And Salima was so young then. Now at least if something went wrong when she was awake, Salima was able to recognize the signs and tell someone if she didn't feel right. But this time it had all happened while she was asleep, so she didn't know herself.

"You scared the hell out of me," Blaise said as she bent to kiss her, and Salima smiled as Simon stood just behind Blaise.

"Sorry I scared you guys," she said in a hoarse voice. "I woke up feeling weird in the night, but I thought I was getting the flu and went right back to sleep. I guess the catheter was already out and I didn't know it." Blaise knew she still wasn't feeling well when she didn't insist on going home right away. Salima hated hospitals, but she needed to be there now, at least for a day, until she recovered from the shock to her system. She could easily have died, and Blaise was so grateful she hadn't. She thought about calling Harry to tell him what had happened, but she knew there was no point. He didn't care.

They sat with her for a little while, and then the nurse told them that they couldn't stay continuously in the ICU, and Salima needed to get some sleep. Her color was already better, and Blaise was relieved as she kissed her again, and promised to be back in a few hours.

"Bring my laptop and my iPod," she told Simon, and he grinned. She was obviously feeling a lot better than when she came in with the siren screaming. She had youth on her side.

"With pleasure." He was beaming when he said it. He was so relieved.

Blaise left all her numbers at the nurse's station, and the nurse took down the information and then looked up at Simon. "Your daughter's going to be fine," she reassured them again. "Would you like to leave your numbers too, or just your wife's?" the nurse asked, and Simon stared at her, not sure what to say. It seemed complicated to explain that he wasn't Salima's father and Blaise wasn't his wife. He hesitated for a moment before he answered.

"Just my wife's will be fine. We'll be together. And we'll be back in a couple of hours. Call us immediately if she has a problem."

"She's all right now. We just want to get her levels regulated, and she needs to rest. She can go home tomorrow." The doctor had already told them, and they thanked her and left. They both looked like they'd been in a car wreck.

"I must really look like shit," Simon said to Blaise in the elevator. "She thought I was old enough to be Salima's father. I feel like I am."

"I must look like her grandmother, or yours," Blaise said with a tired smile. It hadn't even occurred to the nurse that they weren't a couple. "She terrified me when I found her," Blaise said, still shaken by it, and then she looked at him sadly. "I'm sorry I blamed you for this, even indirectly. I felt so guilty that we'd been making love, and she was dying."

"So did I," he admitted, even though they both knew now that it had happened later, after they might have checked. But the reality that she had almost died had hit them both like a bomb. Blaise was infinitely grateful she hadn't, and so was Simon.

"I'm sorry if I was mean to you," Blaise said sheepishly as they left the hospital, and he stopped walking and looked at her.

"You thought your kid was dying, and I was the guy 'screwing' you last night, as you put it. You had every right to get mad, or freak out, and blame me. I would have done the same thing. You get a pass." He put an arm around her then, and they hailed a cab at the curb. They went back to the apartment and climbed into Blaise's bed and just clung to each other. He could feel that Blaise was shaking. They didn't make love this time, and held each other, silently thanking God that Salima was alive.

* * *

Salima came home the next day, and she was tired but felt almost normal again. The doctor had said it might take another day to feel entirely like herself. And he suggested she stay at home, without running around. She didn't even feel like singing or practicing, which was a sign that she wasn't fully recovered from what had happened. And she went to bed when they got home. She said she was just tired. Simon called Lucianna to cancel Salima's lesson that day, and she was shocked and burst into tears. She was still crying after Simon explained it all and they hung up.

He went to make them lunch, while Blaise kept Salima company in her room. She didn't need supervision, but Blaise was so relieved to have her home that she didn't want to leave her. Blaise was sitting on the foot of the bed, when Salima looked in her mother's direction.

"Can I ask you something, Mom?"

"Sure, sweetheart. What is it?" Salima had a serious look on her face, as though she were about to ask an important question, and Blaise had no idea what was on her mind.

"It was nice of Simon to come to the hospital with you," she said quietly. "I like him a lot, Mom. When you guys left, the nurse thought you were my parents. I thought it was funny at first, and then I wondered about something. Maybe you two looked like my parents, or acted like it in some way for them to think that. Mom, are you dating Simon? I mean . . . you know . . . I know you guys don't go anywhere together . . . I mean . . . like . . . are you in love with him, Mom? Are you a couple?" It was a big question, and she could see that Salima wanted an answer. They had been careful not to let Salima know about their relationship. Blaise still wanted time for them to get used to it before they told her. But they had just run out of time.

"Kind of," Blaise said honestly. "It's very new. It just happened, since Thanksgiving. It's only been a few weeks."

"Is it serious?"

"I don't know yet. We're trying to figure it out. I like him a lot." And then she decided to be more honest with her than she'd just been. "I love him, I just don't know if it's the right thing for both of us. Simon should be with someone closer to your age than mine. I don't want to deprive him of that and everything that goes with it."

"You mean like babies?"

"Yes, among other things. He's fifteen years younger than I am. That's a lot." She was looking intently at her daughter. Salima didn't seem upset, she looked puzzled.

"I kind of suspected something was happening."

"How?" How could a nonsighted person be aware of the subtleties of a budding relationship that had only just happened? Salima always amazed her.

"There are a lot more silences than there used to be.

You must be looking at each other, or holding hands, kissing, or something." She smiled at her mother.

Blaise smiled back at her, and then her face grew serious again. "How do you feel about it?" Salima was silent for a long time and looked like she was thinking.

"I'm not sure. I really like him. I'm not used to sharing you with anyone, and that might be weird. Or it could be nice too, when you're busy. He's good company and he's smart." Blaise couldn't help smiling again.

"That's how I feel about him too."

"Is he cute?" Salima grinned at her.

"Very. Are you shocked? About us, I mean?"

"A little. But I guess you have a right to someone in your life. And I think I kind of like it that he's younger. It's more fun for me." That was one aspect Blaise hadn't thought of.

"Well, we'll see what happens. We might get tired of each other by the time you go back to school," she said lightly. She wasn't going to tell her any more. That was more information than she needed. She knew enough now, and Blaise was relieved that she had no serious objections. And she felt better being honest with her. She thought Simon would prefer it too. In the end, it was a blessing. Her pump failing had been terrifying, but they had come through the crisis together, and now Salima knew that her mother was in love with Simon. A lot had happened in twenty-four hours. But Salima was looking troubled again. She had something to tell her mother, and she'd been waiting for the right time. She hoped this was it.

"I don't want to go back to school," she said softly. "I want to stay here and take lessons with Lucianna. She helped me apply to Juilliard for September," she confessed. "She's going to write me a recommendation, and she could help me get ready for my audition." She couldn't see her mother's face but she was praying that she'd agree. She had outgrown living at Caldwell, and they both knew it.

"We'd have to figure out who would take care of you, when Simon goes back."

"Can't he stay?" Salima sounded worried. She was used to him now, and he was great with her. She still missed Abby, but she did a lot more with Simon, and she had grown up immeasurably in the past two months, and could do more for herself than she ever had before. And she liked it.

"I don't know," Blaise answered honestly. "I think he has to finish out his contract. At least till the end of the school year. They might let him quit, but he'll have to want that too. Let's not worry about it now. We haven't even heard from school about when they're going to reopen. What about your college classes? Don't you want to finish that?" Salima shook her head. She was sure.

"I want to study music." And Blaise knew she had never been happier than since she'd started studying singing with Lucianna.

"Well, we have a lot to think about, don't we?" Blaise said, and reached out to pat Salima's hand.

"Is that a yes?" Salima pressed her, and Blaise laughed.

"It's a strong maybe," she said honestly. But Salima could hear that her mother wasn't against it.

"I really want to get in to Juilliard. And I like living at home with you."

"I love having you at home too." She had been gone for long enough. Too long. Eleven years. And she was great company. But what Blaise would need to make it work was someone to take care of her when Simon left to go back to Caldwell. He would have to finish out the school year when they reopened. "I think we're getting ahead of ourselves. Let's try to figure all this out after Christmas."

"Will Simon stay with us if he leaves Caldwell? I mean like live with us?" Salima looked intrigued by the idea.

"Maybe. I'd like that. It's up to him."

"Have you asked him to?" She was curious about them now.

"Not yet," Blaise laughed, just as Simon walked into Salima's bedroom carrying a tray.

"Am I interrupting anything?" he asked. He could see that they'd been having a serious conversation, but both mother and daughter looked pleased.

"I was telling Salima about us," Blaise said quietly, and for a minute he looked as though he were going to drop the tray. "Actually, she guessed, when the nurses thought you were her father."

"I think it would be nice for you both," Salima said generously. "What's for lunch?" She clearly wasn't having a problem with it, and Simon looked relieved.

"Caesar salad and an omelet. I'll do better tonight. But let's check your blood glucose and adjust the bolus before you eat."

"Okay," Salima said, sitting up in bed and smiling at him, as he set the tray down on her desk, and took care of the necessary routines. Salima was used to it. "Just think, if you stay with me and Mom, we'll have great food all the time," she said when she was ready to eat.

"I'm sure that's the only reason your mom wants me," he said, smiling at Blaise. He set the tray down next to Salima and touched her hand so she would know it was there. "Our lunch is in the kitchen," he said to Blaise, and after kissing Salima again, she told her they'd be back in a little while. Salima grabbed her iPod then and put the earpiece in.

"Have a nice lunch," she said to her mother, as Blaise followed Simon back into the kitchen.

"How did that go?" Simon asked her, as they sat down at the kitchen table. He had made the same for them, and had covered it to keep it warm.

"Amazingly well. I think she was startled at first, but not really surprised. She said she suspected it."

"She's very sharp."

Blaise nodded. "And she likes you. A lot. She isn't

bothered by the difference in our age at all. She doesn't want to go back to Caldwell. She wants to stay and go to Juilliard in the fall."

He wasn't surprised to hear it. He knew Lucianna had been lobbying heavily for the school. "How do you feel about it?"

"I think it's the right thing for her. She's too old for Caldwell. And she loves her singing lessons. Juilliard would be good for her."

"Are you willing to keep her at home?"

"Only if I can find someone for her after you leave. I can't take care of her alone. I'm out all day, and I travel too much."

"We'll figure it out, Blaise. Right now, let's just eat lunch." They had covered a lot of ground in two days. They had hit some heavy bumps but were closer than ever. And their relationship had come out of it unscathed. They had told Salima about their relationship, and she didn't object to it. And she wanted to drop out of school, stay home, and study music. It was a lot to digest. Simon leaned over and kissed her, and they dug into their omelets, and for now everything seemed to be on track.

Chapter 12

The Christmas that Blaise, Simon, and Salima shared was perfect. They all loved their presents, and opened them on Christmas Eve after a delicious dinner. They went to midnight mass at St. Patrick's Cathedral, and as she always did when she went to church now, Salima lit a candle for Abby. It was hard to believe she'd been gone for almost three months. Salima knew she'd never forget her, but so much had changed in Salima's life since she died. It made it seem like much longer.

They stayed up late that night, and Blaise put Salima to bed. And afterward she found Simon already waiting in her bedroom. He thanked her for the beautiful Christmas and the lovely presents. And he had given Blaise a narrow gold bangle to wear with the one she always wore now, from Dubai. She loved Simon's more. He had had a message engraved inside: "Merry Christmas, I love you, S." And she had given him a watch. It was a Rolex he could wear every day, and he loved it. And she loved the ivory bangle from Salima too. And Salima loved all her gifts. Simon had recorded some wonderful music for her, and made a number of CDs, compiled from his own music collection.

The next morning Simon made them an enormous breakfast, including the homemade whole wheat waffles Salima loved, with the diabetic maple syrup. He had given her her own waffle iron for Christmas along with a stack of books in Braille that she wanted to read.

They were just finishing breakfast when Simon's cell phone rang. He grabbed it from where it was sitting on the counter, and Blaise saw him frown as he answered. She knew instantly it was Megan. He sounded tense when he told her they were eating, and then he paused for a long time as he listened, and as he did, he left the kitchen and stayed on the phone and walked back to his room.

Blaise made idle chitchat with Salima after he left and tried not to sound as distracted as she was. She could tell that whatever Megan was saying, she must have been upset about something, and Simon had looked worried when he left the room.

"Something wrong, Mom?" Salima asked her. She could hear the tension in her mother's voice, and Blaise didn't want her to know that she was upset, nor that Simon had been involved with a teacher at school. He didn't want Salima to know, and Blaise had promised him she wouldn't tell her. His affair with Megan was a breach of school rules, and he was embarrassed by their situation. Romances among faculty members were frowned on, but inevitably some occurred. But he didn't want Salima to know he had spent three years with a married woman. He was ashamed.

"No, I'm fine," Blaise lied to her as they talked about what to do that afternoon. Christmas was always a casual day for them, usually spent in pajamas, watching old movies or football, and Simon had promised to make them his famous turkey hash, from turkey left over from the night before.

It was a full twenty minutes before Simon walked back into the room, and he pretended to be cheerful, and said nothing about the phone call until Blaise was alone with him.

"What happened?" She couldn't wait to ask him, she was nervous about the call and how long it had been.

"Nothing. She just wanted to wish me a merry Christmas, and she was upset because her middle son broke his arm." Simon sounded concerned and had already told Blaise he loved her sons. They hadn't lied to him. She had.

"Did his father hurt him?" Blaise asked, looking worried about a child she didn't know.

"No, he fell off his new bike," Simon said, and seemed uncomfortable. Blaise had the distinct impression that he didn't want to discuss Megan with her.

"Anything else?" She didn't know why, but she had the feeling there was more, and he took a moment to answer.

"No, it was fine," he said vaguely, and loaded the dishwasher. Blaise walked over to him and kissed him then. The look on his face reminded her of when Andrew called her. She could see the pain in Simon's eyes.

"I love you," she said simply, and put her arms around him.

"I love you too," he said sadly, and then he kissed her, and she thought she saw tears in his eyes. But he said nothing more about Megan, and they spent the rest of the afternoon reading the paper, relaxing, and watching football on TV, until Simon went to start dinner and produced the promised hash. And he was in better spirits by then, and had recovered from Megan's call. She was the ghost of Christmas past, or at least Blaise hoped so. The three of them had a good time at dinner. They were still being circumspect around Salima, and didn't want to shock her. She had no idea that Simon spent every night in her mother's room, and Blaise didn't tell her. She didn't need to know.

When she and Simon went to bed that night, they agreed that it had been a lovely Christmas, their first. She said something about it, and he was quick to correct her.

"The first of many."

"I hope so," she said softly. He slept in her arms that

night, and all she could hope was that he wasn't dreaming of Megan.

Blaise was off for the week between Christmas and New Year, and she spent time with Salima and Simon. They went to concerts and out to dinner, and took Salima skating in Central Park. She loved it. The three of them had a great time together, and Salima went to two recitals at Juilliard with Lucianna and met some of the students. She came back more excited than ever about the school and could hardly wait to audition. The time flew by, and Blaise's vacation ended all too quickly.

The first two weeks of January were totally crazy for Blaise once she went back to work. She had three major trips planned, one to California and two to Europe, and each of them only for a few days. And as always now, Teresa stayed at the apartment to help Simon with Salima, and each time Blaise returned, he was thrilled to see her. And by midmonth she was exhausted. She was traveling too much, but the interviews she was doing were important. All of her recent ones had already been aired, and had done well. And the night she got home from her last trip, Susie Quentin's live special was on, with her interview with the first lady. It had been the talk of the network for weeks. Blaise sat down to watch it with trepidation, and Simon joined her a few minutes later right before it came on. He didn't want to miss it either. He knew how nervous Blaise was about it. Andrew had sent Blaise a text about it, as though she wouldn't know it would be on. She particularly wanted to see it to see how stiff her competition was. This was the big opportunity the network had given Susie to shine, and Blaise knew that if Susie did well with it, her own future could be impacted. A star could be born that night, if Susie knocked their socks off. Blaise knew she would be fighting for her position at the network every day from then on. It was tough enough as it was, without adding more pressure. Blaise looked intent and tense as Susie and the first lady came on, from a sitting room at the White House.

The interview opened with Susie explaining who she was, and saying how happy she was to be at the White House with the first lady, which Blaise told Simon she thought was hokey. No one cared who the reporter was, she explained, especially at Susie's stage of the game, they were just a vehicle to draw out their subjects, and ask the questions everyone wanted to know. She was the mouthpiece for the viewing public, their alter ego. But she had a massive ego of her own, and it leaped at the viewers right through the TV. She was all about Susie, and eventually addressed the first lady. Her first question was inane. Her second one was worse. And for her third one, she made a blunder and asked the first lady how she had liked living in Virginia before the White House, and what that time had meant to her. The question was only interesting because the first lady had never lived there, her predecessor had. Susie was an administration late.

"Oh my God," Blaise said, wincing, "how did she

manage to screw that up, and who the hell did the research?" The first lady looked confused on the air. Simon was amused by the flow of editorial comments from Blaise.

Susie then went on to ask her if she thought her husband had ever had an affair. Blaise nearly choked and stared at the TV in disbelief. She had done nothing to warm up her subject and put her at ease. So far she had bored her, made a ridiculous mistake about her living in Virginia, and had just embarrassed her on prime-time national TV in front of millions of people. The first lady did not look pleased, to say the least. She looked poised but pissed. And Susie was clueless, as she waited for an answer to her question.

The current president was a seriously religious man, who was known for his moral standards and puritanical values. He might have been a hypocrite, but Blaise didn't think so, and his wife sure as hell wouldn't admit it if he was. He was a very straitlaced man, and all Susie had accomplished was seriously angering the president's wife, who looked stunned after Susie asked the question and quietly answered, "No."

"I'll say one thing, she's got balls," Blaise said about her rival. She was beginning to look seriously foolish, and Blaise nearly fell off the couch when she asked the first lady if she'd ever had an affair herself. She was turning her special into tabloid TV and had copied Blaise's occasional harsher, controversial edge without the judgment, brains, and charm.

"Oh my God," Blaise groaned with both hands on

her head. "She belongs in an institution. Is she nuts?" The first lady was sealed up tight as a drum after answering no to that question too, and the interview might as well have ended there. From then on, she answered in monosyllables, and fielded every question as she'd been taught to do by experts.

The questions droned on after that, and Blaise wondered how much more the first lady would take. Susie had the guts to ask her if she had smoked dope in college, to which she answered no again, and then, looking at her sympathetically, Susie asked if her husband left her and she was suddenly no longer the first lady, what would she do? The first lady responded that the question was irrelevant and waited for the next one, with the look of someone who has been publicly betrayed.

Susie then outdid herself on the next one, as Blaise held her breath and waited. Susie said she understood that the first lady had a gay brother, and how did she feel about same-sex marriage? And with that, the first lady smiled at her graciously, carefully unclipped her mike off the lapel of her stylish black suit, stood up, and walked off the set, as Susie stared at her in amazement. It had never occurred to her that that could happen, and it never had before. It was a first, and had never happened to Blaise once in her career, with any subject. She always respected them, even when she asked tough questions. But Blaise's were questions in the context of their politics and careers, not about their spouses' extramarital affairs or gay relations, geared to the sensational, with no useful purpose. She never went too far. Unlike Susie, who had burned all her bridges and torched her career in just under twelve minutes. Blaise burst out laughing. She was grinning from ear to ear and could just imagine pandemonium at the network, as Susie burbled incoherently, paddling desperately to cover what had happened, and they cut to commercial. During the break, Blaise tried to explain to Simon that he had just seen television history at its best. Blaise was thrilled at Susie's monumental stupidity, and even more so when the first lady did not return to the set after the break. There had obviously been a rapid conference with Charlie and maybe even Zack, and Susie made a brief statement about how sorry she was to have offended the first lady, and how grateful she was for the interview, while she looked like she was about to cry. They cut to commercial again, and then acted as though the interview had run its expected amount of time, which was not the case. It was supposed to run an hour, and the next thing Blaise saw was a taped interview she had done the previous week with a granddaughter of Bobby Kennedy who was running for a congressional seat in Massachusetts and was said to be a presidential hopeful. She was a terrific young woman, and with enough commercials, they managed to fill the hour. And unexpectedly, with the taped Kennedy piece not yet aired, Blaise had saved the day. Her star in the network heavens was assured, and Charlie called her at the end of the show. He sounded like he was ready to have a stroke, and Blaise managed not to laugh, as Simon smiled. It had been quite an evening, and thanks to Blaise a terrific show, though not the one they'd planned. It had been Charlie's idea to run the young Kennedy piece to fill the time and save their ass, and it had.

"Holy shit, did you watch that?" Charlie asked in a shaken voice. "I damn near had a heart attack."

"I loved it," Blaise admitted honestly, as Charlie groaned.

"You would, you bitch." And then he laughed. "I would too, in your shoes. She submitted a whole different list of questions to programming, and started ad-libbing on the air. You do too, but you never asked a first lady about her husband cheating on her, even when they had, or about her gay brother."

"I'll bet Zack loved it," she said evilly.

"I think he'll drive Susie back to Miami himself, or her lifeless body after he kills her. Thank God we had your Kennedy piece in the can, or I'd have been on the air singing songs from *The King and I* or *Sound of Music.* Shit, Blaise, I'm too old for this job. Tonight nearly killed me. You saved our ass," he said again with fervor.

"I hope Zack gets that," she said seriously, but they both knew that the first lady walking out on Susie's interview would be top of the news the next day, and all over YouTube on the Internet for months to come. Susie Q had committed a cardinal sin that had ended her career: "Thou shalt not cause a first lady to walk off the set."

"Tomorrow should be fun at work, for a change," Blaise said gleefully.

"For you maybe. If I hadn't had that piece of yours to run, my ass would be out the door too. Zack must have called me fifteen times."

"Don't worry. The ratings will be through the roof on this." He knew she was right. The ratings loved television disasters.

"So is my blood pressure," he said mournfully, and a few minutes later they hung up. Mark called her after that, and he was thrilled for her. Susie Q was history. And Blaise was safe.

She and Simon talked about it for hours afterward and Salima came in to comment. She couldn't believe what she'd heard. Nor could the entire country as they watched it replayed again and again. It was breaking news.

Blaise managed to look serious and dignified the next day at work, although she was laughing inside. Susie appeared briefly to pack up her things and disappeared without saying goodbye. The whole station talked of nothing else, and Charlie looked like he had survived electric shock therapy. He met with Zack for an hour, who now understood that live interviews of sensitive major subjects, like presidents or their wives, were not a good idea, and why.

Blaise went quietly about her work throughout the day, doing research in her office, and offering no comment about Susie. Blaise had dodged a bullet yet again.

She was in great spirits that night, telling Simon everything that had happened that day at the network, when the phone rang. She could tell by the way Simon spoke that it was work related, and it sounded important. It took her a few minutes to figure out that it was Eric, the head of the school.

"What did Eric say?" Blaise asked, looking relaxed, after a great day at work. It had been a total victory for her, and her first stress-free day in months. The heat would be on her again sooner or later, but for now she had a major reprieve that would last a while, until the next Susie Quentin came along.

Simon's face was pale when he answered her question. "They're reopening next Monday. I have to go back this weekend." He looked devastated.

"So soon?" She felt like she'd been punched in the stomach and was suddenly panicked. Her joy over Susie Q's demise was short-lived. "You're going back?" She had been hoping he'd stay in New York with her and Salima. It was what Salima wanted too. Blaise knew he had a contract he had to honor, but she hadn't wanted to think about his leaving, and hoped they could figure out something so he could stay, or come back very quickly.

"I have to," he said simply. "My contract doesn't end till May. What about Salima?"

"She wants to stay here. And she was hoping you'd stay with us."

"I can't," he said, looking miserable, and Blaise was thinking it would be a long time till he returned in May. And now Salima wouldn't be at the school, so she had no excuse to go up there to see him. She wished there was some way for Simon to stay, but knew there wasn't.

"I'm going to miss you," she said sadly, as his eyes met hers.

"It's more complicated than that," Simon said slowly.

"How's that?" She could see something more in his eyes, but she didn't know what it was.

"I didn't want to tell you and ruin Christmas." He swallowed before he spoke again. He could hardly get the words out. "Megan left her husband on Christmas Day. She finally did it." Blaise nearly felt her heart stop at his words.

"What does that mean for us?" Blaise held her breath as she waited for his answer.

"I don't know yet," he said honestly. "I want to see her when I go back, and talk about it. I have to finish it cleanly and figure out what I'm doing."

"I thought we knew what we were doing," she said with a devastated expression. She had trusted him and given him her heart, and now he no longer sounded sure.

"I love you, Blaise. But I spent three years waiting for her to do this. She did it for me. I have a responsibility here, to her and her children." He looked agonized as he said it, and Blaise as if he'd hit her.

"And she wants to have your baby, of course," Blaise said with sudden irony in her voice. It was a tone he'd never heard her use, of defeat and bitterness. She could already see what was going to happen. He would go back to Meg, marry her, and have kids. She knew it was what she should have expected him to do at his age. But neither of them had believed that Meg would finally get free, after three years of empty promises. Her husband had finally crossed the line once too often, and her fear of losing Simon forever had given her the courage she'd never had before. "Do you love her?" Blaise asked him in a pained tone. She had expected better than this from him, or hoped for it at least. He had been so sure that he wanted a life with Blaise, no matter how unusual, and he had convinced her. But there was no fighting the fact that he still had feelings for Megan. He had waited three years for her, and she had been everything he wanted then. Now, torn between two women, he was confused.

"I just need to figure this out," he said with a look of desperation. "I don't want to lose you. I love you." She could see that he meant it, but as he had said, it was complicated. She could see now that he didn't want to lose Meg either. He wasn't ready. He had waited so long for this, and she had finally left her husband.

"And what am I supposed to do here in the meantime?" He was going back to school, and now possibly to Megan. Blaise felt as though her life had just fallen apart. Her situation at the network was secure. And now her love life was disintegrating. Again. It had come apart in an instant.

"Give me the time I need to figure out what I'm going to do with my life, and end it cleanly with Meg, if it's right for me to be with you. I need some time to sort this out."

"I thought we already knew that it's right for us," she said unhappily. But now nothing was clear, and Simon looked confused. He had known about Megan leaving her husband since Christmas. And his confusion was the difference between being thirty-two and being forty-seven. Blaise knew what she wanted now, but he was torn. "What do I do with Salima, if you have to leave this weekend?" She had to deal with the practical aspects too now. She had no one to help her, and she was going to Lebanon for two days the following week. But the real problem was not Salima, it was them.

"Eric thought I'd be bringing her with me. I'll talk to him about it tomorrow." It was the least of their problems. Blaise couldn't believe what had just happened. Not only was he leaving almost immediately, but Megan was suddenly front and center again. She was angry he hadn't told her sooner.

She sat looking at him for a long moment and said nothing. There were tears bulging in her eyes, but she didn't want him to see her crying. She refused to be pathetic. She was too proud to beg him to choose her, and she knew she couldn't. He had to make the decision on his own and follow his heart, wherever it led him.

"Let me see if I understand this clearly," she said, sounding like the woman he saw on television, not the woman he had come to love. "You want time to talk to Meg and figure out if you still love her, and who you want to spend your life with. Does that pretty much sum it up? And during that time, you'd like me to wait here, hoping that you pick me, with no idea of what you're going to do."

"I don't know what else to do," he said, looking acutely unhappy. He hated hurting her, but he didn't want to make a mistake. He had to be sure he was making the right decision. "I never thought she'd leave him. I honestly thought it was over, Blaise. I swear. She rocked my world when she told me she left him. And she did it for me."

"What if she's lying to you again, or to him? Or what if she goes back to him after you lose me?" She was trying to be calm, but all she wanted to do was lie on the floor and scream. How could she have done this to herself again? She realized now that they had gotten involved prematurely. He wasn't ready. And maybe he never would be. Or he'd wind up marrying Megan. She felt like a total loser.

"I don't want to lose you," he said clearly again. "I'm in love with you, Blaise." But he had three years of history with Megan, a sense of responsibility to her, and the possibility of having a baby, none of which he had with Blaise. And their relationship was brand new.

"I think that's the same thing Andrew said when I left him, that he loved me and didn't want to lose me," Blaise said coldly, and Simon could see clearly just how hurt she was, and he hated being the one to do it this time. "You can't have it both ways, at least not for long. Go figure out what you want," she said, and stood up, but she didn't approach him. "And I've got some serious thinking to do in the meantime. Maybe fifteen years really does make a difference. You have a right to be with the woman you want, Simon. I was just hoping that woman was me. Apparently, that's not the case."

"I don't know that. I don't know anything right now. I'm confused. She threw me a curve here. She left him after I told her it was over."

"She sounds like a prime manipulator to me." That was one thing Blaise wasn't, and he knew that. He didn't blame her for being upset or even angry with him. But he couldn't tell her something he didn't know for sure. He knew he needed to see Meg again and clear the air before he could go any further with Blaise. It wasn't finished with Megan.

"You talked to Andrew for four years after it was over," he reminded her gently. "You still do. You said it was unfinished business. So is this for me. I need to see her, and either cut the cord completely or make it work. I don't want to wonder about this in five or ten years. I need to know that this is where I want to be, with you. You lead a big life, Blaise. You're a big person. You have a gigantic career. And if we're together, we're going to be in the press. You have Salima. I have to figure out if I'm big enough to take this on, and that I can bring enough to the table. And part of that is knowing if Meg is past history for me, or if there's something left. I can't come to you cleanly until I know where I stand with her."

"That all makes sense," Blaise said quietly, feeling as though her heart had turned to stone inside her. "I just don't want to live through that. I've been there. It's not a good situation for me." And she thought it unlikely that he'd choose a woman fifteen years older instead of one his own age. She was fighting a losing battle, and she knew it. And she'd rather bow out gracefully than wait for him to reject her later. She didn't feel like she could win against Megan. She was sixteen years younger, and willing to have kids. And he had loved her for three years.

"I'm sorry to do this to you. You don't deserve it," he said miserably.

"No, I don't," she agreed with him. "And neither do you. You deserve to be with a woman who really loves you. Just make sure she does, before you take on a woman who lied to everyone for three years and has three kids by someone else. That doesn't sound like a good situation to me."

"I've never been happier in my life than I've been with you for the past three months. I wanted it to go on forever." He looked heartbroken as he said it, and so did she.

"So did I. I was beginning to think it would. I

thought we had it all figured out, but I guess we didn't." She had already resigned herself to the idea that he was going back to Meg. She was sure he would, and stay there. He had been loyal to Meg for three years before he left, to the point of obsession. How could she compete with that? And their relationship was healthy and sane, despite the age difference, not obsessed. And then she thought of something. "If you're really leaving, and planning to work it out with Meg, don't wait until the weekend. Have Eric send someone immediately. I don't want to drag this out any longer than we have to. If you're going to break my heart, and that appears to be the plan, make it quick. Don't linger. It'll just make it worse for both of us," and particularly for her. He had someone else waiting for him, she didn't. And knowing that Megan was back in his life was agony for her.

"Blaise, I told you I need time. I'm not telling you I'm going back to her for sure. I need to see her and be sure of what I want. If I didn't do that, it wouldn't be fair to you, or to me."

"I understand. I'm just not as optimistic as you are. And to be honest, this is humiliating. I don't want to stand around, while you figure it out, sample the merchandise, and decide who you love better. I have to compete every day at work and fight for my life. I don't want to do that with you too. If you're unclear enough to want to check it out with her again, I doubt very much that you'll be coming back to me. And you probably shouldn't. She can offer you a much more normal situation, with a house full of kids, hers and your own. That's pretty hard to resist, particularly at your age. All I can offer you is my very grown-up life and Salima."

"I love you both, you and Salima." He looked honest as he said it.

"I'm grateful for everything you did for us for the past three months. It was amazing, particularly for Salima, and for me too," she said sadly. She had never been as happy in her life. And now she had to pay the piper. She had been a fool to think their ages didn't make a difference, and she knew it. They did. She was trying to be reasonable, but she was hurt and angry, and sounded bitter.

"I'll call Eric in the morning," he said quietly, and stood up to go back to his room. He wanted to spend the night with her, now more than ever, but he sensed that she wouldn't let him. She didn't say another word to him and walked back to her suite. And when she got there, she lay on the bed and sobbed. Her worst fears had just come true.

Chapter 13

The two days after Eric's call telling Simon the school was reopening were a blur for both Simon and Blaise. He continued keeping Salima busy, they were on a museum binge, and had been to three in the past week, while Simon explained both the visual and historical aspects of the shows to her. Salima loved it. And he had taken her to the LightHouse for the Blind too, and two concerts in the evening. But his mind was somewhere else. Several times Salima had to press him to get an answer to a question. His mind kept drifting as he thought of the situation he was in.

"Is something wrong?" she asked him finally as they left the Whitney. He hadn't told her yet that he was leaving for Caldwell that Sunday, or sooner if Eric sent his replacement. Blaise wanted to break the news to Salima herself. She knew how much Salima would miss him. Her life, under Simon's care, had been totally transformed. She had grown up in a mere three months. He had worked magic. And with Blaise as well. He made everything better, for each of them, and had brought both women out of their shell. When Blaise had talked to Simon about it, she told him he wasn't an enabler but an enhancer. It was an apt description of him.

"Are you sick?" Salima put a hand on his forehead to check for fever, and he grinned. He had just hailed a taxi for them, but usually they took the bus or subway. They were going to Zabar's to pick up food he needed for dinner. If nothing else, he thought he could feed them decently until he left. Blaise was no longer willing to let him do much more than that, except take care of Salima. Blaise had skipped dinner and gone straight to her room the night before, claiming she had a headache. But Simon knew better. Her heart was aching, not her head, and he felt guilty for it. He had been honest with her about how confused he was, after Megan finally came through after all this time, claiming she had done it for him. She made a major point of telling him she had left her husband for him, and he couldn't abandon her now. He had to at least give her a chance. He felt he had no other choice. He wanted to be fair to both women, and himself, but inevitably, one of them was going to get hurt, or maybe they all would.

"I'm fine. I was just thinking about Caldwell," he said, which was partially true, but he'd really been thinking about Megan. "I'm going to have to go back soon," he tried to warn her, without letting the cat out of the bag, that he'd be leaving on Sunday. He thought Blaise was wrong not to tell her sooner. She wanted to find his replacement first, and then she would drop the bomb.

"I want you to stay here with us. Who cares about your contract?" Salima said, pouting.

"The board of trustees," he said with a rueful grin as they got out at Zabar's, the West Side delicatessen and delicacy shop he had discovered when he first got to New York. He went there often to buy the things they liked, and Salima liked going with him. She loved the hearty food smells of the shop. "Even if I decide not to renew my contract, I have to finish out the school year." He already had applications to the two best schools for the blind in New York sitting on his desk, and planned to complete both before he left. He'd already sent one back to the Perkins School in Massachusetts. "You've got to finish what you start in life," he said cryptically to Salima, as he selected two of Blaise's favorite cheeses and asked for a thick slab of foie gras. But he didn't think that foie gras was going to soothe Blaise's aching heart, or his own. He hated to leave her, but he knew that if he turned his back on Megan now, he would always wonder what might have happened. He had waited for her to leave her husband for so long. Blaise was a much more exciting woman and a better person, but Megan was the kind of girl he'd always thought he'd wanted. And now she said she wanted a baby with him. Just one, since she already had three, but she was suggesting they get married as soon as her divorce came through, and get pregnant as soon as possible. He knew that the life he'd have with her would be completely different from the one he'd shared with Blaise. He loved his life with Blaise, but was still unsure what he could contribute to it, and felt inadequate and overwhelmed at times.

He had never expected someone like Blaise to come along. She was a star and such a huge success. What could he give her? That had haunted him since the beginning. She claimed that all she wanted from him was love, but he wanted to give her more, and he couldn't. Materially, he had nothing to offer, no matter how fancy his mother's family was. Some of that would be his one day, but for now he had nothing. He was an underpaid teacher, and their relationship was still so new. It was hard to commit his future to a woman he had known and loved for three months. With Megan, it had been three years, albeit disappointing ones. But now that she'd left her husband, it would be different. Or at least he hoped so, and they wouldn't have to meet in cheap motels. But when he thought of Blaise and how much he loved her, he was totally confused. Each woman offered him a different life and world. His head was spinning.

"I think you're sick," Salima said as they wandered aimlessly through Zabar's among the pungent smells, and Simon kept forgetting what he needed. He wanted truffle oil for Blaise's favorite pizza, if she'd eat it. His cooking for her was an expression of his love too. And it seemed like the least he could do.

When they got back to the apartment, Blaise was home from work, in her office, working on her computer. She had come home early. For once all was peaceful at the network, now that Susie had left, but her personal life was a disaster. She glanced up as Simon walked into the room and set a cup of French vanilla tea down on her desk. She smiled as she thanked him, but the atmosphere between them now was cool, and the look in Blaise's eyes said "don't come near me." A door had already closed, and Blaise was trying hard to lock it and throw away the key. He hadn't touched her since Eric's call two days before, and didn't dare approach her. Once wounded and chilly, Blaise was suddenly intimidating.

"Thank you," she said formally, as he looked at her with sad eyes.

"I'm sorry, Blaise." It was all he could think of to say, and he meant it.

"Me too. Don't worry about it. You'll feel better when you're back in Massachusetts." She didn't add "with Megan," but the words were written on her face.

"That's not a sure thing," he reminded her. She looked as though for her it was over, but for him it wasn't. "I just need to answer some questions, and figure out what I want to do with the rest of my life." The way he said it reminded her again of how young he was. At her age, she had been on a path for years, but he was still looking for the right one. It was a vast difference between them, and also was a reminder to her that sometimes love was not enough.

Simon knew he needed more, he needed a job that inspired him, a career he felt passionate about, and a woman to share it with him. He didn't want to be Blaise's boy toy or look like one. His own life had to have substance and meaning, before he could join her. With Megan, he would always be the pathfinder and leader. He knew she didn't enjoy her work and wanted to stay home with the kids. With Blaise, she would always be the more successful one. In some ways, it didn't bother him, but if he came back to her, he wanted to do so on solid ground, standing on his own two feet, if she even let him come back, which looking at her now, he strongly doubted. She had put as much distance between them as she could, living in the same apartment, since he had told her about Megan.

"Is something wrong between you and Mom?" Salima asked him that night at dinner. Blaise had skipped dinner again and claimed she had another headache. "Did you have a fight or something?" Simon hesitated and put another slice of pizza on her plate. It was the one he had made for Blaise, with the truffle oil. He had tried to bring it to her in her bedroom, but her door was locked, and she didn't answer when he knocked. He texted her, and she didn't respond. The message was clear. She was suffering in private, while trying to appear "fine" to him. She was anything but.

"I'm worried about her," Simon said to Salima, not wanting to share with her what was going on. He didn't know what Blaise was going to tell her, how little or how much. But Salima correctly sensed there was something major going on. She hoped it would blow over soon. Simon wasn't being much fun, nor was her mother, who was isolated in her room, pretending to be busy.

Eric called Simon that night to tell him he had found a relief teacher they'd used several years before. She had just gotten divorced, had no kids, and was willing to step into Simon's shoes in New York, temporarily at least. She thought it sounded like fun, and was excited to do it. She was three years younger than Simon, but Eric thought she could handle the job, and Simon knew her and could brief her on what she had to do for Salima.

"How soon can she start?" Blaise asked Eric when he called her after speaking to Simon.

"As soon as you like. Tomorrow if you want. She's all set to go, if you want her. I think she should spend a day with Simon so he can brief her, but she's familiar with all our procedures, and she's a bright girl. She'll catch on fast."

"Fine. Then have her come down tomorrow," Blaise said in a strained voice. "Simon can come back to you the day after. I'm sure you're anxious to have him at school." He had told her that the students were returning Sunday. A few had dropped out or made other arrangements, like Salima, but most were coming back to Caldwell. He was very sorry that Salima was not returning after so many years, but he understood. And it was good for her to be at home.

"I'm glad it worked out so well with Simon. I was sure it would, once everyone adjusted. I think Rebecca will work out well for you too." They discussed the financial arrangements. She was going to work directly for Blaise, since Salima was not returning to Caldwell. She was giving up the cottage on the grounds too. Eric had found Rebecca for Blaise as a favor, so as not to leave her in the lurch when Simon left. He knew how busy Blaise was, and that she needed someone with Salima at all times, particularly when she traveled. She had told him she was going to Lebanon the following week and Morocco in a month. But there was no way she could go to Lebanon now and leave Salima with a new person.

Eric agreed to have Becky at the apartment at noon the next day. She would come to the city by bus in the morning and take a cab to the apartment. As soon as Blaise hung up, Simon called her. It was the only way to reach her. She was holed up in her room with the door locked. She had been crying before Eric called her, and didn't want Simon to see her. The situation was miserable enough without his feeling sorry for her on top of it. She didn't want to look pathetic to him, and hadn't felt this vulnerable in years. Not since Andrew. And the irony was that she had finally trusted someone and opened up, and now he was leaving too, for another woman. It wasn't quite as simple as that, but it felt that way to her.

"You talked to Eric?" Simon asked her when she answered her cell phone. He hadn't even been sure she would do that, since she hadn't answered his texts. "I know Becky, and she's pretty good. I think she and Salima should get along. Don't let Becky baby her, though. I'd hate to see Salima lose all the ground she's gained." But he doubted that would happen now. Salima had become her own person in a mere three months.

"You could stay and do the job yourself," Blaise said sadly. In her heart of hearts, she was hoping he would change his mind and stay, she wished he could, but she knew it was out of the question. He had a contract to fulfill, and he was a responsible person. And he had a woman he felt he had to go back to, in fairness to all three of them. That was the part Blaise hated. She could sense that she'd already lost him, and knew how it would turn out. She honestly believed Megan was the woman he should be with, and that she wasn't. His relationship with Blaise had been a long shot, given their age difference, and she had lost. She had taken her chips off the table, and gone home. Now all she wanted was for him to leave as soon as possible, and end the torture of their situation as quickly as they could. She didn't want him to linger. It was too painful knowing he was right there, and no longer hers. He was already Megan's, and now she realized he always had been. She had won him back by leaving her husband.

"I wish I could stay," Simon said, and meant it. But

he had to go back and face reality on all fronts, at work, and with Megan. "I'm sorry, Blaise," he said, wanting to hold her in his arms again and sleep with her before he left, and make love together. But he was too respectful to do so. He knew how much he was hurting her, and he loved her too much to make it worse. He wished he could have them both. It was an age-old dilemma, and she'd been there before.

"I'm sorry too," she said, as tears filled her eyes, and he could hear it in her voice. "That's life, I guess. Things don't always work out. It'll be better for you this way." She had already given him up in her mind. And he knew she was thinking about children for him again. "And your mom will be happy. She won't have to worry about how old I am."

"That never mattered to me, your age, or my mom." She knew that was true. But Megan still had a hold on him that he hadn't freed himself of yet, and maybe never would. He had no idea now which woman was right for him, Meg or Blaise. And Blaise had taken herself out of the running, out of pride and self-preservation, if nothing else.

"When are you leaving?" she asked in a choked voice.

"Tomorrow." He had just finished packing when he called her. "Tomorrow night, if Becky seems okay to you."

"I don't have any other choice. Eric says he doesn't know anyone else."

"She'll be okay." But he wasn't as sure that Blaise

would be, which worried him. She was taking his leaving very hard. "I'll stay in touch with Salima," he promised. "We can text each other on her voice-texting phone, or she can call me. And you can call me whenever you want." He hoped she would, but he had the feeling she wouldn't, and he was right. She knew she had to let him go now to lead his life and find his path, with the woman he wanted. She wished it had been her. She was certain he would stay with Megan. He had invested too much time in her not to.

After they hung up, it was strange knowing that she was in the apartment with him, and not together. Her bed was so empty now. He might as well have been back at Caldwell. He had already left her life, and she was setting him free, because she loved him. All that remained now were the last agonizing details. She lay awake for hours that night, thinking about him. And in his room, Simon was thinking about her too. He had never felt worse in his life. He missed her acutely, even before he left, and he cried himself to sleep that night, as Blaise lay silent and awake in the moonlight in her room. They were worlds apart.

Blaise ran into Simon in the kitchen the next morning when she went to get a cup of coffee. He handed it to her out of habit. She suddenly felt a thousand years old, and assumed she probably looked it, and no longer cared. Simon hated to see her so miserable but didn't tell her how beautiful she looked or how much he loved her. And Salima came in seeming depressed while they were talking. Her mother had told her the night before that Simon was going back to Caldwell, and a new girl was replacing him, and Salima had cried when she told her. But she was relieved that her mother was letting her stay home instead of going to Caldwell. But she was heartbroken to be losing Simon from her daily life. Salima went to see him in his room after her mother told her.

"What about you and my mom?" she asked him bluntly.

"That's kind of on hold for now," he said vaguely, in an apologetic tone.

"You mean it's over?" Salima looked sorely disappointed and even more so that he was leaving and on such short notice.

"I don't know. It's complicated. I have to work some things out, and your mom probably won't want to wait while I do. It'll take some time."

"I think she loves you, Simon," Salima said softly. She could hear how sad he was, and her mother's cheeks had been wet when Salima hugged her after she explained that Simon was going.

"I love her too. And I loved my three months with you. I'll send you text messages every day." She could write hers by phone, and receive his by voice.

"Will you come to visit?" May seemed an eternity away to her, when he finished the school year.

"If it's okay with your mother," he said respectfully. "We're going to miss you at Caldwell. It won't be the same without you." But Salima was happy to be staying in New York. She had a wonderful new life there, thanks to Simon. And she didn't want to go back to the cottage there when Abby died. But she was worried about his replacement.

"What if Becky is a drip and we don't get along? I had so much fun with you."

"So did I." He smiled. "Your mom can find someone else if she has to, from one of the schools here. But I think Becky will be fine. Give her a chance. You weren't all that happy about me in the beginning either." They both smiled at the memory of Salima's early defiance.

Becky arrived while all three of them were in the kitchen, carrying one small suitcase, and she looked daunted by the group. She said hello to Simon, he introduced her to Salima and they shook hands, and then he introduced her to Blaise, who looked somber as she looked her over. She was too upset to give her a warm welcome, and Salima was no better. Becky looked worried when Simon showed her to her room next to his.

"Did someone die, or is that because you're leaving? They look really sad," Becky commented as she set down her suitcase, and looked around the tiny room, and then back at Simon. "I guess they don't want you to go."

"I'm sad too. They're really nice people. Just give them some time. They'll warm up. This is a big change for them. It was an adjustment for them to have Salima at home, and when Abby died. Now they're used to me, so you just have to keep her busy, and establish a relationship with her yourself."

"I'll try," Becky said shyly. Her personality was more like Abby's than his.

"Don't baby her," he warned her. "She likes to get out. And she still won't use a cane, or a dog. You can work on that with her." Becky nodded. She had long blond hair she wore in a braid down her back, and big, frightened eyes.

"What's Miss McCarthy like? Is she scary?" Becky had thought so when she walked in, but Simon knew she was just sad.

"Not if you do your job well. That's all she wants. And she travels a lot, so you have to be fully responsible while she's away, and all the time." He took her out to the kitchen then and showed her where things were. He walked her around the apartment, pointing out the piano where Salima had her lessons, indicated Blaise's suite, and then walked down the hall to Salima's room. Becky already seemed lost. It was all more than a little frightening to her. She was a simple girl who had grown up on a farm in New Hampshire, and got into working with blind children when her mother went blind. Most of the staff had some kind of personal tie to their work.

Salima was listening to music in her room and looked up when they walked in. She had recognized Simon's step, and she had heard Becky's, so she knew he wasn't alone. Salima looked sad, and her mother's door had been closed when they walked by it. Simon's heart felt like a rock in his chest.

They went back to the kitchen, and he told Becky all the things Salima liked to do, and about her insulin pump, her aspirations for Juilliard, and how talented she was. He sounded proud of her when he said it. And for a minute, Becky felt like he was a member of the family, not an employee. He was fiercely protective of both Salima and Blaise and raved about them both.

Blaise asked him to come to her office at the end of the afternoon. She had been there all day, and she was tired and pale when he walked in. But he didn't look much better. They both looked strained, and he knew leaving was going to be hard. He was trying not to think of that as he looked at Blaise, and she invited him to sit down. He did, with a sigh.

"What do you think of Becky?" she asked him directly. He had been with her all afternoon, describing the job.

"I think she's competent and smart. I know she's reliable from working with her before, although it's been a while. I think she's scared, and it'll take her time to feel comfortable. But once she does, I think she'll do a good job. She's not an exciting person, or as fun as Abby, but she's nice, she knows what she's doing, and you can rely on her."

"She looks terrified," Blaise commented, looking worn out.

"You're a pretty impressive figure," he said gently, and Blaise smiled.

"Is that what you thought when you came here?"

"For a short time. I knew you wanted a woman in the job, but you made me feel at home very quickly. And I really wanted to make it work. Becky's more hesitant as a person. But I think she and Salima will warm up to each other with time. And Salima doesn't need as much help as she used to."

"Thanks to you." Blaise looked at him for a long time, and he nodded. And he had won them over in the beginning.

"I don't know what to say. . . . You know how I feel," he said, choking on the words, and she nodded as her eyes filled with tears.

"Yeah . . . me too . . ." she said softly. There was nothing left to say, about Megan, and all the rest.

Blaise went to ask Salima then how she felt about Becky, and Salima said she was okay. She wasn't excited about her, and she wasn't Abby or Simon. She shrugged. She had no specific objections to her, she just wasn't enthused and neither was Blaise, and Becky could sense it, but she had a feeling there was something else going on, and she didn't know what it was. Simon looked as distressed as they did, and Becky felt like she was intruding on all of them at a bad time.

Blaise ordered pizza for dinner, and Simon had a slice before he left. He couldn't even finish it, he was too upset, and then he looked at Blaise, who sat at the table eating nothing, while Salima toyed with her salad, and Becky was embarrassed as she took a second slice. No one was eating but her, and she was starving. She hadn't eaten all day.

"I'd better get going," Simon said, looking at Blaise, and she nodded. He had rented a car for the return trip to Massachusetts.

He wished Becky luck and told her to call him if she had any questions, and then he hugged Salima hard. She burst into tears, and he told her to call or text him whenever she wanted. Blaise had walked into the front hall by then and was waiting for him near the door where he had left his bags. The others stayed in the kitchen, and Simon looked down at her and wanted to forget everything and stay, but he didn't say it and knew he couldn't.

He took Blaise in his arms, and she didn't resist. She was soaking up the last feel of him, as she smelled the familiar aftershave on his neck and felt his powerful arms around her for the last time. "Take care of yourself, Blaise. . . . Call me if you need me. . . ."

She nodded and pulled away a little to look at him with a sad smile. "Be a good boy, figure your life out . . . you deserve wonderful things in your life, and a great woman." She felt as though she were giving up her child and the man she loved.

"I love you," he said in a choked voice, with tears in his eyes.

"I love you too," she said in the saddest voice he'd ever heard. Because she loved him, she was letting him go. Somewhere in her heart she thought it was right for him to go back to Megan, and what he wanted, so she wasn't trying to hold on to him, or stop him, or convince him otherwise. Besides, she was too proud. It seemed cleaner to just release him, with no strings.

He picked up his bags then, opened the front door, and rang for the elevator, and a minute later he was standing in it and looking at her. She gave him a small wave as he stared at her, and the door closed. She almost fainted as she walked back into the apartment. She wanted to scream. She had never been in so much pain in her life. It was a powerful reminder to her not to fall in love again.

Chapter 14

The days dragged by after Simon left, and Blaise filled them as she always did, with work. With Susie Quentin back in Miami, there was no one else lusting after her job for the moment, and she was working on upcoming specials, doing her morning segment, and planning interviews abroad. She put off the trip to Lebanon. She wanted to stay home for a few weeks to make sure that Becky was working out with Salima. Neither Blaise nor Salima had any real objection to her, although Salima said she was boring. She had the personality of a mouse, and she started off on the wrong foot.

She took Salima's clothes out for her in the morning and put the toothpaste on her brush for her, trying to be helpful, and Salima snapped at her that she wasn't a child, she was almost twenty years old. Abby had done it for her, and Salima had liked it, but Simon had led her into a whole other world and treated her like an adult. Salima texted him several times a day, and he always responded. Salima always went discreetly into another room to listen to his texts, so she could hear them in private and not upset her mother. But Blaise didn't hear a word from him after he left, and was sure she wouldn't. She didn't call or write to him either, and hearing the sorrow in her mother's voice, Salima didn't mention him anymore, or tell her about the texts.

"I'm sorry, Mom, about Simon," she said one Sunday night, when Blaise was trying to cook them dinner. She was roasting a chicken, and attempting one of his recipes for risotto. She burned the chicken beyond recognition, and the rice turned into cement.

"I'm fine," she said about Simon, trying to believe it. She had to be. He wasn't coming back, and she had to take care of Salima and work. She couldn't afford the luxury of falling apart over a man, no matter how much she had loved him. She had learned that lesson with Andrew. And as though he had radar, Andrew had called the day after Simon left. Blaise didn't take the call and didn't even care. And for the first time, she knew she would never answer his calls again. She had no desire to talk to Andrew. She was finally healed. Loving Simon had freed her, no matter how it worked out in the end.

"I guess I need a class at Cordon Bleu," Blaise said when they ordered sushi after she threw away the charred chicken and inedible rice. The smell was awful.

Becky had offered to cook for Salima, but her cooking was even worse than Blaise's. Blaise felt like they had lost so much when Simon left. The laughter in their house. The excitement for Salima over their outings. Delicious dinners. Someone for her to talk to at night, who cared about her. Now Blaise was left with silent evenings, too much work, and no one to ask her how she was. The only thing that made the atmosphere a little better was Salima singing with Lucianna or practicing every night.

By Valentine's Day, he had been gone for three weeks, and it felt like a year to Blaise. Salima was starting to adjust to Becky, who was trying hard. They had made Valentine cupcakes that afternoon, for Salima to give to her mother to cheer her up. She knew how sad she was even though she didn't talk about it or mention Simon's name. And when Becky said something about him in passing, Blaise always fell silent and changed the subject, or left the room. She had bought a special Valentine cake for Salima, made with artificial sweeteners. It was a big chocolate heart with pink icing, which was a rare treat for her. But with careful planning, Salima could indulge from time to time. And Salima had bought her tulips too.

Lucianna joined them in eating the cake after their lesson, and she asked Salima with some concern if her mother wasn't feeling well. Blaise was so depressed she looked sick. In her office, Mark was worried about it too and tried urging her to see her doctor, which she refused to do.

"I don't need a doctor," she told him. "I'm just feeling down. No one ever died from that."

"You look too sad," he told her. "You're starting to turn green. You either need a vacation, or a visit to the doctor to make sure you're okay, or a new boyfriend."

"I'll settle for my trip to Morocco to interview King Mohammed VI in two weeks." It would be the first trip she'd taken since Simon left. She felt confident she could trust Becky with Salima now. Becky was both knowledgeable and diligent about Salima's pump. She was going to interview the king and do a special on his fabulous fleet of fancy cars. He had priceless Aston Martins that he flew to England for maintenance and repair. And a lovely wife whom Blaise was going to interview as well.

But a week before the trip, she was in bed with the flu and felt like death. She missed two days of work, which wasn't like her, and when she went back to the office, Mark put his foot down.

"Let's talk straight here. I don't care how fine you say you are. You look like someone exhumed you. You never miss work, and you just did. I don't think you've eaten in three weeks, and to be honest, Blaise, you look like shit. If you get any thinner, you'll disappear. And I can tell you don't feel good. And you think you're going to make it to Morocco and back? I like my job, and if you drop dead in Rabat, I'll be out of work." She smiled at what he said, and she wouldn't admit it to him, but she felt as bad as she looked. Her stomach had been somewhere around her knees since Simon left, and she never ate dinner anymore. She was so exhausted that she came home and went to bed. "I'm so sorry Simon left and things didn't work out." He hated her being alone again, and he could see how bad she felt.

"I'm just depressed," she said again, dismissing what he said.

"Then take antidepressants. You won't be able to do a good interview feeling like that, and it's a long trip." They had plans to go out to the desert so he could show off his cars and the kind of speeds they could reach. Just thinking about the heat made her feel sick.

Blaise knew she had to go on with her life. She was stunned to realize how much she loved Simon, and how empty her life was without him. It felt like a wasteland, and she tried to put up a good front for Salima, but she couldn't even do that anymore. She was exhausted, and all she did was sleep when she went home, which she knew was a sign of depression too. She had all the symptoms, and it didn't take a doctor to figure out why. She was sad about Simon, but she insisted to Mark in the office and herself she'd get over it. She had no other choice. He belonged to someone else. And she was an adult. She had to live through it. But she was concerned about the trip to Morocco too. She didn't know how she was going to do it, the flu was hanging on, and she thought maybe vitamins would help. She didn't think she needed anti-depressants, just time. She'd been through it with Andrew. But somehow this felt worse. Because this time she had lost a good man, a great one, not a bad one who had lied to her.

She dragged herself to the doctor on Tuesday afternoon. She was leaving for Morocco that weekend.

Her doctor pointed out that he hadn't seen her for a year, which he thought was a good sign. "How've you been?" He was a pleasant man in his fifties, whom she only called on rare occasions, or for insurance exams for the network when she renewed her contract every few years.

"Fine." She was not going to confess to him that she was suffering from a broken romance, only that she was working too hard and was tired.

"Anything I should know about?"

"I'm exhausted," she said honestly, "and I've had the flu off and on for the last month. I'm leaving for Morocco this weekend, and I thought I should check in before I left." He had a feeling that she wouldn't have done so unless she felt really bad. He told her there were a lot of bad flus around, and she might have picked up some bug on a trip, or a plane. She told him she had been in the Middle East several times recently, but was always careful what she ate and drank bottled water. But she admitted that her stomach was a mess.

"Have you lost weight?"

"Probably a few pounds." It was more like ten, but she didn't tell him. She knew why. She wasn't eating. She had had no appetite since Simon left.

The doctor checked her blood pressure and told her it was low, but not dangerously so. "That could be from the flu," he reassured her. "You don't need medication for it. I'm going to check you for anemia too. That could account for how you're feeling. Anything else I should know?"

"Nothing I can think of." Just Simon, she thought but didn't say. She felt stupid knowing that by now he was with Megan, probably happy, and she was pining for him and wasting away. She told herself she had to get a grip.

"Are you sexually active?" He went down a list of standard questions.

"Not at the moment. I was."

"How recently?" His pen was poised over the paper to write her answer as she thought about it.

"A month ago. I just ended a relationship a few weeks ago." But she didn't tell him how heartbroken she was. It was none of his business.

"Could you be pregnant?"

"Hardly, at my age. I think I'm a little too old to get pregnant, without technical help," she said, and he nodded. It was true. But accidents did happen, even at her age. She wasn't that old. Forty-seven wasn't entirely out of the realm of the possible, even if unlikely, as she said, "We used protection." They hadn't the first time, but it had been their only slip, and after that they'd been careful. Simon had thought they should be, for her sake, although she wasn't worried about it with him.

"Condoms?" She nodded. "You're not on the Pill?" She shook her head, although she knew there were accidents with that too. But she'd never had a mistake of that kind in her life, except for Salima. She had always been careful and was responsible about it, and Simon had been too, even though she thought it unlikely she'd get pregnant. They hadn't taken the chance.

"I don't think that's it," she said firmly.

"Probably not. But it doesn't hurt to check. I'll run some hormone levels on you. Your estrogen may be low. This could be the beginning of menopause." That sounded even more depressing, and she said her periods were still regular, except less so since the shock of his leaving, and her depression, and she'd been sick.

"I think I'm anemic, or just run-down."

"You look fine," he said after he examined her. "And I'll have the results of the bloodwork tomorrow. Give me a call." She left his office a few minutes later and went home. But she felt no better that night and went straight to bed. Salima came in to see her after dinner.

"I'm sorry I'm such a bore at the moment. I can't seem to shake this flu. How was dinner?" Blaise asked her in a lifeless tone.

"Okay. Nothing fabulous. I'm trying to teach her to make pasta like Simon, and soufflé. She's not much of a cook." Salima had learned a lot from him and was trying to direct Becky. She had all his recipes written down in Braille and a Braille cookbook he had given her.

"Soufflé may be asking a lot." Blaise grinned. Simon had real talent in the kitchen, not just recipes. They talked for a little while, and then Salima went back to her room to chat with her friends on Facebook, and

Blaise went to sleep. She woke up on schedule at four A.M. the next day and felt like death again. She was beginning to get worried and wondered what the doctor would say. Maybe he was right and she had picked up some nasty virus on a plane, or in a foreign country. She felt like she was dying, or at the very least seriously ill. She began thinking about leukemia or lupus.

But in spite of how she felt, she did an excellent segment about the Middle East that morning. And the makeup artist thought she looked pretty, although she felt disconnected and dull, and the only time she seemed like herself now was on the air. She felt like an old well-trained horse who only came alive when she worked.

And she was so busy that afternoon that she forgot to call the doctor. It completely slipped her mind. And at five o'clock, after he saw his last patient, he called her.

"Well, I think we're getting there. You're definitely anemic. I'm going to prescribe some iron for you, Blaise. And I think you may have picked up a virus on a trip. There's not much we can do about it, a virus won't respond to antibiotics, so you'll just have to wait it out. You'll probably feel better in another week. Most viruses don't last much longer than that, and you said you've been feeling rotten for about a month." It had been that long. She had felt fluish the week he left, and totally awful for the three weeks since. She was relieved by what the doctor said, at least it wasn't something really awful. She had to be able to do her job. Salima depended on her.

"Thank you, doctor," she said, sounding more relaxed. She'd been slightly worried about the tests. At least he had a reason why she felt sick. Anemia and a virus.

"And there's one other thing," he continued as her heart skipped a beat. What if it was something terrible after all and he had saved it for last?

"Serious?"

"That depends on how you feel about it. You're pregnant." He said it, and Blaise stared at her office wall, trying to comprehend what he had said.

"I am?" She couldn't believe it.

"Yes, your HCG levels are quite high, which is a good sign if you want to keep it. From the dates you gave me for your last normal period, you're ten weeks the way we figure it, eight from the date of conception, which must have been in early January. You're two months pregnant. And if that's not what you want, then you'll have to do something about it in the next month." He said it matter-of-factly. Blaise felt like the air had been sucked out of her lungs. What in hell was she going to do? "You should call your gynecologist for a visit soon. She'll want to get an early sonogram, but apparently you haven't had any problems." And as he said it, Blaise realized that she had missed a period in January, right at the time Simon left, and she thought it was because she was upset and not eating. And she had just missed one again. She had paid no attention. "You should be able to hear a heartbeat by now when you see your doctor." Oh my God. She almost threw up. No wonder her stomach had been so upset. She was panicked as she thanked the doctor, hung up, picked up her bag and coat, and started to leave the office, as Mark looked up from his desk.

"What did the doctor say?" He hadn't had time to ask her since the day before, and he looked concerned.

"I'm anemic, and I picked up some kind of virus on one of my trips." There was no way she was going to tell him that she was two months pregnant. She was not going to have another baby, especially now, with Simon back with Megan. It was unthinkable. His silence confirmed that he'd gone back to her and stayed. She hadn't even wanted a baby while he was with her.

"Well, at least you know what's wrong. Your doctor faxed over a prescription, by the way. I'll fill it for you tomorrow."

"Thanks," she said, and flew out the door. She wanted to run away from everyone, but where could she go?

Much to her relief, there was no one in the apartment when she got home. She had forgotten that Salima was going to a Mozart concert at Carnegie Hall with Lucianna, and they had taken Becky with them. Salima wanted to expose her to the cultural events she knew nothing about and had never experienced before. Becky was starting to really enjoy New York, and although she wasn't Simon, Salima liked her. She was an honest, decent, kind girl, wanted to learn, and tried hard. And Blaise agreed.

When Blaise walked into her room, she stared out

the window at Central Park. There was still snow on the ground, and she tried to keep from calculating seven months forward to when this baby would be born. It was due the first of October. She didn't want to give it a birthday. She didn't want it at all. She thought of calling Simon, but that seemed so wrong. She was sure he was back with Megan. His silence since he'd left confirmed it to her, and she'd been very firm about letting him go and not trying to hang on to him. And even if she was having his baby, she didn't want to use it to lure him back to her. He needed to be with someone his own age. But this was a disaster for her. The last thing she wanted was to have a baby alone at her age. It had been hard enough with Harry, who was never there and an uninterested father, although his real lack of interest had only happened when Salima got sick. Before that, he'd been sweet with her, when he was home, which wasn't often. And Blaise had traveled just as much as he did, and now she traveled more. There was no room for a baby in her life. And what would Salima think? And the network. A thousand things were racing through her mind as she lay down on her bed and started to cry. And then she told herself that there was nothing to be scared of. She would have an abortion, and no one would ever know. But what about Simon? Didn't he have a right to know? Her mind was whirling, as she lay in tears on the bed, utterly exhausted and overwrought, and fell asleep.

Chapter 15

Blaise told no one what she had discovered, and didn't intend to. The only one she would have told was Simon, and that was out of the question. Blaise was sure that if he hadn't gotten involved with Megan again, or had broken up with her, he would have called her. Simon had said he loved her when he left, but by now everything could have changed. He was young and had been very confused. But his total silence for the last weeks confirmed to Blaise that he was out of her life for good. And now she had a decision of her own to make.

At first, it seemed so simple. There was no room for a baby in her life. She was too busy. She had a daughter who needed her full attention and help when she wasn't working. She traveled all the time. She had no one to lean on, or take care of this baby if something happened to her. And most of all, she felt she was too old. But apparently, God didn't think so if she had gotten pregnant. Or was it just an accident of fate? A cruel joke life had played on her? She was forty-seven years old, pregnant, and alone. What the hell was she going to do? She didn't even know why she kept asking herself that question. She knew what she was going to do. So why did she keep asking herself? she wondered. And all she could think of was how sad Simon would be if he knew what she was going to do. She felt as though she was stealing this baby from him. But he was out of her life, with Megan. Of that she was sure. It canceled his rights to her body, her life, and their child. Or did it?

Blaise was still torturing herself over it when she left for Morocco. And if she hadn't felt so tired and queasy, it would have been a fabulous trip. King Mohammed VI and his wife, Princess Lalla Salma, were a charming couple. They did everything possible to honor and entertain her. The princess was a huge fan and showed Blaise all over Rabat. They had beautiful children, and the palace was incredible. She stayed at the Latour Hassan Hotel and had dinner at the palace every night. And the taping they did in the desert with thirty of his fabulous cars, and the king driving at full speed, and even driving Blaise in one of his Aston Martins, was a segment she knew all their male viewers would love. And the tour of the palace with the queen was spectacular and magical as well. Blaise thought it was one of the best shows she had done in a long time, and her crew agreed with her. The only problem she had was that she felt sick a lot of the time, but she overrode it with determination and will power. She was a pro, and managed to get everything done. She remembered now that she had been just as sick and worked just as hard before Salima was born. For Blaise, work always came first, and she had even more reason to stick to her routine this time. She was not about to jeopardize her job.

She went to Marrakech for a few days on the way home, to relax, and stayed at the newly redone Hotel Mamounia. And she spent a day in Paris, and a night at the Ritz. It was the first break she'd taken in a while, and she strolled through the Place Vendôme and down the rue de la Paix, thinking of the decision she had to make when she went home. She kept telling herself she still had time, but not much. She wished that she could talk to Simon, but she knew that that would be wrong. She had no hold on him now, nor should she. She had had no word from him, nor any contact since he left. She had encouraged him to go back to his own life and find out how he felt about Megan, and that was what he had done. She had no right to reach out to him now, if he had shown no desire to contact her. He had a right to his freedom, and she had to deal with this on her own.

Blaise didn't know it, but Salima had told him, in the many texts they exchanged daily, that her mother was in Morocco, interviewing the king and queen, and then a few days later that she was in Paris on the way home. Simon didn't comment, but Salima liked to give him news of her sometimes. And as Simon read the texts from Salima, he thought about the life Blaise led. It was one of the great differences between them. She was a world-famous, glamorous network star, a woman of great accomplishments, and he had done so little compared to her, but even if he was satisfied with his life, he had enjoyed hers. He missed being part of it and being with her and Salima. He always told Salima how much he missed her, and she told him she was teaching Becky to cook from the recipes he had left. Salima quipped to him about her, "I cook better, and I'm blind." And he told her to be nice. He loved her texts and e-mails, and they communicated daily, often many times. Salima respected his opinions about everything, and his advice. He was her hero.

But she was getting on well with Becky after a month with her. She just wasn't an exciting person, or as much fun as Simon, but she was willing to learn.

Salima was busy every day now with Lucianna, preparing for her audition at Juilliard. She had taken a tour of the school with Lucianna, and all Salima wanted now was to get in. Lucianna had written a recommendation for her, which Salima hoped would carry some weight. Her audition was scheduled at the end of March, and she texted Simon that she was worried about that too. Hearing what she was doing made Simon miss them all the more.

Blaise was startled when her BlackBerry rang in Paris, it was from a blocked number, so she answered. It was

Andrew. She hadn't talked to him in a long time and didn't want to now, but he had caught her by surprise, and she didn't want to be rude and hang up.

"Where are you now?" he asked her, envisioning her in New York. He was at his office, and it was morning for him. For Blaise, it was the end of the day. And his voice sounded as sultry and sexy as it always had, when it made her knees go weak. But this time it didn't. She was bored listening to him.

"I'm walking around the Faubourg St. Honoré in Paris, to do some shopping," she said matter-of-factly.

"You lead a golden life," he said, aware that she didn't sound excited to hear him, or even interested in what he said.

"I guess I do." The trip to Morocco had done her good. She felt a little better physically, and being in Paris even for a day was exciting. She had just spent three days with a king and princess visiting a gorgeous palace, had a rest in Marrakech, lying in the sun and exploring the Soukh, the bazaar filled with treasures, and she had bought a mountain of fun things for Salima, including a vest with little bells she knew she'd love, and now she was in Paris, about to do some shopping, and staying at the Ritz. Simon had told her once, when she was agonizing over the threat of Susie Quentin, not to forget who she was. And now Susie was gone, Blaise was still herself, a successful, powerful woman with a "golden life," as Andrew said. The only thing missing was Simon. But not Andrew anymore. She didn't miss him at all.

"Why don't I call you later?" he suggested. "You sound busy." He could hear the traffic noises behind her as she crossed the street toward Hermès.

"I don't think that's a good idea," she said, standing in the late-afternoon March sunshine on the Faubourg.

"Are you there with someone?" he asked, pretending to sound jealous, but she doubted that he really was. It was just an act he put on, like everything else. Suddenly, he sounded sleazy, and none of her memories of him were good. At least Simon had been a decent person and genuinely loved her, even if he was young and confused.

"No, I'm not," she said in answer to his question. "I'm alone and enjoying it thoroughly." She didn't ask him about his wife this time. She didn't care. It had taken her almost five years to get there, but she had finally arrived. "Don't call me later, Andrew. I have nothing to say. And neither do you." He was shocked when he responded a minute later after a startled pause.

"What's gotten into you?" He sounded hurt, but she knew he wasn't. Only his ego was bruised. He had no heart.

"I guess I finally got over you. It was long overdue." He didn't know what to say, so for a moment he said nothing, sure that she'd warm up to him again. She had loved him so much. But that was old news. "Thanks for the call," she said, "but don't do it again." And before he could say another word, she hung up. She stood outside Hermès laughing to herself out loud and feeling great. She walked into Hermès then and bought herself a gorgeous yellow bag, a Birkin, three scarves, and a bottle of perfume. And for once, finally, as Simon had suggested, she knew exactly who she was.

When Blaise got back to the apartment in New York, from the airport, Salima was practicing with Lucianna, and Becky was in the kitchen with an anxious expression, trying to make a soufflé. For a fraction of an instant, it made Blaise sad and reminded her of Simon. But poor Becky looked so incongruous, and so stressed, that Blaise laughed.

"Don't feel bad," she reassured her. "I can't make one either. How's everything?" she said, putting her travel bag down, and taking off her coat. She looked well and was feeling better, and she had slept on the plane. "Salima okay?"

"She's fine," Becky said as she slid the ceramic dish into the oven and smiled at Blaise. "We had a nice time while you were gone. We went to see a Broadway musical. I'd never been to one before, it was great." She was discovering a whole new world in New York, and this time Salima was playing teacher and enjoying it a lot. Becky was only ten years older than she was, but they looked about the same age. She was a nice, wholesome country girl, and Blaise had grown fond of her in the past eight weeks.

* * *

Blaise went to change her clothes and unpack the things she'd brought home for Salima, and she had brought a sweater home from Paris for Becky, in a pale blue the color of her eyes. And by the time Salima finished her lesson with Lucianna, Becky was pulling the soufflé out of the oven with a terrified look, and then a groan of dismay. Blaise had just walked back into the kitchen and smiled. Half the soufflé had risen perfectly, and the other half had fallen, so she was improving, but not there yet. Salima told her what she'd done wrong, when Becky explained the situation to her. She had gotten strict advice from Simon on it. And Blaise said it didn't matter, it would taste good anyway, and it did.

The three women chatted at the kitchen table, and for the first time in nearly two months since Simon had left, the atmosphere was lighter. All three of them laughed, and Blaise told them about her trip, and then gave them their presents. It felt like home again, and not because of Simon this time, but because of the three people who were there.

Becky loved her sweater and thanked Blaise profusely. She had never had anything from Paris. And Salima loved the Moroccan vest with the little bells.

It was the first night that Blaise hadn't gone to bed early, feeling crushed. The trip to Morocco and Paris had done her good. And Mark could see it the next day. She looked fresh and alive on the air, and when she strode into her office, Mark told her how great she looked.

"Those vitamins must have really helped," he said, looking relieved.

"No, I think Paris did. I had fun. I went shopping all by myself." And then she giggled evilly. "And when Andrew called, I blew him off."

"Hallelujah," Mark said, celebrating the victory, and then Blaise got to work. She wanted to see the interview she'd done in Morocco and check how they edited it.

Blaise spent a nice weekend with Salima and Becky. She took them out to dinner, and they had fun, and in quiet moments alone, she wrestled with her decision. She knew she still had time, but not too much. She had already made up her mind to have the abortion, but she was dragging her feet and hadn't called her gynecologist to schedule it yet. She was planning to, but now and then she'd wonder for a minute what it would be like to have a baby there, with her and Salima, if they could manage it, or if it would be more than she could cope with. She had always thought it would be, but the subject had never come up for her again since Salima, nor did it have any appeal. Now, for only brief seconds, she let herself fantasize about it, and then shut down again. She wondered if she was sentimental because of her feelings for Simon. But she knew that if she had this baby, it would be hers, not theirs. He had the life he had begun with Megan, and would have the children he had with her.

If she had it, which wasn't even a possibility in her mind, she planned to notify him when it was born, and make some kind of visitation arrangement. She wouldn't share the pregnancy with him, and she had no desire to be a burden to him, or use it to create a bond he didn't want, if he was involved with someone else, which was the case. His silence for the last two months made that clear. She had told him not to call her when he left, assuming he'd be with Megan. She didn't want to be the other woman in his life, or older ex-girlfriend he felt sorry for. She had wanted him all to herself. But she realized now what a loss it was not to hear from him at all.

And at this point, he had inadvertently become a sperm donor and nothing more. Her feelings for him were irrelevant. She still loved him, but in a distant benevolent way, knowing he had moved on. The agonizing pain of the first few weeks after he left had begun to dull. It was more of a chronic ache now, one that she could live with, a void she'd have to learn to fill with other things. And if by some insanity, she had the baby, he could see it and spend time with it, but she no longer expected to have a relationship with him or even hoped for one.

All she had to do now was make the decision about whether to have the baby. She called her doctor on Monday, a week after she got back to work. All weekend, it had been gnawing at her that maybe at her age it was a miracle she had no right to reject. She just wasn't sure. And there surely wouldn't be another opportunity.

"What are you going to do, Blaise?" her gynecologist asked her when Blaise left work early to see her on Tuesday afternoon. She had been awake the night before until the sun came up, wondering what to do.

"I don't know. I feel a little crazy and conflicted about having it. I've never wanted another baby." She didn't tell her that she hadn't wanted the first one either. Both pregnancies had been accidents, and she felt like at her age she should have known better, but they had been careful every time but once. "My daughter is type 1 diabetic, and all the genetic counselors we saw told us that it would probably never happen again. I really wouldn't want to go through it. And she lives at home now, and is blind. So I have a lot on my plate already, and a big career. And I'm not involved with this baby's father. We broke up two months ago." The gynecologist looked sorry to hear it.

"Is he a nice guy?"

"Very. He wanted a baby, and I told him I couldn't get pregnant at my age, and I thought it was true," she said ruefully. "He's involved with someone else now, so if I do this, I'd be on my own."

"I had a fifty-one-year-old woman in here last week who thought she couldn't get pregnant either. Nature surprises us sometimes. You have to do what's best for you. Particularly if you're doing it alone."

"What's she doing about it?" Blaise asked about the fifty-one-year-old woman.

"She's having the baby. But she's married, and her husband is thrilled. They'd even considered adopting, so this works for them. What about you? Have you told the father?"

"No, and I'm not going to. We're not in contact. I think it's best that way. I'll tell him if I have it. But I want to make the decision on my own, because if I have it, he won't be around to help me. I don't know why I'm even thinking about it. I was sure I was going to have an abortion, and I probably am. But I keep wondering if it's some kind of gift. At my age, maybe it is." The doctor smiled, looking noncommittal. She didn't want to interfere.

"You have about two weeks if you want an abortion," she said simply, just to let Blaise know the time frame. "And if you decide to keep the pregnancy, you should have a CVS next week, to check for genetic anomalies. It wouldn't be recommended after that, and in that case you could have amniocentesis. But I think CVS would be a good idea. So you should try to make the decision this week." She was two and a half months pregnant. And the sonogram the doctor did after that showed a strong heartbeat, and Blaise could see the baby on the screen. She tried not to think about it after she left the doctor's office. This was not about the baby and what had caused it, her love for Simon. It was about her life, and what she thought she could handle or not. Her responsibility for Salima was huge, and Harry was no help. She did it all alone. And she would this time too. She was sad again that Simon had gone back to Megan, but he had. Now she had to figure out what to do about this baby—abort it or have it on her own. She lay on her bed when she got home, and all she could think of was having a baby in her arms again. Simon's baby. Even though she kept telling herself that he would never be part of her life again and he belonged to someone else, she knew that the baby was his, and the result of their love. And even if they had only been together for a brief time, and weren't meant to be together forever, they had loved each other deeply. And the baby that had happened as a result was undeniably a gift.

"You're so quiet, Mom," Salima said on Sunday morning when she walked into the kitchen, and Blaise was sitting there, staring into space.

"I was just thinking."

"What about?" She thought her mother sounded in better spirits lately, and that she had had a hard time at first when Simon left, but recently she seemed more like herself.

"I don't know . . . I was thinking about work . . . the show I did in Morocco, nothing special," she lied to her. She had to make the decision by the next day. Salima was sure she was thinking about Simon but didn't want to ask. Salima had already had two text messages from him that morning. He had remained faithful in their correspondence for the past two months. But he never mentioned Blaise. He wanted to keep his relationship with Salima pure and untainted. He wondered about her and missed her but didn't want to use Salima for information or to pass messages to Blaise. If he'd had something to say to her, he would have said it himself.

Blaise went back to her room after breakfast and spent the day in her office at home doing work, while Salima and Becky went out. And by the end of the day, when they met for dinner, Blaise looked exhausted. She was torturing herself about the decision and hadn't made it yet. And as she lay in bed and looked at the moon that night, she was still undecided, torn either way. And she lay there thinking about when Simon had been in that bed with her, and the wonderful time they'd shared.

She felt peaceful when she fell asleep that night, hoping she'd wake up in the morning, knowing what to do.

And then for no reason, she woke in the middle of the night. The moon was still shining brightly, and she had two more hours to sleep before the alarm went off. And as though someone had spoken the words clearly, she heard a voice in her head. "It's a gift." The voice said it so loudly she almost heard it in the room as well. "It's a gift," she said to herself, as she went back to sleep, remembering Simon in her bed. The decision had been made.

Chapter 16

Blaise had the CVS test the doctor had recommended, the following week, and she went to have the test alone. It was invasive, and there was some risk of miscarriage, but it would give them the information that the baby was genetically healthy, and if she wanted to know the sex of the baby, they could tell her that too. She told them she wanted to know, and she had three or four weeks to wait until the result. And she was nervous about it. Now that she had decided to go forward with it, she hoped everything would be all right. The baby was due on the first of October, and she had decided to tell Salima when it showed, which it didn't yet. She was very slim and in good shape, and she was only three months pregnant. And she wanted to keep it from the network for as long as possible. She suspected they wouldn't be thrilled, but she was going to take very little maternity leave, just as she had done with Salima. She didn't want to take a lot of time. There were too many projects to finish, and someone else would be taking her place if she did.

And she was still adjusting to the idea of having a baby. She was somewhat in shock. She covered a story in South Africa the week after she had the CVS test, and from there she went to London and attended a royal wedding as a guest. She was back in New York ten days after she left, with lots of stories to tell Becky and Salima. She was continuing her busy life, unhampered by the pregnancy.

"You lead such a glamorous life," Becky said, still in awe of her.

"No, she doesn't," Salima interjected. "She still hangs out with us." And to prove it, they went bowling that night, and they all had fun. Salima said she deserved a handicap, and Blaise said she would probably play just as badly if she wasn't blind.

"Yeah, just like you can't cook," she teased her mother. "And neither can Becky!"

"Yes, I can. I finally got the soufflé right last week." It had become an obsession with her. Her trial by fire. A rite of initiation, and she had passed.

"Yeah, with Simon walking us through it. That's like painting by number," Salima said, teasing her, but she'd been impressed. And the soufflé was good.

"Well, it worked, and I did it," Becky said victoriously. Blaise was getting to like her more and more, and so was Salima. And Blaise tried to ignore the fact that her heart gave a little flutter when Salima mentioned Simon. She knew he was still very much in touch with Salima, although he had vanished completely out of her life, except for the baby in her womb. She was going to tell Salima that Simon was the baby's father, but no one else. And Simon, of course, when it was born. But she wanted to keep any press interest in her pregnancy as minimal as possible. And she was hoping to keep it from the network till May or June. Her doctor said she could travel till August, and sitting at a desk during her morning segment, the viewers wouldn't have to know until she gave birth.

Blaise had plenty to keep her busy. Salima was preparing ardently for her recital on the Memorial Day weekend in May, now that the audition for Juilliard was over. Lucianna had taken her to her audition when Blaise was in London. Salima was hoping for a response by May or June. She was desperate to get into the school, located at Lincoln Center, with three students to every teacher, small classes, fabulous instructors, and dedication to handicapped students.

And Blaise had sweeps week to think of in May for the ratings, which had the whole network in an uproar twice a year. They were planning to show her interview with the king of Morocco during that time, because the producers of her show thought it was so good.

She was going over a stack of research for her new projects toward the end of April when her doctor called, and Mark put the call through to Blaise.

"Blaise McCarthy," she said in a clipped voice, sounding distracted.

"Hi, Blaise." It was her doctor, which brought Blaise rapidly back to earth. "I have your CVS results. Everything is perfect." She said it quickly, to allay any worry, and Blaise heaved a sigh of relief. She hadn't realized how anxious about it she was.

"That's great. Thank you."

"Do you still want to know the baby's sex?" She checked before she told her.

"I'd like that very much," she said with tears in her eyes. It was an important moment. Her baby was healthy. The rest was icing on the cake.

"It's a boy," the doctor said, smiling. She loved delivering that kind of news. A healthy baby and a happy mom. Blaise had had no preference about sex. She just liked the idea of knowing, but hearing that it was a boy suddenly made it all the more real now. She was going to have a son. She hoped he'd look just like Simon, and as she thought it, the tears rolled down her cheeks. She hadn't seen him come in, but Mark had walked into her office when she hung up, and he looked shocked to see her crying.

"Are you okay? Is something wrong?" He knew the doctor had called, and hoped nothing serious was going on.

"I'm fine." He handed her research on a British politician involved in an international money-laundering scandal, and she gave him back some of the earlier research with her notes on it, and then he stopped and turned around on the way out of the room.

"I almost forgot to tell you. You get all the plum jobs around here. They're sending you to the Cannes Film Festival to do a special. It's the third week in May, followed by the Monaco Grand Prix the week after. You can stay over for the Memorial Day weekend at the end of it if you want. I'll book you a reservation at Hotel du Cap." And as he said it, instead of pleased, she looked horrified and almost cried again.

"Oh my God . . . I can't stay over. . . . Salima's recital is that Friday night, the last day of the Grand Prix race. She's been preparing for it for six months. I can't miss it, no matter what. I do it to her every time." She had missed her high school graduation, interviewing the president of South Korea. She couldn't do it to her again. "Mark, I have to be back in New York on Friday afternoon."

"I'll book the reservation, but you'll have to work it out, and leave the morning of the last day of the race, or wrap things up the day before." Mark looked sympathetic. He knew how much the recital meant to Salima. Blaise had been telling him all about it for months.

"I have to. Salima would never forgive me, and I don't want to let her down." She was going to fix this right away and e-mailed Charlie about it immediately, to warn him of when she'd have to leave the Grand Prix. Whatever she did, no matter how important they thought it was, this time she couldn't fail Salima.

* * *

Once Blaise knew the baby was a boy and that it was healthy, she found herself thinking about Simon more and more often. She questioned if it had been a mistake to find out what the sex was. Now she kept wondering if he would look like Simon, and what Simon would say when she told him. She still had no intention of telling him during the pregnancy. She wasn't going to intrude on his life. And she was only four months pregnant. It was still a long way off. But he seemed to be constantly on her mind.

When the ratings came out in May, Blaise's were stronger than they'd ever been. Zack came down to her office to congratulate her personally. And Charlie gave her a bottle of champagne, which she took home to Becky and Salima that night. They opened it, and Blaise poured a glass for the two girls. They toasted her with it, and she clinked a glass with a tiny sip in it. Somehow Salima could tell and asked her mother why she wasn't drinking more. Blaise was always amazed by everything she noticed. Her hearing was so acute, she could tell it wasn't a full glass.

"Somebody has to stay sober around here." Blaise laughed and changed the subject. But she was very happy about her ratings too. It would relieve some of the pressure on her, for now at least.

And two weeks later, she left to cover the Cannes Film Festival and then the Monaco Grand Prix. She stayed at the Hotel du Cap Eden-Roc during the Film

Festival, and then moved to the Hermitage in Monte Carlo for the Grand Prix. Both hotels were superb. There wasn't a luxury hotel around the world that Blaise hadn't been in, a resort or spa where she hadn't stayed while doing an interview or a special. And there were a number of celebrities staying at both hotels. She enjoyed the Film Festival, and the car race using the streets of Monaco was always exciting. She was invited to parties on yachts and in fabulous villas, and one at the palace hosted by the prince and princess. And on that particular assignment, she had to admit that her life was as glamorous as people said. She was constantly surrounded by movie stars and royalty, and she told Salima about it when she called her every day. Salima was diligently preparing for her recital, and pressed Blaise again to make sure she'd be there.

"I'm flying back that morning," Blaise reminded her again. "I'm taking the early flight and with the time difference, I'll be there by noon. I'll be back in plenty of time for the recital. I can even help you dress." They had picked out a long white silk dress that looked beautiful on Salima, and it had been hanging in her closet for the last month. And she and Lucianna had designed the program and what Salima would be singing. They had chosen all the pieces that best showed off her voice. And she had texted Simon that she wished he could be there too. They had graduation at Caldwell that weekend, and he had to attend. But he couldn't have gone to the recital because of her mother anyway. After four months of silence between them, he felt awkward about seeing her. He thought about Blaise frequently, and when he asked about her, Salima said that her mother was okay, and he hoped that that was true.

Blaise called Salima from the South of France every day, and reported on the stars she'd seen and the events she'd been to, but by the end of her trip, Salima could only focus on her recital. By the time Blaise was ready to come home, Salima was in a panic over it.

"You have to calm down. It's going to be fine," her mother told her.

"No, it's not, I'll be awful. And you better not miss your plane. You won't, Mom, right? They won't make you stay longer, or send you somewhere else?" It had happened so often before that Salima was afraid she wouldn't make it this time, and Blaise was terrified of that too. She was so nervous about it that she got up two hours earlier than she needed to, to get to the airport in time to make her plane. And she was leaving her crew at the Hermitage in Monte Carlo to fly home later that day. Blaise was going home early for Salima, and had warned the network that she would.

Blaise checked out of the hotel in plenty of time, and a limousine drove her to the Nice airport. She was catching a direct flight that only ran twice a day from Nice to New York on Air France. And she handed her ticket and passport to an Air France agent at the first-class counter when she arrived. She knew that everything was in order, and she was half an hour early, which was rare for her. Her plans had gone with the precision of a Swiss clock so far that day.

"I'm sorry," the ticket agent looked at her with regret. "Your flight has been canceled. We had a mechanical problem, and the plane didn't get here from New York."

"No," Blaise said, panicking. "That's not possible. I have to get to New York." This couldn't be happening to her. She wouldn't let it.

"I understand," the agent said pleasantly. "We'll have another plane here in three hours. Your flight to New York will leave at noon." Blaise made a rapid calculation, and with the time difference, getting through customs and leaving the airport, she could be at the apartment by two o'clock, three at the latest. It was later than she'd promised Salima, but the recital wasn't until seven o'clock, and Salima didn't have to leave the house until six. Tully was driving them. And a hairdresser was coming to do Salima's hair at three.

"All right, that'll work," Blaise said, determined not to get excited about it. Even with the delay, she would be there for Salima. Charlie had been very nice about her not being there for the last day of the race. Her crew was covering it for her. Blaise had been at everything else all week, and she had told Charlie she had enough film to give them more than they needed. She went to the first-class lounge then to wait for the flight that was leaving at noon.

She went to the desk in the lounge at eleven, to make sure that everything was on schedule. The woman looked at her computer, and then back at Blaise with a reassuring smile.

"You're fine."

"What time will we be boarding?" All Blaise wanted to do was get on the plane. She hadn't texted Salima about the delay. She didn't want to worry her, and she would still be home with plenty of time, or just enough to help Salima get ready and dress her.

"Eleven-fifty," the Air France agent said, still smiling. But the dazzling airline smiles were beginning to look fake.

"Then the flight must be late. It's supposed to leave at noon. If you board three hundred passengers starting at eleven-fifty, we're going to leave an hour late."

"We always make it up in the air," the woman said. They were the kind of answers that were supposed to lull naïve passengers into believing they were on time when they weren't. Blaise knew better. She traveled too much not to know the pat phrases they used when they were lying to their passengers. Blaise did not want to be lied to this time.

"Is the plane here?" Blaise asked, sounding curt, and the woman in the Air France uniform got instantly defensive. Passengers like Blaise who demanded real information were their least favorite to deal with.

"Of course," she said with a haughty look. But at twelve-fifteen they hadn't boarded yet, and Blaise was beginning to seriously panic.

"Look, I have to get to New York as soon as possible. I have the feeling you don't have the plane here yet. I can't play around here. If I fly back to Paris, what can I get on, to get me to New York?" It would slow her down, she knew, but maybe less than a flight from Nice that might not leave for several hours, and she no longer believed a word the woman said. History had proven her right too many times before, and this time it really mattered to her. She would rather have kept the president of the United States waiting than be late for Salima's recital or, worse, miss it entirely. She shuddered at the thought.

The agent checked her computer again. She said that she had a flight leaving for Paris in ten minutes, and the doors weren't closed yet, but she said that Blaise's bags were on the direct flight, and they couldn't put her on the Paris flight until they got her bags off the one she had already checked into.

"Which means I can't make the Paris flight. Okay, let's get my bags off now. What *can* you get me onto after you do?"

"I have a flight leaving for Paris in an hour."

"Perfect." She was reminding herself to breathe and not lose control.

"But it's full, except for one coach seat in the back row. Will you take it?" she asked with an evil grin, delighted to be punishing Blaise for the trouble she was causing.

"I'll take it," Blaise said without hesitation. The woman punched something into the computer, and then shook her head, while Blaise tried to resist the overwhelming urge to strangle her.

"Sorry. There was an error in the computer. There's an infant in that seat. The flight is completely booked."

"When can you get me to Paris, and from there to New York?"

"We have a three o'clock," she said primly. "You can connect with our five-forty flight to Kennedy."

"What time does it land?" Blaise asked through clenched teeth.

"It lands at seven fifty-five P.M. local time." Eight o'clock. Blaise did a rapid calculation. If she landed at eight, she'd get her bags and be out of customs by nine, and in the city at ten, completely missing the recital.

"That won't work," Blaise said with a deep sigh of exasperation. "What other city can you get me out of? London, Zurich, Frankfurt. Anything you've got. I have to be in New York City by six P.M., which means I can land no later than four." It was one P.M. in Nice by then, and the direct flight was going nowhere. They weren't even boarding the plane. "I still need to get my bags off this plane."

"We have a baggage handler strike here today, just a partial one. One out of three baggage handlers didn't come to work." Welcome to France.

"Terrific." She was ready to kill somebody and would have gladly left her bags in France if she could just get to New York, with or without them. She didn't care. But even that wasn't possible because of security.

And with that, they announced that her original nine A.M. flight was leaving at three P.M. from Nice, and would be boarding at two ten. Blaise did another rapid calculation. The flight would arrive at five P.M. local time. She could be in the city at seven. But she couldn't get Salima ready and take her to the concert. She'd have to meet her there, and it would be close. If there were any further delays, she would be screwed, and despite the best of intentions, she would miss the recital Salima had prepared for for months.

"It sounds like the three o'clock from here is going to be my best bet," Blaise said to the agent.

"I always thought so, madam," she said with pursed lips.

"No, you thought so when it was leaving at noon, and before that at nine A.M. It hasn't done either. And if the damn plane isn't here from Paris now, so we can board at two ten, I'm going to have hysterics in the airport," Blaise said, beginning to seriously lose her cool. "I *have* to get to New York."

"I'm sure you will, madam. Try to be patient."

"Look," Blaise said, willing to lie through her teeth if it would impress them, "my name is Blaise McCarthy, I am a journalist in network news, and I have a meeting in New York to interview the president of the United States tonight. And I need you to get me there." Blaise was willing to do anything to get on a plane to New York. Even lie. She couldn't disappoint Salima again.

"Very well, we'll preboard you," she said, as though preboarded seats would leave sooner than the others. It made no difference, Blaise knew, except that you got a jump start on the champagne, and she couldn't drink now anyway, which might have helped. She hadn't had this frustrating a day in years. And all that mattered to her was Salima and being there for her recital. She would have paid double for the seat on the plane if they could guarantee getting her there on time.

"Shall I still take your bags off, Miss McCarthy?" she said with a vacant smile.

"Of course not. We just agreed that I'm taking this flight to New York. Why would you take my bags off now, especially when you didn't before, when I did want them taken off and you said you had a strike."

"We do."

"Fine. Just leave my bags on." She had the ticket stubs for her checked luggage in her purse. She texted Salima then that her flight had been delayed, but she would get there. She couldn't meet her at the apartment, and would meet her at the concert hall. She would be there no matter what. It was seven A.M. in New York by then, and she was sure that Salima was still asleep. Instead, she texted back within seconds.

"Please, please, please get there. I need you." Her words ripped Blaise's heart out, and she started to feel sick. It had been a stressful morning, and she was terrified there would be some further delay.

"I promise I'll be there," she texted back, and Salima answered back with "ok." Blaise prayed she was telling Salima the truth.

After that, Blaise waited tensely until they announced the flight to New York, which began boarding at two fifteen, another five minutes late. Blaise headed toward her gate, and already exhausted, she boarded the plane and took her seat, and turned down magazines, newspapers, pajamas, toiletries, orange juice, and champagne. It felt like a bazaar with everything they offered. She accepted a bottle of water and sank back into her seat, praying they would close the doors soon. She texted Salima that she was on the plane, and then had to turn off her phone before she got a response. And at three fifteen they slowly rolled away from the gate. She should have been landing in New York by then. If she had, it would have worked perfectly. Now she wasn't sure.

They finally took off and headed toward New York, and Blaise sat nervously, glancing at her watch for the first two hours and then gave up. There was nothing more she could do. She would have to do all her rushing on the ground at JFK. And before she took a nap in the comfortable seat, she told the purser that she needed to verify VIP assistance on the ground, to get through the terminal and customs quickly. She told him the story about interviewing the president too. She didn't know if he believed her or not, but he said he'd check what he could do. And after that she watched a movie for a while and fell asleep. She didn't wake up until they were serving the meal, most of which she didn't eat. And after that three different flight attendants asked her for autographs. She wasn't in the mood but signed them anyway. She was tense for the rest of the flight, checking every half hour on their ETA.

"I thought you were supposed to make up time in the air," she said, looking anxious.

"Yes, but we're fighting headwinds today." Blaise felt like she was fighting all of Air France, headwinds, and the universe. It had been a nightmare so far, of contradictions, delays, and lies, which were standard fare these days for flying on all airlines in every part of the world. It wasn't unique to Air France.

She went back to sleep then under the blanket, and felt the gentle roundness of her stomach. She would be five months pregnant in a few days, and she was wearing loose shirts and tops that covered the slight bulge. Unless you looked very carefully, it really didn't show yet, but she knew it would soon. She had managed to conceal Salima until she was six months pregnant, but after that the cat was out of the bag. She had been a young network star then, just starting out, and people thought it was cute, even her producers. She had been twenty-seven years old. She didn't know how cute anyone would think it was at forty-seven and unmarried. She suspected that Zack would be less than amused, particularly if it caused a problem for them. Blaise intended to see that it didn't, but she was concerned. It could even start Zack on a bad roll again, looking for another Susie Quentin. Or worse, another Blaise McCarthy. But there was nothing she could do—she would have to take a few weeks off to have the baby. She smoothed her shirt over her belly, and lay in her seat, "praying" the plane toward New York. So far they were on time, and the only thing that could delay them further now was if they had to circle the airport in New York instead of land, due to storms or traffic.

She had tea and a light meal before they landed—it was foie gras, smoked salmon, cheese, and champagne. She skipped the champagne and ate the cheese and foie gras, and twenty minutes before they landed, the flight attendants put everything away and asked them to bring up their seats. Blaise went to brush her hair and suddenly realized that she was going to have to wear the dark blue linen slacks and white shirt she had on, and sandals, to the recital in New York. She wouldn't have time to go home and change. She quickly brushed her teeth, combed her hair, and put on makeup, and she looked very chic and impeccable when she went back to her seat. Even in casual clothes, she looked like a star. But she was chic for the French Riviera, not New York. At least Salima didn't care, as long as she was there for the performance, and she prayed God she would be.

It was 5:01 in New York when they landed, and there was an Air France VIP escort waiting for her. They took her off the plane first and literally ran with her to immigration, and stayed with her while she waited for her bags. A porter and the VIP person took her to customs, and she said she had nothing to declare. It was 5:29 when she left customs and raced outside to the curb. Mark had arranged a town car for her since Tully was with Salima, and Blaise texted her as soon as she got in the car, or tried to, only to discover that her cell phone was dead. So Salima had no idea that her mother had landed and was in the car. She tried to call her from the car phone, but Salima's phone was off.

The driver wove her expertly through traffic, and it was six forty-five when they approached Lincoln Center in rush-hour traffic, where Salima would be singing at Alice Tully Hall. Blaise got out and literally ran across the plaza, to the theater, and produced the ticket she had fortunately put in her purse in Nice. She was so glad she had it with her. Lucianna had arranged a front-row seat for her, as well as seats for Becky and Mark. Blaise was out of breath when she took her place between them, and Mark looked relieved when she got there and beamed. Blaise glanced up at the empty stage, with the grand piano on it. There were two other students performing after Salima, and she was scheduled to go on first. Blaise had just made it by the skin of her teeth, but she suddenly realized that this was the first time she ever had. And she had never tried this hard to come home. Something had changed. Suddenly not being there for Salima seemed wrong, and moving heaven and earth to be there for her was right. And Blaise certainly had.

The audience took their places and the stage manager turned down the lights, as Blaise held her breath, and a moment later Salima walked onto the stage with Lucianna, who left her front and center, close to the edge of the stage. She was wearing a sad, worried look, and Blaise realized that Salima still didn't know her mother was there. And with a sudden surprising gesture, Blaise left her seat, took two steps toward the stage, and said just loudly enough for Salima to hear, "I'm here," and suddenly Salima beamed. She had heard her. And a moment later the performance began. She sang like an angel, the crowd applauded thunderously when she took her bow, and Lucianna led her proudly off the stage into the wings. The thrill of victory was on Salima's face, and Blaise hadn't stopped crying while she sang. It had been the most beautiful night of her life.

Blaise found her backstage afterward, and Salima threw herself into her arms.

"You came! You did it! I didn't think you would."

"I damn near had to hijack a plane to do it. I nearly assaulted a ticket agent in Nice in the first-class lounge. I got here two minutes before you walked onstage."

"Thank you for telling me you were here," she said to her mother. "My performance wouldn't have been the same if I didn't know you were. I did it all for you, Mom." And as she said it, Blaise started crying again. She was so proud of her, and so was Lucianna. And Salima went back to take another bow at the end.

Blaise took Salima, Mark, and Becky to Harry's Cipriani afterward, and Lucianna joined them a little while later. Salima said she was ravenous, she had eaten very little all day, she'd been so nervous. And Blaise told her again how beautiful it had been. Lucianna had had the performance videotaped, and Blaise couldn't wait to see it again.

And on the way to the restaurant, Salima had texted Simon to tell him how well it had gone. She stood outside the restaurant for a minute to listen to his text, and he told her that he was proud of her too, and he wanted her to send him one of the CDs. She texted him back and promised she would. And she told him that her mom had been there, and made it just in time.

The white silk dress they had gotten for the recital looked beautiful on Salima, and Becky had bought a new dress too, at Barneys, and Blaise laughed about what a mess she was, in shirt and slacks and gold sandals, wrinkled beyond belief after eight hours on the plane.

"I don't care if you showed up naked, Mom. I'm so happy you were there." Salima beamed.

"Me too," Blaise said, as they held hands. Blaise leaned over and kissed her then. She had never been prouder in her life, of Salima for her accomplishments, hard work, and outstanding performance, and of herself for finally showing up when it counted. For once, network news had taken a backseat to her family, and Salima had come first. It was the happiest night of Salima's life, and Blaise's too. And as she sat smiling at Salima, Blaise felt the baby move for the first time.

Chapter 17

Salima was coasting on the excitement of her recital all weekend. Lucianna called to tell her again how fantastic she had been. Blaise sent Lucianna two dozen red roses to thank her, and two dozen pink ones to Salima, and all of them were in high spirits. They went to the park on Saturday, and out to dinner in the West Village, at a noisy new place Salima had heard about that was full of young people. And the three of them celebrated all over again. And on Sunday, Salima and Becky went out, to the park for a concert, and Blaise finally got some time to unpack from her trip. There were clothes lying all over her room and she looked disheveled in a big white shirt, bare feet, and jeans, with her bright red hair flying loose after she'd washed it that morning. She was trying to make order out of chaos when the doorbell rang, right after they left. She thought it was Salima and Becky, having forgotten something and left their key in the apartment, since the doorman didn't call from downstairs to announce a guest.

Blaise pulled the front door open with a smile, expecting to see the girls. "Forget your key, ladies?" she teased them, and found herself looking at Simon in khaki slacks and a white shirt, with a blazer over his arm. She had no idea what to say when she saw him. It was like opening a door and seeing a ghost. And he could see it on her face, as she went suddenly pale.

"Oh . . . I'm sorry . . . I thought it was the girls. What are you doing here, and why didn't they announce you downstairs?" Blaise said. She wasn't angry, just surprised, and she was so stunned, she didn't invite him to come in. They just stood there in the doorway, staring at each other, and Blaise felt a wave of emotion wash over her, which she tried to conceal. But Simon had seen a glimpse of it in her eyes.

"I guess the doorman still thinks I live here, or likes me or something. . . ." Simon looked at her with gentle eyes. "Are you busy, or can I come in?" he asked cautiously, not sure if she would let him.

"Sorry, yes . . . to both . . . I'm busy, and you can come in. I just got back from France on Friday. I was unpacking." And she was still awash with the good feelings of Friday night.

"I hear Salima's performance was a smash hit," Simon said as he followed Blaise into the familiar hall and then into the living room where she led him. They had sat there before, though very rarely. It felt too formal to him. He preferred hanging out in the kitchen with her, her home office, or her bedroom. But he was an outsider now, he didn't live there. Blaise tried not to think of it as they sat down. She had no idea why he'd come, except maybe to see Salima, which she couldn't help thinking was presumptuous of him, without even calling first to ask if he could. It seemed unlike him. He was generally better behaved.

"She was fantastic," Blaise said with a smile. "I suppose you've come to see her. She and Becky just went out. That's why I thought you were them. I don't think they'll be back for a while." She was treating him like a guest or an old friend, not a man she had once loved, and still did.

"I came to see you," he said quietly. "And I apologize for not calling first. I was afraid if I did, you wouldn't see me." He was right, she wouldn't have, she thought to herself, but she didn't say it to him, she just nodded.

"When did you get back to New York?" she asked politely.

"Last night. We had commencement yesterday. I'm through at Caldwell. I wanted to see you in person. I apologize for my silence. I know it was wrong not to at least e-mail you. I just had to work things out, and it took time. I didn't want to call you until I sorted it out. All of it," he said, looking her in the eye. He was as direct and honest with her as he had always been.

"You don't need to apologize, Simon," she said softly, and looked away. "I knew it was over when you left. I guess it was foolish of me to think it could work with us. I know now it couldn't, but it took me a while to realize it and accept it. I hope everything worked out well for you." She was trying to be gracious, but she really didn't want to hear the details about Megan. It would have hurt too much, even now. Especially now, with the baby.

"Things worked out the way they were meant to. I really questioned if I wanted to stay in this kind of work. Eric and I talked a lot about it. He thinks I have a gift, so I took the job at the Institute for Special Education for the fall. Eric thought it would be a good fit. He was great. It was really time for me to move on to something bigger. And I didn't want to just take a job because of you. I had to do it for myself, and make sure this is the career I want. I know that now. I had some doubts about it for a while." The school for the blind he was referring to was in New York.

"What else would you have done?" She was startled to hear that he had considered other lines of work, and would have given this one up. Eric was right. He had a gift. And Salima and countless others were proof of that. Even her singing studies were thanks to him. He had made both their lives better while he was there, even with his soufflés. She smiled at the memory of the time they'd shared, and their brief affair.

"I thought about opening a restaurant. Or working in one, if I couldn't afford my own. I mean a great restaurant, like La Grenouille. I've never done anything with the training I have, except for friends." He smiled at her. "I have a gift for that too, and I had a secret dream of being a chef. I've put that away for now, but at least I'm clear about it, and it doesn't feel like a sacrifice. I'm excited about the new job. I outgrew Caldwell a while ago."

"I thought so too," she agreed, surprised by what he was saying. She had never realized that he was serious about being a chef. She thought he was just having fun. But he was very good at that too. He was a man of many talents.

"And I've always wanted to live in France and work in my uncle's vineyards. I think the wine business is fascinating. I was thinking about moving to Bordeaux. But I decided not to do that either. Actually, my uncle was less enthused about it than I was. I worked for him for two summers in my teens, and I almost burned the place down once with fireworks. He was afraid I'd screw up his business and burn down the château." He grinned and she laughed.

"Well, you certainly had some interesting options. And you can always do either of those later, the restaurant, and the family wine business. But it sounds like you made the right choice for now." It hurt looking at him and making idle conversation. She hoped it didn't show. He was as beautiful and appealing as ever.

"I hope so," he said about his career decision, looking very young. The age difference between them seemed vast to Blaise now, and she felt foolish for ever thinking he'd want a life with her. He hadn't even figured out what he wanted to be when he grew up, and was only just beginning to. He needed a woman his age to go in different directions and try things out with him. Her life was already established and not as fluid and flexible as his. "And I can always work as a *sous chef* somewhere on weekends if I want. It might be fun. And the family business isn't going anywhere. My mother thought I'd hate living in Bordeaux. She couldn't wait to leave when she was young. I'm going over this summer for a few weeks to visit family at the end of June." She knew he spoke French fluently, which made it easy for him. It was a real advantage she didn't have when she was there.

"I just came back from the South of France, the Cannes Film Festival and the Monaco Grand Prix. It's always crazy, but I love it there," she said, keeping things light.

"What are you doing this summer?" he asked her. His eyes never left hers for an instant. And he looked as though he wanted to say something else, but didn't dare.

"We're trying to decide between Cape Cod, the Vineyard, and the Hamptons." He nodded. They sounded like reasonable choices for her and Salima and a nice vacation for them.

"And Becky worked out well," he confirmed. He could tell Salima liked her, from her texts, and she had reported that her mother did too.

"Very. She's not exciting but she's very sweet, and they're like two kids together. I think Salima has taught her more than she's taught Salima. But it seems to work. And she's very responsible when I'm gone." She didn't say that it was nothing like when he was there. There was no point. Nothing in her life was the same without him, and wouldn't be again, but she didn't want to look back, only forward. They both had to move on, and he already had. And she had something important to look forward to now too. He had mentioned looking for an apartment in New York, and she assumed it was for him, Megan, and her three boys.

"Blaise, I wanted to tell you how sorry I am about how confused I was when I left—" She stopped him before he could say more.

"That's all over, Simon. We don't need to talk about it." And she didn't want to. Just seeing him was painful enough.

"After a while, I figured if I called, you'd hang up on me. And I didn't want to write an e-mail. I wanted to come and see you and talk to you myself. But I couldn't leave Caldwell till now. I got here last night, so I came to see you today." He had walked around all morning before he did, trying to decide what to say to her, and how.

"It doesn't matter," she said gently.

"It does to me. It all matters. How I left, what happened when I got there, you have a right to know."

"You look happy," she said, trying not to remember how much she'd loved him, or that his son was in her belly, which he didn't know and couldn't see, but she would tell him later, in four more months. "I'm fine too. You gave us enormous gifts while you were here, both of us. You gave Salima independence, which is an incredible gift. And what we shared was wonderful. But some things aren't meant to last. What we had didn't. Let's leave it there. You have Megan, and a new job to look forward to. You have a lot of life ahead of you, and I'm happy as I am." She was trying to convince both him and herself as she said it, and he shook his head with a pained expression. He could see in her eyes how much he had hurt her.

"I left Megan three days after I got back to Caldwell." He was staring at her intensely as he said it. "And I found out everything I needed to know. I can't be with a woman that dishonest, even if she did leave Jack for me in the end. I don't think she did. She left him for herself, which was the right thing to do. But that doesn't obligate me to spend my life with her. I couldn't. I'd have been miserable with her. I knew it after the first dinner I had with her. Nothing happened with Megan, Blaise. I wasn't clear about it until I saw her, and then it was crystal clear. I wasn't in love with her anymore. I was in love with you, and I still am. You may not want me anymore, and I don't blame you if you feel that way, after four months of silence. But I needed to know more than that. I wanted to come back to you with a job I'm excited about, to know that I could bring something to the table other than truffle pasta and cheese soufflé. And I needed to be sure about one other thing, and I am. I wanted to be sure that I don't care about having children, so I wouldn't regret it later. I don't need to have babies. I'd rather be with Salima and you. I love you, Blaise." She saw all the pain he'd been through, and it was mirrored by her own, but they had both come out of it better people, whatever happened now. "I love you, and I don't expect you to take me back. I just wanted you to know it, and that I wasn't wasting my time for these four months. I was quiet because I needed to know how I really felt, about everything. I grew up. Maybe too late for you, but I did. And if you're happy now, I'm glad. I can't imagine the pain I must have caused you for the past four months while I was growing up." She sat looking at him for a long time, and she wasn't sure what to say. They had each grown and moved on, and had wound up in a different place. It was ironic, and she smiled at him.

"What made you decide to give up having kids?" she asked him.

"Because I love you more than any child, and I'd rather be with you. I wanted to be sure that I was okay about giving that up, and I am. I understand why you don't want them, and I'm fine with it." He had come to all the right conclusions, the ones she had hoped to hear, but he had arrived a little late.

"It's strange how life works. I've been doing a lot of thinking too. I came to kind of a crossroads in March when I had to make a big decision, one of those life-changing moments when what you decide will affect the rest of your life. And I landed in the opposite place you did. I wish you had told me about Megan, by the way. It might have helped. I made all my decisions based on the assumption that you were back with her for good. It would have been nice to know you ended it with her after three days." It would have spared her a lot of pain and suffering, but he hadn't called. He hadn't been ready for her yet, and maybe it was for the best, she realized now. Because she had made the right choice for herself, not for them, or him.

"I'm sorry," he said humbly. "So what decision did you make in March?" A chill ran down his spine as he wondered if she was involved with someone else now, someone she loved more than him, maybe someone her own age who was more mature. He thought she looked more beautiful than ever, and wondered if that was why. "Are you involved with someone now, in a serious way?" His heart nearly stopped while he waited for the answer, and she nodded. He closed his eyes for a moment when she did. "I was such a fool," he said softly, and then looked at her again with deep regret.

"Maybe I was too. I expected you to know all the answers immediately, because I thought I did. We both had some growing up to do. You were smarter than I was about that. And I'm not involved with someone the way you think I am, although it's very serious and very long term. Forever actually. I came to a different conclusion than you did about having babies. I decided that I want to have another child." She looked peaceful as she said it.

He looked shocked. "When did you decide that?" She waited an eternity before she answered, while he could feel his heart pounding in his chest. He looked at her, and she looked no different, except even lovelier than before, and all he wanted was to take her in his arms.

"I decided it when I found out I was pregnant with your baby, a little boy." He looked like he'd been shot out of a cannon as he stared at her.

"Why didn't you tell me? When did that happen?"

"In January apparently. I found out at the end of February. I thought you were with Megan, and had made your decision, so I decided not to tell you until the baby was born. I always planned to tell you then. But I didn't want to impose on you, or intrude while I was pregnant." He looked like he was going to cry when she said it, and he moved closer to where she sat.

"Does Salima know?" He was horrified that he had known nothing about it, and hadn't been there for her.

"Not yet. I'll have to tell her soon, though, probably by next month. She knows how much I love you. She'll be okay with it. I haven't told anyone until you right now. I decided it was a gift, and I accepted the gift. That's what I decided in March."

"How could you not tell me and do this all by yourself?" There was accusation in his voice as well as guilt. What if she had never told him? He would have been deprived of his son, and her.

"You didn't need to know before he was born if you were with Megan, or whoever else. You can have visitation and see him whenever you want. He's your son too." As he sat next to her, he put a gentle hand on her white shirt, and felt the baby move. He looked at Blaise with tears in his eyes.

"I don't deserve you, but I love you so much. When are you having him?"

"End of September, beginning of October. I'll call you the minute he comes," she promised, and Simon looked heartbroken as he sat next to her.

"Is it over for you, with us, I mean?"

"In some ways, it's just beginning, with him. We have a lot of years ahead of us to share this child. If nothing else, we can be friends, and should be for his sake." She was at peace about it.

"I want more than that, Blaise. I want what we had before"—he sounded determined as he said it—"even if I was an idiot and didn't deserve you, probably still don't, and maybe never will." He looked at her humbly and she shook her head and smiled.

"I'm not sure I deserved you." She smiled. "I'm too old for you, too settled in my life. I know what I want and who I am, you reminded me of that, to never forget who I am. I did forget, for a long time, with Andrew, and even with you. All I wanted was to be with you, at any price. I wanted to forget how old I was, how young you are, the difference in our ages, where we were in our lives. You left because you wanted Megan. You thought you wanted someone your own age, and you were right. You don't need someone like me."

"I loved her the way you loved Andrew, even though he was wrong for you. You got taken in by him. Megan fooled me. She has no integrity, no soul, no heart. You are everything I want and I've been looking for all my life, and I don't give a damn how old you are. You're young enough to be having my baby, so don't give me that." And with that, he took her in his arms and kissed her, and her head swam as he did. She wanted to forget all the reasons why it didn't seem right to her anymore, but she wasn't sure she could.

"Besides, your mother would kill you," she said after they kissed, and he laughed.

"I don't care what she thinks. After pretending to be so bohemian all her life, she turns out to be a lot more bourgeois than she thinks. You and I love each other. That's all. No time. No years. No age. It worked when we were together. And now we have a baby. Blaise, give us a chance. Please. It won't be perfect. Nothing ever is. But let's try, for all three of our sakes, and even Salima. I didn't even know about the baby, and I came here today to tell you how much I love you, on the off, crazy, wonderful chance that you still love me too and are nuts enough to try again."

"I do love you," she said, smiling at him. "I never stopped, especially once I knew about the baby."

"Well, then?"

"And what happens when some young girl comes along in two or ten or twenty years, and you fall in love with her?"

"You're the only woman I want. Now and in twenty years. Fifty years. I didn't come back for the baby I didn't even know about. I came back for you." She didn't answer him, and he kissed her again, and she could feel all the hurt of the past four months slipping away from her and disappearing into the mist. He pulled her to her feet then and put his arms around her. "I love you. I will always love you. No matter how old you are." What he was saying was what she had wanted to hear, what she had hoped he would come back to say, even when she told him to leave. It was what she had wanted from Andrew, and Harry before that. And Simon was the only man who had ever said it, and been there for the right reasons. He was there for her, not the trappings, or the stardom, or her job. He only wanted her.

"You know we're crazy if we do this. I'm fifteen years older than you are. When I'm fifty, you'll be thirty-five. When I'm sixty, you'll be forty-five and still gorgeous."

"It's okay, I may have been an idiot for the past four months, but I can count. And I don't give a damn about what anyone thinks or says, except you and Salima. To hell with everyone else. I've never found anyone like you, and I know I never will again. I'm not willing to give that up."

"Neither am I," she said softly, as she looked up at him and smiled. They were there because they loved each other truly and profoundly, and she knew that now, and so did he. There were no doubts, no questions that needed to be answered. There were just the two of them, solidly on their path. He was smiling at her, and he had never been so sure of anything in his life, and so was she.

Chapter 18

Simon, Blaise, and Salima went to Bordeaux to visit his uncle and cousins in July. They had a wonderful time and they stopped in Paris on the way back. Salima had never been there before, and they took her everywhere, and she loved it. They walked all over Paris, went to Notre Dame and Sacre Coeur, the Louvre, Versailles, ate lunch in bistros and walked through the Tuileries Gardens and Bois de Boulogne and went shopping. And Salima slept in her own room at the Ritz. They didn't take Becky. It was a family trip, and she went home to New Hampshire for three weeks while they were away.

Blaise had told Salima about the baby in June, and she was wonderful about it and promised to help. She was thrilled when Simon came back. And just before they left for Europe, she got accepted to Juilliard. She and Simon both had new adventures to look forward to in September, and the baby right after that. The network was fine about the pregnancy, and wanted Blaise to take at least four weeks off after the birth, and she negotiated them down to three. She had already hired a baby nurse who was going to sleep in the room next to Becky's, and she had offered to help with Salima too. But Salima didn't need a lot of help, and she would be busy at school. And she and Simon argued about a guide dog on the plane on the way back. They were an even match. And he was with Blaise too. After the trip, he had promised to teach them both French, and teach Salima to cook. They each brought something to the table, their special talents and gifts.

August whizzed by, with a heat wave that made Blaise uncomfortable as she got bigger. She was determined to work as hard as ever and continued taping interviews. She even impressed Zack with her energy and determination, despite her pregnancy. She finally admitted to it on air during one of her morning segments, and the network was flooded with gifts for the baby, which really touched her.

Simon, Blaise, and Salima rented a house in the Hamptons and went out every weekend. And some weeks, Becky and Salima stayed there and had a ball. And Becky was off on Saturdays and Sundays, which gave her time to spend with a new boyfriend she had met while they were in Europe. He was a struggling artist and a very nice guy, and Salima liked him too.

Simon started his new job at the end of August,

before Salima began at Juilliard. It was very exciting for him. The school was in the Bronx. The students were from age three to twenty-one, and Simon worked with the older ones, which was his strength, as he had demonstrated with Salima. The program was more extensive than what he had been able to do at Caldwell, and he showed Blaise and Salima around the second week he was there. He was ecstatic and he could hardly wait for the baby to come. His life was complete, with Salima and Blaise, their baby, and his new job.

The week after he started at the New York Institute for Special Education, Salima started at Juilliard. She had a wonderful adviser whose main job was to keep Salima from signing up for every class they offered. She signed up for a heavy course load, and Becky took her to school on the bus every day. And Salima used her white cane while she was there and didn't care. All she could think of were the music classes she was taking, two of them with Lucianna, who was incredibly proud of her. She joined a church choir in Harlem for extra course credit, and she was so busy with classes and after-school activities that Simon and Blaise hardly saw her. And she had a thousand new things to tell them every night.

Blaise was still working at the network on her due date on the first of October, and she felt huge by then. The baby was a good size, and in the last days of her pregnancy, she looked like she was going to pop any minute.

Simon happened to be watching her morning segment before he left for school, on the baby's scheduled due date. She was talking about a recent scandal in the Senate when he saw an odd expression cross her face. She maintained her concentration, but he had the sense that something was wrong, and called her immediately when she came off the air. She answered her cell phone as soon as she saw it was him.

"Are you okay?" he asked, feeling nervous, about to leave for school, but he wanted to be sure she was all right first. She had looked odd to him.

"I think so," she said hesitantly. "My water broke while I was on the air. I was going to call the doctor in a minute. I'm glad you called." And he was startled to realize she sounded scared. It was so unlike her that all he wanted to do was get to her and reassure her and take her in his arms.

"I'll be right over," he said immediately. He had already warned the school that they were expecting a baby any day, and they had been very nice about it.

"I'm not so sure that's a good idea," Blaise said in a strained voice. "I don't know what happened, but I'm having contractions every four minutes." He tried not to panic when she said it, and made an effort to sound calmer than he felt, for her.

"That's okay, sweetheart. Get Mark or Charlie to take you to the hospital with Tully. I'll meet you there in ten minutes. Have Mark call the doctor. *Right away!*"

"Okay," she said meekly. She was having trouble talking through a contraction, and Mark appeared as it was happening and was terrified at the look on her face as she handed her BlackBerry to him and Simon told him what to do.

"Call the doctor and bring her to the hospital immediately. She's having the baby," he told Mark with a calm he didn't feel, as he ran out of the apartment, and Mark promised to get her to the hospital as fast as Tully could drive them there.

Everyone who saw her leave cheered as Mark and Charlie led her away, and Blaise waved and smiled wanly. She really had stayed until the last minute.

"Christ, were you planning to have it at your desk between meetings?" Charlie scolded her as they crossed the lobby and found Tully outside. But Blaise didn't say a word. She was in too much pain. It had all happened so fast. And on his way to the hospital, Simon called Becky and told her to pick up Salima at Juilliard. She wanted to be there too, and after some hesitation, Blaise had agreed.

After that Simon got minute-by-minute reports from Mark in the car with her, while Tully drove through midtown morning traffic as fast as possible, praying he wouldn't have to deliver the baby. Mark told Simon the doctor was on her way.

It took them twenty minutes to get to the hospital, and Simon was on the sidewalk waiting for them when Tully pulled up and Mark hopped out immediately, looking panicked.

"Get a doctor fast! She's going to have it really soon!" Blaise could no longer walk or talk by then and looked relieved when Simon got in the car with her and gently helped her out. Mark had gotten a nurse with a wheelchair, who sized the situation up immediately and literally ran the wheelchair with Blaise in it into the building, saying only, "Let's get you upstairs," as Simon ran beside them and Blaise clutched his hand in a viselike grip.

"I love you," she managed to say between contractions.

"I love you too," Simon said, trying to reassure her. But everything was happening so fast it was hard to say anything. The doctor was waiting for them when the elevator opened at labor and delivery. She took one look at Blaise, and they took her straight to a birthing room, and Simon and a nurse had her clothes off in less than a minute. There was no time for drugs or an epidural, explanations, or anything except Simon telling her he loved her and Blaise moaning with the pain as they got her on the delivery table, and the doctor checked her with a look of satisfaction, and smiled at Simon and Blaise.

"I think we're ready for a birthday party," she said, and told Blaise to push as Simon watched in wonder and Blaise gave a terrifying scream, as their son's head emerged from between her legs, and he looked at his parents with surprise. He was born with the next contraction, as Simon and Blaise cried and laughed and watched with amazement as the doctor lifted him onto her stomach, and the baby looked around as the doctor cut the cord. The baby was beautiful, looked like Simon, had Blaise's red hair, and was totally alert. Less than an hour before, Blaise had been on the air. None of them had expected him to come so fast, and he weighed just under nine pounds. Salima arrived just minutes after he'd been born, and Blaise was holding him by then. A nurse led Salima to her mother, and she cried when she kissed her and touched the baby's cheek.

"I came as fast as I could," she said apologetically.

"If your mom had done this any faster, she'd have had him during a commercial on the air," Simon said, still in awe of the miracle they had just seen. They took Blaise to a room a little while later, and the three of them spent the day together, taking turns holding the baby. And in between the baby nursed.

Becky came to take Salima home that evening, and Simon spent the night with Blaise, and in the morning they went home. They were a family and had welcomed Edmond Charles Ward into their midst. He was named after Simon's uncle in Bordeaux.

The apartment was filled with flowers when they got home, and gifts continued to arrive all day. The network had sent her an antique bassinet filled with baby clothes and teddy bears. Harry had sent enormous flowers and balloons. The baby's birth had been announced on the evening news. As a result, there were so many gifts and flowers in the apartment, they could hardly walk around. Teresa the housekeeper, Natalie the baby nurse, and Becky were in the kitchen, Salima was hanging out with Simon and her mother in the bedroom with the baby, and by dinnertime, Simon had realized the obvious.

"I think we may have to move," he said to Blaise with a look of astonishment. They were exploding out of her pristine apartment, and she laughed.

"I thought we might." She looked peaceful and ecstatic as the baby nursed, and Simon lay next to her to admire them both. He had never seen anything so beautiful in his life.

Simon's mother waited until the day after they got home to come and visit them from Boston. Simon's father was too busy, but he promised he'd come to meet the baby soon. The minute Isabelle walked through the door, she commented that they were living like gypsies and she hoped they were planning to move.

"We just figured that out ourselves," Simon said. The apartment was bursting at the seams. But his mother looked awestruck when she saw the baby, and smiled proudly at her son. She had been knitting tiny blue booties and caps for the last month and had written him a poem that had no point and made no sense, which she read them that afternoon.

She held the baby and he slept peacefully in her arms, and when she handed him back to Blaise, she spoke to Simon in a disapproving tone.

"I hope you're planning to marry her now," Isabelle

said about Blaise, as though she weren't in the room. She looked sleepy as she nursed.

"I thought you thought she was too old for me," Simon teased his mother.

"You have a child now, Simon. You can't just live together like artists or poets. She has a respectable job, and so do you."

"Don't be so bourgeois, Maman. What kind of bohemian are you?" he said, and laughed as she sat down on the bed next to Blaise, whom he loved with all his heart, even if she was not his wife. They hadn't gotten married, and didn't see why they should, despite what his mother thought. Or if they decided to, they would do it in their own time, for reasons that mattered to them.

"It's a shame the baby has red hair," Isabelle said wistfully as she gazed at him. "Let's hope it turns dark." Blaise laughed. The comment was so like her.

"We can always dye it," Blaise suggested.

"I don't think that's a good idea," Isabelle said in a worried tone.

The baby nurse and Teresa were trying to get organized. Becky was helping wherever possible. And Salima picked the baby up as soon as Isabelle set him down. It was easy to tell that he was always going to be in someone's hands. He had doting parents and a loving sister, and a grandmother who loved him despite the color of his hair. Isabelle held him in her arms again before she left the next day.

"At least his hair is not quite as red as yours," she

said to Blaise reassuringly, looking at her daughter-in-law affectionately. Isabelle was thrilled with her new grandson. And she reminded them again to get married, as though they might forget. Blaise and Simon didn't share her concern. "L'amour n'a pas d'âge," she said, referring to Simon and Blaise. Love has no age. And she looked pensive for a moment as she said goodbye to Blaise.

"Do you realize that when Simon is fifty-five, you'll be seventy years old?" Isabelle said to her. Blaise had just turned forty-eight and Simon thirty-three that summer. And the fact that they were together and had Edmond was miracle enough for Blaise. They didn't care about the math.

"We can all count, Mother," Simon said with a look of exasperation as he escorted his mother out. And Salima bent over the baby to stroke his cheek again. She loved holding him and feeling his face next to hers.

"And when you're eighty-five, I'll be a hundred," Blaise whispered to Simon with a grin, when he came back into the room and she was nursing his son. Edmond looked drunk with delight and his father grinned.

"That sounds good to me," he said, smiling at her. They had each found the person that they had always wanted and needed. It had just come in a different package than they'd expected. They had been wise enough to see it, and brave enough to grab it, and know it was a gift. The numbers were of no importance. Only the people and the love they shared.

Simon had given her everything she'd ever wanted and longed for in her life. And Blaise was the woman he'd been looking for and hadn't known it till he saw her. They completed each other, and each was better and had a fuller life because of the other. And with all the humanity that made it special and unique, it wasn't perfect, and they didn't need it to be. But it was very, very close to perfect. It was exactly the life they wanted it to be.

About the Author

DANIELLE STEEL has been hailed as one of the world's most popular authors, with over 650 million copies of her novels sold. Her many international bestsellers include *Country, Prodigal Son, Pegasus, A Perfect Life, Power Play, Winners, First Sight, Until the End of Time, The Sins of the Mother, Friends Forever,* and other highly acclaimed novels. She is also the author of *His Bright Light,* the story of her son Nick Traina's life and death; *A Gift of Hope,* a memoir of her work with the homeless; *Pure Joy,* about the dogs she and her family have loved; and the children's book, *Pretty Minnie in Paris*.

Visit the Danielle Steel Web Site at
www.daniellesteel.com

On Sale in Hardcover
September 2015

978-0-345-53104-9

Chapter 1

The birds calling to each other in the early morning just after the dawn heralded another perfect day in the lush jungle south of Bogotá. Pablo Echeverría, his skin a deep tan, his eyes the darkest brown, his hair almost to his shoulders, pushed back behind his ears, and his beard slightly overgrown, walked out of the hut where he and Paloma lived. She was expecting their first child, and the date was coming near. Paloma was as fair and light-skinned as he was dark, and her name suited her. In Spanish Paloma meant "Dove." She was a bird of peace in the jungle where they lived and Pablo worked. He was her brother's right-hand man. Raul Vásquez López was one of the most powerful men in Colombia, despite the simple way they lived. Pablo had been with him for three years, working his way up through the ranks since he had come from Ecuador, and gaining Raul's trust.

They called Raul "El Lobo," the Wolf. He was cunning, daring, and quick, like a wolf.

Pablo was the son of an Ecuadorian general who had been killed in a military coup, assassinated by rebels. Pablo had turned to the drug trade, and after three years of working on a smaller scale in Ecuador, he had found his way to Raul. And the three years he had spent working for him since had been a satisfying and productive alliance.

Pablo and Paloma weren't married, and no one cared, he was planning to marry her soon, after the baby was born. For now, he and Raul had other things on their minds. Raul liked the idea of Pablo being with his younger sister. Pablo was not only smart, capable, and trustworthy, he was a good man. Paloma had had no medical care through the eight months of the pregnancy, but at nineteen she was fine. And she was planning to give birth at the camp. Pablo had been reading books about how to help her, and if things started to go wrong, he could drive her the two hours to Bogotá. Her brother was twenty years older than she was, and Pablo was twenty-eight, young to have risen so high in Raul's operation, but Raul knew pure talent when he saw it, and his inquiries about Pablo in Ecuador had proved him right. He prided himself on his infallible judgment about his men, and Pablo had never let him down. He executed Raul's orders flawlessly, and handled their purchasing and transport operations brilliantly. There had been no problems, and no slips in the three years he'd been there.

Their simple life at the camp suited him. Pablo went to both Bogotá and Cartagena for Raul regularly, but he was always happy to get back, meet with Raul, who was like a brother to him now, live with the other men, and come home to Paloma, waiting for him in their hut. He had built it for them himself. In his first year at the camp, he had lived in a military surplus tent with the other men, but once he was with Paloma, they wanted privacy and a space for themselves. She had grown up in Raul's camps, after their parents died. Her three other brothers worked for Raul as well. And Pablo had rapidly caught her eye, as she had inevitably caught his. Raul had defended her virtue fiercely until then. It was a sign of his deep respect for Pablo that he had entrusted her to him, and given him his consent. To Pablo, she was the ultimate prize. He loved the sweet scent of her skin as he nestled with her at night, her gentleness in all things, and her full belly now, heavy with their child. Raul wanted it to be a boy. Pablo didn't say it, but he didn't care. He just wanted it to go easily for her, and the baby to be healthy when it was born. She was a brave girl, used to the primitive conditions in which they lived, and said she wasn't afraid. Pablo could feel the baby kick him, when she slept behind him with an arm gently cast over him, in the cool night air of the jungle.

Pablo was wearing his old military jacket from

Ecuador, with an undershirt, fatigue pants, and his old army boots, as he lit his first cigarette of the day, and took a long drag. He had slipped out, as he always did, without waking Paloma, and had his first cup of coffee with Raul every morning, while they discussed the missions of the day, and the state of their activities in process. They had dealings in Panama, Ecuador, Aruba, Venezuela, Bolivia, and Mexico, and exported literally tons of cocaine to Mexico, Canada, Africa, Europe, and the United States. Raul ran the largest and most successful drug operation in South America. They exported it by land, air, and sea via ships and speedboats out of Cartagena. Pablo was in charge of coordinating their transport operation at the highest level. While Raul ran everything from their camp, Pablo slipped quietly into the two cities, checked on operations, conveyed Raul's orders, and then came back to the camp to report to El Lobo, who ran his vast empire with military precision. Raul was a man worthy of respect and admiration, for the sheer efficiency with which he ran his business. And he had built it all himself, adding one piece of the giant operation to the next, until his arms encompassed much of South America. Pablo was his most trusted legman, but they all knew that Raul was the heart and soul and brains of their business, and ran it all on a grand scale.

Pablo finished the last of his cigarette as he walked into the clearing where Raul made camp. His tent was military and heavily camouflaged, but no one was ever sure where he slept at night. The location was always kept secret even from Pablo, although they met at his tent in the morning to discuss work. But the joke in the camp was that El Lobo slept with the other wolves. The women he slept with were temporary and of no consequence to him, he considered them more of a liability than an asset, and he teased Pablo that he didn't have his romantic ideas. But it was a weakness he tolerated in him, since it benefited his sister, and Pablo treated her well. Raul was all about business, nothing else mattered to him, except the loyalty of his men. He considered their total dedication to him a sacred trust. And those who failed him in some way rapidly disappeared. Their families, attachments to women, and personal lives were of no interest to him.

He was smoking a Romeo y Julieta limited edition Havana cigar, as he did every morning, when Pablo arrived. He offered one to Pablo from the box on his desk every day, and Pablo always declined. He smoked a cigar with Raul sometimes before he went home at night, but didn't have the stomach for it first thing in the morning. But he liked the familiar, pungent smell when he walked into the tent, and often brought the cigars for Raul from Bogotá. They were common here, for men like Raul. Despite the way he lived in order to run his business, he was a man of distinguished tastes. He had been educated in Europe, and had gone to Oxford for two years. It made for interesting conversations with Pablo, when they shared a brandy and a cigar late at night. Pablo had been well educated too, from a respectable family. It gave them something more in common than the business interests they shared.

The moment Raul saw Pablo, there was a brotherly light in his eyes. He clapped him on the shoulder, and they embraced. The two men even looked somewhat alike, although Pablo was younger and taller and in flawless shape. Their coloring was similar, as was their military style.

"How is my fat sister?" Raul said, teasing him, as Pablo helped himself to the strong dark brew of coffee that Raul made himself, and drank gallons of, every day. His coffee cup was never empty.

"Getting bigger," Pablo said proudly. "I think it will be soon." He was mildly worried about it, but knew better than to say it to Raul, who called him an old woman when he did. Raul knew that Pablo's soft spot was Paloma, which he always considered a dangerous thing. It was why he never allied himself with any woman, he just used them. He thought women were too risky for that reason, and easily became an Achilles' heel, but it was a flaw he forgave Pablo, only because Paloma was his sister.

Raul had been sitting, looking at a table full of maps and a list of transport ships, when Pablo walked in. He pushed the list toward Pablo as soon as he sat down, pointing the cigar in the direction of the maps.

"So what do you think? We ship to North Africa tomorrow? And Europe at the end of the week?" He liked to keep things moving and not let the shipments sit for too long after they came in. They had gotten a huge shipment in Cartagena from their supplier the day before, and he wanted to get it out quickly. Despite what they paid in bribes to government officials at all levels, El Lobo knew better than to let the goods sit in warehouses longer than they had to.

"That sounds right," Pablo said, studying the maps. "I don't see why we can't ship to Europe tomorrow too. Why wait till the end of the week?" He pointed to the name of a ship that was smaller than the others but had served them well before. "And Miami, when the next shipment comes in." Raul nodded. Pablo always planned ahead and was as careful as Raul was himself about moving and storing the goods. They wanted to ship it out as fast as they could on ships they knew were safe.

As they discussed the details and mechanics of it, four other men walked in. Two were in camouflage, the other two in garb similar to what Raul and Pablo wore. They were the silent army of the dark side. And a few minutes later, six more men arrived in the tent, awaiting instructions. Pablo dispatched five of the ten to Bogotá for operations there, and he was planning to take two of the men to Cartagena with him. He didn't need more. He was an expert marksman, and he preferred traveling in smaller groups. Raul listened while Pablo gave the men instructions, nodded, and silently approved as he relit his cigar. He didn't offer his cigars to the others, only to Pablo when they were alone, as a mark of the brotherhood they shared.

Half an hour later, five of the men were gone. Three were staying at the camp, with another dozen peppered through the jungle, part of the protection of the camp. Pablo and El Lobo exchanged a few last words then, and Raul nodded as Pablo left with the two men he wanted with him.

"See you tonight," Pablo said over his shoulder. Pablo always reported in when he got back, to let Raul know how things had gone. They had a vast communication network that functioned efficiently, but Raul and Pablo communicated by phone and e-mail as little as possible, and both preferred it that way. They met in person before and after Pablo's missions.

Pablo trudged silently through the fierce brush of the jungle for half an hour, until they reached a heavily concealed Jeep. Pablo got behind the wheel, as the two men took away its protective covering, and then they both got in. They drove along a barely serviceable dirt track for a while, and eventually joined a battered narrow road, and stayed on it for half an hour, until they reached a clearing with a narrow airstrip that was barely more than a dirt track but was just long enough for the small plane that landed ten minutes later. Pablo had radioed for it before he left the camp, and it would make it possible for them to cover the thousand miles to Cartagena and return by that night. None of the three men spoke on the flight, and Pablo didn't say a word to them until they reached the landing strip they used regularly on the outskirts of Cartagena. Pablo was a man of few words.

He was thinking about their various operations being carried out that day, shipments coming in to several cities, others waiting to be moved. They picked up a car at the airstrip that was parked for them there, and drove to a warehouse just outside the city, and from there to a small battered building, which housed their office. It looked completely innocuous, and no one would have suspected the millions of dollars of business being conducted there. Pablo parked the car behind a neighboring house, with chickens wandering through the yard, and walked into the first building through a back door. One of Pablo's men stayed at the back door, the other moved to the front door. All three of them were armed. And Pablo walked up the creaking stairs to meet three men waiting for him there. He met with them for just under an hour, delivered all of Raul's instructions, and ascertained that the plan was clear and that they were ready to carry it out. The cocaine was being shipped, concealed in farm equipment, to North Africa, which worked well for them. And the shipment to Europe was being sent with textiles going into Marseilles. It had all been successfully done before without a problem.

Less than an hour later, Pablo was back on the road, to the airstrip, and in the air minutes after they arrived. The mission had gone well. When they reached the camp that night, they carefully concealed the Jeep where it had been before. Raul was waiting for him. Pablo assured him that all had gone according to plan. They handled all their shipping through Cartagena. Raul told him he needed him to go to Bogotá the next day, which was standard procedure for Pablo. He went to one of the cities where they did business almost every day.

"Did you eat?" El Lobo asked him with concern. One of the men had bought sandwiches on the way to the airstrip outside Cartagena. They had other things to occupy them than to worry about meals.

"We ate." Pablo smiled at him, touched by the fraternal gesture. When they were alone, Raul treated him like a younger brother. And with that, he poured a glass of brandy, pushed it toward him, and offered him a cigar, which this time Pablo accepted. Raul was pleased with how things had gone. He knew he could always count on Pablo to execute his orders to perfection. He had earned the brandy and cigar and El Lobo's praise.

"My sister can wait," El Lobo said, as the leader of their operation, and Pablo smiled. Whenever Pablo came back to the hut, Paloma was happy to see him, asked no questions, and never complained. Her life with Pablo had been a little piece of heaven for the past two years, in the rigors of their world. It was a hardcore man's world with no room in it for women's needs and demands, which she knew well.

The two men enjoyed the brandy and cigars, in a

civilized moment at the end of their day. The business Raul ran was a high-stress operation where millions of dollars were involved on a daily basis, and there was no margin for mistakes. There had been none so far, which had won Pablo El Lobo's trust.

It was nearly midnight when Pablo went back to his hut, and found Paloma half asleep in their bed, which was a thin mattress on the floor. She smiled sleepily in the moonlight as she felt Pablo slip into bed beside her, naked. He pulled aside the covers to look at the velvet of her body, and her belly seemed to get bigger by the hour as their child grew inside her. She put her arms around his neck, and he kissed her and held her as she slipped back to sleep again with a soft purring noise, and he lay admiring her until he fell asleep himself.

The next day, after meeting with Raul in the early morning, as always, Pablo drove the Jeep to Bogotá, and this time he went alone. He met a man at a house in the Macarena district, who handed him a battered suitcase full of money, the fruits of their work a few days before. Pablo often brought large amounts of cash to Raul. He asked no questions about where it went or how it was handled, although he had heard long ago that Raul had personal accounts in Switzerland and in other countries in the Caribbean. But if so, Raul had never shared that information with him. There were some things El Lobo kept to himself, no matter how much he trusted him. Pablo knew where some of the operation's accounts were kept, but he knew better than to ask any details. When Pablo returned to camp that night, Raul told him that he needed him to return to Bogotá, for a smaller operation than the one he had carried out that day. There would be no money pickup this time, but only some directions that needed to be verbally given, and Raul said it wouldn't take him long. He wanted no record of the transaction, and they were laying the groundwork for the transfer to Miami, which usually went smoothly, with operatives they had dealt with for a long time.

The two men chatted for a few minutes, but Pablo was eager to see Paloma, who he knew had dinner waiting for him, since he had told her that he was only going to Bogotá. She was smiling and held her arms out to him in a simple white cotton dress she had made herself, and she was wearing gold sandals he had brought her from the city. He loved bringing her small gifts whenever he could. Raul always warned him about spoiling her, and told him he would regret it one day. Women were like that, according to El Lobo, who had never trusted a woman in his life.

They sat down to dinner to the familiar sounds of the jungle, and Pablo could hear a small plane droning overhead. He knew that there were several men coming in that night from Ecuador. They were part of Raul's empire, and Pablo knew he would be meeting with them and Raul the next day when he got back from his mission in the city.

Paloma didn't ask him what he'd done that day. She never did. Her brother had trained her well. They had other things to talk about, and for now, all she could think about was the baby. She hardly ate that night, she was too big. And after dinner, they lay down on the bed, listening to the noises around them, and were comfortable lying side by side. He rubbed her back, and she fell asleep, after she tossed the white cotton dress onto the floor beside the bed. Her body was so spectacularly beautiful, even now with the enormous bump that made him smile each time he saw it, and her breasts were large and full, bigger than they'd been before, and she had long graceful legs, which hadn't changed. In another world, she would have been considered a remarkably beautiful girl, but here she lived concealed and isolated in her brother's jungle camp, in a place that paid no attention to her, except as an occasional object of envy or admiration. As Raul's sister, she was unattainable, except to Pablo. And only he really appreciated how beautiful she was, and what a kind, gentle girl. Here, no one cared.

She was still asleep when he left the camp early the next morning, when he went back to Bogotá, to carry out the mission he'd been assigned. It was a brief meeting with a man he knew well and had met with many times before. They agreed to the amount of cocaine to be transferred to Miami, and how much it would cost. The funds would change hands later on.

After the meeting, Pablo walked for a little while, and stopped at a café. He ordered a cup of strong black coffee, which the waiter served him, as he sat on the terrace in the sun. When he finished it, he ordered a second cup, although the brew was strong, and the waiter spilled it accidentally, as he was about to set the cup down. The hot coffee spread across the table but missed Pablo. The server apologetically mopped it up, with an embarrassed look. Pablo didn't look like the sort of man one would want to annoy. There was a tension about him that was reminiscent of a lion ready to strike.

And as the waiter wiped up the last of the coffee, he whispered almost inaudibly, "Now." Pablo's eyes grew steely the moment he said it, and he glanced back at the waiter with a murderous look, then looked away. Pablo stood up and threw a few coins on the table, as the waiter watched him mournfully, and just as inaudibly, Pablo said, "No," strode away from the table, and walked to the Jeep. He was back on the road a few minutes later, and his eyes were cold and hard as he drove.